Face Value

Books by Michael A. Kahn

The Rachel Gold Mysteries
Grave Designs
Death Benefits
Firm Ambitions
Due Diligence
Sheer Gall
Bearing Witness
Trophy Widow
The Flinch Factor
Face Value

Writing as Michael Baron
The Mourning Sexton

Face Value

A Rachel Gold Mystery

Michael A. Kahn

Poisoned Pen Press

Copyright © 2014 by Michael A. Kahn

First Edition 2014

10 9 8 7 6 5 4 3 2 1

Library of Congress Catalog Card Number: 2014931581

ISBN: 9781464202780   Hardcover
      9781464202803   Trade Paperback

Poisoned Pen Press
6962 E. First Ave., Ste. 103
Scottsdale, AZ 85251
www.poisonedpenpress.com
info@poisonedpenpress.com

Printed in the United States of America

In loving memory of my father, Bill Kahn.
All but six, Dad.

Acknowledgments

A heartfelt thanks to Barbara Peters, my editor and my navigator.

Prologue

Tommy Flynn leaned over the body, hands on his knees.

This was hardly his first. He'd averaged more than one a year during his thirty-three years as a St. Louis cop. Though he'd retired from the force twelve years ago, he could still recall each one. Shooting victims mostly, and mostly men. A few knifings, including a barroom brawler known as Battleship who'd died with a knife jammed up to the hilt in his right eye socket. Two floaters. Several traffic fatalities—the most memorable being a husband and what turned out to be his mistress, both decapitated in a collision with a garbage truck. He'd been driving a Porsche 911, top down. By the time Tommy and his partner arrived at the scene, a drunk bystander had retrieved the heads and put them on the corpses' laps—although he'd placed the man's on the woman's lap, and vice versa. Generated some crude jokes back at the station.

This wasn't his first jumper, either. He'd had two others—both men, both in their thirties, both hitting the sidewalk headfirst after falls of several stories. Hard to forget those two. From the neck up, Hamburger Helper.

But this was the first corpse he'd known.

Not including Muriel, God bless her, who didn't really count because he was off duty at the time and she'd been in a coma in the ICU for more than two weeks, hooked up to all kinds of machines, when he'd given the doctor the okay to pull the plug.

And he knew this one, poor gal.

He'd spotted the body in the alley on his midnight smoke break, which had started twenty minutes late because the move-out of the insurance agency on the third floor took longer than expected. He couldn't leave the front desk until the movers signed out. Tapping his pen, he'd watched on his closed-circuit TV monitor as the two knuckleheads exited, finally, through the freight entrance.

At 12:20 he'd stepped out into the warm October evening, fired up a Camel, and started off on his usual stroll east down Olive toward Broadway. His knees had ached. They always did after sitting. Arthritis. Walking helped loosen things.

An alley separated his office building, the Chouteau Tower, from the parking garage to the east. He'd glanced over as he passed by the alley. That's when he saw the corpse—or what appeared to be a corpse. He'd seen bodies in the alley before, but they'd turned out to be drunks passed out or homeless people bundled in rags.

From habit instilled by all those years on the force, he'd checked his watch before stepping into the alley.

12:24 a.m.

As he approached, he could tell it was a woman. Facedown, head turned away from him. Dressed in business attire—dark skirt, pale blouse. Although the light was too dim to see colors, he knew that the fluid pooled around her head was blood. There was also blood darkening the back of her blouse. He could tell she'd fallen from a great height—her skull was partially crushed, her right arm clearly broken, a splintered piece of bone had pierced through the skin on her right leg. He surveyed the area. Her open purse was about ten feet from her body, and some of its contents were scattered about, including a set of keys and a wallet.

He stepped around the body and looked down at her.

Jesus.

He bent over to get a better look.

Jesus H. Christ.

He knew her.

Not well, but better than he knew most of the lawyers at Warner & Olsen, the main tenant in the Chouteau Tower. The firm took up the top four floors. Worked crazy hours, those lawyers. Especially the younger ones. Like this gal. She worked late most nights, which is how he got to know her. Back before they opened the sixth-floor crosswalk to the parking garage, his duties had included escorting any female leaving the building after eight o'clock to the parking garage. He'd escorted her several nights a week, every week.

She'd been a bashful one. A foreigner—an Arab or maybe one of those Pakistanis—but spoke perfect English, no accent. Pretty gal, too, in that modest foreign style. Seemed embarrassed about taking him away from the front desk so many nights, but was always grateful and thanked him in such a heartfelt way that he ended up the embarrassed one, shrugging it off, telling her no big deal.

Even after they opened the crosswalk to the garage, he occasionally saw her. Sometimes she'd come down through the main lobby around seven to go pick up dinner from Subway or Quiznos or the St. Louis Bread Company. Always stopped at the front desk to say hello and ask him how he was doing. Last Christmas she gave him a tin of homemade cookies she called barazeh. Told him she made them from her aunt's recipe. They were delicious—crunchy sesame cookies with honey and pistachio.

He realized he hadn't seen her for awhile. Maybe two weeks. And now look at the poor thing. Side of her face crushed in, blood oozing out of her ear and nose, body shattered.

Jesus Christ.

Tommy straightened with a wince and looked around. The Chouteau Tower, which was on the west side of the alley, rose twenty-four stories, all steel and glass. The parking garage on the east side of the alley was ten stories of concrete. The elevated walkway connecting the two structures spanned the alley overhead about thirty yards south of where he stood. Her body lay on the garage side of the alley, about ten feet from the outer wall. He looked up, visualizing the interior of the garage, the cars parked against the wall. The outer wall on each floor rose about two feet above the parking surface, leaving about eight feet of open space between the top of the wall and the ceiling. He looked down at her and shook his head.

Jesus.

He reached into his pocket, pulled out his cell phone, and flipped it open. He frowned, trying to remember the number for the nearest police station. He couldn't, so he punched in 9-1-1.

Part 1

Whether Stanley Plotkin shall turn out to be the hero of his own life, or whether that station will be held by anybody else, these pages must show.

Tony Manghini
Manager of Office Support Services
Warner & Olsen, LLP

Chapter One

They held the memorial service in Graham Chapel on the campus of Washington University. Although Sari Bashir had died only eight days before, her funeral had already taken place in Detroit. Even with the autopsy, she'd been buried just five days after her death, which is actually a long time lapse for someone of the Moslem faith.

I glanced around the chapel. Warner & Olsen had closed the office for the service, and it appeared that most of that firm's lawyers and staff were in the chapel that morning, along with many others. I recognized a few professors from the Washington University Law School. I spotted Tommy Flynn, the Chouteau Tower's late-shift security guard, seated near the aisle in a row toward the rear of the chapel. I'd heard he'd been the one to discover her body.

Like many in the chapel crowd, I knew firsthand that the long hours and demanding tasks (and taskmasters) of Big Law take their toll on young associates. Some turn to booze or drugs, some develop medical problems, some lose their marriages. A few quit their jobs, a few (including me) quit Big Law, a few quit the profession, and every once in a while one quits altogether. According to the medical examiner, Sari Bashir had quit altogether on the third Thursday in October, somewhere between nine and eleven that night. That's when she fell to her death from the eighth floor of the downtown garage where she parked her car. The police concluded that she'd taken her own life—a conclusion that haunted me, and no doubt others, in the chapel that day.

Sari and I met during her third year of law school, when she'd worked for me part-time as a law clerk. She was a lovely person—quiet, sweet, diligent. The first member of her family to go to college, Sari had grown up in Detroit. Her mother had died of cancer when Sari was in elementary school. Her father worked on the assembly line at the Ford Motor plant in Dearborn. I'd met him at her law school graduation. I still have the photo I took of them that day. They stand side by side, Sari in her cap and gown, a diploma in her hand, her father Ameer in a suit and tie. If you look closely, you can see tears of pride on his cheeks.

It was a beautiful memorial service. Sari's cousin Malikah was the first of the four speakers. She described growing up with Sari in Detroit—from Barbie doll parties at grade school sleepovers to band camp at Interlochen in high school.

The next two speakers were the founding partners of Sari's law firm: Donald Warner and Len Olsen. Except for their ages—both were in their early sixties—they were a study in contrasts. Many believed those contrasts were the key to the law firm's success as one of the dominant firms in the Midwest. Donald Warner was tall and gaunt, with the build and gait of a retired basketball center, a position he'd played forty years ago at the University of Illinois. Len Olsen, though nearly six feet tall, seemed short by comparison. He looked more like a former quarterback, which he'd been at Southeast Missouri State in Cape Girardeau. Warner's expertise was in the esoteric realm of international corporate finance, while Olsen had made his name in courtrooms throughout Missouri and the surrounding states.

Both men had apparently worked with Sari during her six years at the firm, and each shared a touching vignette that highlighted her dedication to the profession—and each did so in a manner that highlighted the contrast in personal styles. Donald Warner stood at the podium and delivered his eulogy from prepared remarks in the deliberate, measured tones of a local TV news anchorman.

Then came Len Olsen. He removed the microphone from the stand, walked around the stage as he spoke, and eventually came down the stairs and strolled up the main aisle, making eye contact with many of us in the audience. As I recalled, he'd grown up near the Arkansas border in rural Missouri. He spoke with a gentle, musical southern drawl that had been charming juries and judges for decades. We in the audience, like Olsen himself, chuckled occasionally and, toward the end, wiped away a tear.

The last to speak was the dean of the law school, who read aloud remembrances of Sari by several of her professors. He spoke of his own memories of the shy but determined young law student who'd become articles editor for the *Law Review* by her third year. He concluded his remarks with the announcement that Warner & Olsen had established a fifty-thousand-dollar scholarship fund in Sari's memory.

The service ended with the organist playing what the program identified as Sari's favorite song, John Lennon's "Imagine." You could almost hear the sigh of relief throughout the crowd as the first plaintive notes rang out. The music meant that the service was over, and that meant that the most painful aspect of Sari's death—namely, the facts surrounding her death—would not be touched upon.

You may say I'm a dreamer, I sang to myself, thinking of Sari, *but I'm not the only one…*

As I joined the crowd moving down the rows toward the center aisle for the slow stroll to the rear of the chapel, the somber mood was shattered by a strident nasal voice toward the back.

"Shall we focus our attention on the vote count for the Presidential election of 1836?"

I couldn't help but smile.

Stanley Plotkin. Barely five feet tall, bad haircut, horn-rim glasses resting on a big nose. Even those of us who knew Stanley Plotkin were taken aback by his outfit that morning. He had on an ill-fitting black tuxedo, including cummerbund and black bow tie.

Seemingly oblivious to the crowd, he squinted up at the enormous man standing next to him. "Do you recall the victor, Jerry?"

"In 1836?" the big man replied in a near whisper, clearly trying to encourage Stanley to lower his voice. "Andrew Jackson?"

"Jackson?" Stanley Plotkin snorted. "Hardly. Martin Van Buren."

"Okay."

The huge man next to Stanley was Jerry Klunger. He stood at least six-and-a-half feet tall and must have weighed close to three hundred pounds.

"How many votes?" Stanley demanded in a nasal staccato.

"I don't know," Jerry said. "Maybe we should leave now."

"Exactly one hundred and seventy."

"Okay."

One of the women moving up the aisle in front of me shook her head at Stanley and mumbled something. I saw a lawyer from the firm give Jerry a sympathetic smile.

"Second place?" Stanley demanded.

"Maybe we should leave now."

"William Harrison. Seventy-three. And then?"

The big guy shrugged. "Beats me."

I nodded at Stanley as I paused at his aisle.

"Ms. Gold," he stated in greeting, averting his eyes a moment, and then turning back to Jerry. "Hugh White, Daniel Webster, and Willie Magnum, tallying in at twenty-six, fourteen, and eleven, respectively. All Whigs."

Jerry frowned. "They were bald?"

Stanley snorted. "Whigs. W-H-I-G-S, Jerry. An American political party that operated from 1834 to 1856."

Jerry placed his enormous hand on Stanley's shoulder. "Miss Gold is here, Stanley. Time for us to leave."

Chapter Two

Stanley Plotkin and Jerry Klunger followed me to my car. They worked in the mailroom at Warner & Olsen. I had known Stanley—or, more precisely, I had occasionally been in the same room as Stanley—for about a decade. His mother, Bea, was a good friend of my mother. The two women, both widows, had been playing mahjong together on Tuesday nights at the Jewish Community Center for nearly a decade.

Stanley was a difficult person to know. Although he was probably smarter than most attorneys at Warner & Olsen—and certainly smarter than me—his progress through school and life had been disrupted by a version of Asperger's syndrome that fell somewhere along the autism spectrum. According to what Bea told my mother, Jerry Klunger acted as Stanley's protector at work, which is one of the reasons Stanley had lasted so long at the job. He was now in his third year at Warner & Olsen. They were the law firm's odd couple—one a brilliant eccentric, the other a slow-witted giant with a heart of gold. Both were twenty-nine, and both still lived at home with their mothers. Tony Manghini, their sarcastic mailroom boss, referred to them as Master Blaster.

My mother had asked last night if I could take Stanley and Jerry with me to Sari's. They worked the late shift—noon to nine—and normally rode the bus together to and from work. Jerry lived just two stops further down the same bus route. But to get to the memorial service that morning would have meant at least one transfer and nearly an hour-long ride to go just eight miles from their homes. So I picked them up at Stanley's house.

When we arrived at the chapel, they had taken seats in the empty back row, Jerry on the aisle, his massive body effectively blocking anyone else from taking a seat in that row. That's because two was an even number, and Jerry knew that Stanley had a thing about sitting in a row with lots of other people because that increased the chances of an odd number. His mother had told me that Stanley had an obsessive aversion to odd numbers, especially in a row of seats. That was why he couldn't go to the symphony even though he had a huge collection of classical music at home—hundreds and hundreds of vinyl records arranged not by composer but by some combination of musical eras, styles, and keys unfathomable to all but Stanley.

They got into my car, Jerry in the passenger seat, Stanley in back. As we pulled out of the parking lot, I glanced back at Stanley.

"We're going by your house," I said.

Stanley checked his wristwatch. "Now?"

"You need to change out of that tuxedo."

Stanley stared out of the passenger window.

My cell phone rang. I could tell who it was from the caller ID. "Yes?"

I listened for a moment.

"That's not acceptable, Barry," I said. "Your client needs to comply with the judge's order."

He tried to start in again.

"Forget it," I said. "I'll see you in court at two." I pressed End and set the cell phone down.

We drove in silence, Jerry occasionally glancing back at Stanley, who was staring out the side window and moving his neck around in those odd contortions of his. My mother had sensed from her conversation with Stanley's mother that Stanley had had feelings for Sari Bashir. He'd been upset when he learned of her death, although it was beyond me how she could detect that emotion, or any emotion, in Stanley.

We were stopped at a light when Stanley announced, "She was not depressed."

I glanced at him in the rearview mirror. "What do you mean?"

Stanley was staring out the window. He started whistling.

"Stanley?" Jerry said.

Stanley turned toward Jerry and raised his eyebrows.

Jerry said, "What do you mean she wasn't depressed?"

"She was troubled," he said. "More precisely, agitated. But not depressed. Not sad, not melancholic, not despondent."

"When?" I asked.

"The last four days of her life."

"What makes you think that?" I asked.

Stanley rolled his eyes. "It was obvious."

The light changed to green.

"Agitated?" I asked. "About what?"

"Presumably about whatever resulted in her death."

Jerry turned toward Stanley. "She must have been very agitated."

Stanley stared at him.

Jerry shrugged. "You have to be pretty agitated to commit suicide."

Stanley snorted. "Oh, puh-leazse. Do you fail to comprehend, Jerry?"

"What?"

"Sari Bashir did not commit suicide."

I slowed the car and glanced in the rearview mirror. Stanley was squinting and tugging at his black bowtie.

"Then how did she die?" I said.

"How else?"

"Did she slip?" Jerry said.

Stanley gave one of his snorts, which sounded like a dog's bark. "Slipped over a wall two feet high? Not under our current gravitational system."

"What are you saying, Stanley?" I asked.

"Sari Bashir's death was a homicide."

I pulled the car over to the curb and turned to face him. "You think someone killed her?"

Stanley was staring out the window now. He started whistling his tuneless song.

"Murdered?" Jerry said. "Do you have any proof?"

He stopped whistling. "Of course."

"What kind of proof?" I asked.

"The best kind."

"What does that mean?" I asked.

"All in good time. All in good time."

And he started whistling again.

I knew enough not to push Stanley. Jerry made a couple of attempts, but Stanley refused to say anything further.

Chapter Three

Stanley's mother greeted us at the door of her 1950s ranch-style house. Bea Plotkin was a short plump woman in her late sixties. She wore a plaid house dress and white tennis shoes.

"Hello, Mrs. Plotkin," Jerry said.

She gave him a hug, her arms not quite reaching around the big guy's waist.

She turned to me with a big smile. "Rachel, darling. Such a sweetheart."

"Hi, Bea." I leaned over and gave her a kiss on the cheek.

As Stanley went down the hall to change, we followed Bea along the plastic runner over the carpet into the living room.

"Such a tragedy," she said, shaking her head, "and a shanda for her poor father."

Jerry and I were seated on a brown plaid couch that was entirely enclosed in a clear plastic cover that made crinkling noises whenever one of us shifted position. We were facing what Stanley apparently referred to as the Hall of Frames, which included framed photocopies of his brother Harold's diploma from Harvard Medical School, his brother Martin's diploma from the Jewish Theological Seminary, and Stanley's framed Mensa certificate. From the dates on the documents, it was clear that Stanley was the baby brother.

When Stanley appeared in the hallway, he had donned his usual law firm outfit: a short-sleeved dress shirt buttoned all the way to the neck, black pants belted high enough on his waist to expose his argyle socks, and thick-soled black shoes, which he kept buffed to a high shine.

I dropped them off in front of their building. As they came around the front of my car, I rolled down my window.

"Jerry?"

He lumbered over to the window and bent down.

"Yes, ma'am?"

"When do you two break for dinner?"

"Usually around 5:30."

"Where do you go?"

"St. Louis Bread Company."

"I'll meet you there."

"Alright."

"Be sure to tell Stanley I want to see his proof. He needs to bring it with him to the restaurant."

"Yes, Miss Gold."

Chapter Four

Barry Kudar had earned the nickname Barracuda inside the courtroom. This was why he'd been elevated to partner at the venerable Reynolds Price just six years out of law school. It was why, at age thirty-nine, he was on every St. Louis corporate general counsel's short list of litigators for bet-the-company cases. It was why Jimmy O'Brien, the white-haired dean of the plaintiffs' bar, had told him in open court last year, "You are one nasty little prick, Barry, and I mean that as a compliment."

I am quite certain the Barracuda took that as a compliment. Indeed, he acted as if "nasty little prick" was an essential element of his persona. Just check out his photo on his law firm's website. The typical range of lawyer expressions on headshots of law firm bios runs from avuncular smiles to contemplative gazes. In Barry Kudar's photo, he frowns into the camera defiantly, as if channeling Robert DeNiro's Travis Bickle in *Taxi Driver*: "You talkin' to me? You talkin' to me?"

My professional relationship with Barry was hardly collegial. He was an aggressive and obnoxious jerk who turned every conversation into a confrontation. The simple courtesies you expected from opposing counsel—such as consent to a short extension of time due to a family illness or planned vacation—you'd never receive from Barry. You learned early on in a lawsuit with him that every telephone conversation had to be documented with a letter reciting the points discussed, and that your letter would trigger a nasty response disputing your recitation.

A flurry of those back-and-forth letters had brought us today to the afternoon motion docket in Division 2 of the Circuit Court of the City of St. Louis. We were here on my motion to compel the deposition of the Barracuda's client, a prominent heart surgeon that I'd sued for sexual harassment of my client, a nurse at the hospital.

Entering the courtroom, I spotted Barry seated at counsel's table to the left of the bench, scribbling furiously on a legal pad. As usual, he was immaculately attired—today in a navy pinstriped suit, crisp white shirt, navy-and-crimson-striped tie, and gold cufflinks that sparkled in the afternoon sun coming through the courtroom's high windows. His black hair was slicked straight back, which accentuated his angular features and the prominent widow's peak on his forehead.

I took a seat in the front row of the gallery on the right side of the center aisle. There were maybe twenty lawyers in the courtroom for the afternoon motion docket—a few at the two counsel tables, three seated in the jury box, and the rest of us spread around the benches in the gallery. Some were reading newspapers, others were checking messages on their smart-phones, a few were studying court papers, and one elderly male attorney at the end of my row was slumped back on the bench, arms crossed over his chest, sound asleep.

"All rise," the bailiff commanded.

We rose as the door behind the bench opened and Judge Henry Winfield entered. He took his seat in the high leatherback chair behind the bench and nodded toward us.

"Please be seated." He turned to his docket clerk. "Okay, Shirley. Call the first case."

Shirley Garner, his plump, fiftysomething docket clerk, called out, "Browning versus Evans. Defendant's motion to dismiss."

As the lawyers for the parties approached the podium, I opened my briefcase and took out the materials for today's motion.

Twenty minutes later, Shirley announced, "Garcia versus Mason, et al. Plaintiff's motion to compel deposition and for sanctions."

Barry Kudar jumped to his feet and moved quickly to the podium. By the time I joined him, Judge Henry Winfield was leafing through my motion papers. Tall, ruddy, and bald, the judge had played left tackle for the University of Missouri football team in their 1965 Sugar Bowl victory over Florida. The start of many a trial had been delayed as Judge Winfield regaled the trial attorneys with tales of gridiron battles of yore. His chambers were festooned with Tigers memorabilia from his glory days.

Though usually good-natured, Judge Winfield looked up from the papers with a frown. "So you two are still squabbling, eh? Thought we resolved this problem three weeks ago."

"As the Court knows," Barry said, trying to seize control of the argument, "my client is a cardiothoracic surgeon. An esteemed surgeon, I might add. While Miss Gold may think her client's baseless claim for money is the most pressing matter in the world, this Court certainly understands real-world priorities. I would urge Miss Gold to read the final clause in the Court's order. Yes, the Court did order my client to appear at his deposition last week. However, that requirement was, and I quote the Court's order, 'subject to the medical needs of Dr. Mason's patients, which shall take precedence over said deposition.'"

He gave me his best version of a disdainful look, which was somewhat diluted by the fact that I stood two inches taller than him.

He turned back to the judge. "Your Honor, I regret that Miss Gold has wasted all of our time today with yet another discovery motion. May I respectfully suggest that if anyone is deserving of sanctions by the court, it is this lady. Miss Gold needs to be reminded in no uncertain terms that the Court's time and opposing counsel's time are assets not to be squandered."

I'd kept my expression neutral throughout his argument.

I continued to stare at the judge, who turned to me. "Well, Miss Gold? Opposing counsel seems to have a point."

I said, "I assume that opposing counsel has made his point in ignorance of the facts."

"In ignorance?" Barry gave me a snide look and shook his head. "Hardly. I am fully aware of all of the facts."

"In that case, Your Honor, we would request that the court assess sanctions against Dr. Mason *and* his counsel."

Barry turned to me, eyes wide with outrage. "On what possible grounds?"

I continued to gaze at the judge.

"Continue, Ms. Gold," the judge said, leaning forward slightly and rubbing his chin.

"We proposed to depose Mr. Kudar's client last Thursday on the punitive damages issues. Mr. Kudar rejected that date on the ground that, quote, 'the medical needs of his client's patients that day took precedence.' Here is a copy of his letter to me making that contention."

I handed copies of the letter to the judge and Barry, who snatched his copy with a smug grin.

The judge read the two-paragraph letter and looked up. "Okay?"

"My client still works at the hospital," I said. "She told me that Dr. Mason generally takes Thursdays off. When the weather is nice, Dr. Mason plays golf in the morning at St. Louis Country Club. She knows this because Dr. Mason often talks about his golf game in the operating room on Fridays. The weather was nice last Thursday, so on a hunch I drove out to his country club that morning. I parked along the shoulder of a public roadway near one of the greens and waited. I had borrowed a camera with a telephoto lens. I took these shots of Dr. Mason. As you will see, each photograph has an electronic time and date stamp."

I handed one set of three 8 x 10 color photographs to the judge and another to Barry. In the first, Dr. Mason was seated in the golf cart with another man. In the second, he was on the green lining up a putt. In the third, he was laughing in conversation with the other man as they walked back to their golf cart, their putters over their shoulders.

I paused, watching the judge study the photographs. According to the time stamps, the photographs had been taken last Thursday at 10:23 a.m., 10:31 a.m., and 10:42 a.m.

"Because my client still works at the hospital," I said, "she has access to the daily schedule for the operating rooms. Here are copies of those schedules for last Wednesday, Thursday, and Friday."

I handed one set to the judge and another to Barry.

"As Your Honor will see, Dr. Mason had two operations on Wednesday and two on Friday. He had none on Thursday. As the photographs show, on Thursday he was playing golf. Thus, Mr. Kudar's contention is false. There were no medical needs of Dr. Mason's patients last Thursday that took precedence over either his desire to play golf or his obligations under the Court's order."

When Judge Winfield finally looked up, his ruddy complexion was closer to scarlet.

"Your motion will be granted, counsel."

He stared at Barry and shook his head. "How many hours did you spend on your motion, Miss Gold?"

"Counting the trip to the country club, approximately five hours."

"And then your time today. That's another hour of your time that Mr. Kudar and his client have wasted. What is your hourly rate?"

"Four hundred dollars."

"Include in your order an award of sanctions against Dr. Mason *and* his attorney in the amount of two-thousand four-hundred dollars. That is a bargain, Mr. Kudar. You pull these shenanigans again, sir, and I will personally report you to the disciplinary committee."

"Thank you, Your Honor," I said.

"Be sure to include in the order," the judge said, staring at Kudar, "the date for the deposition. That date can be any date you please, Miss Gold. Any date. If the good doctor has to rearrange his schedule to accommodate yours, so be it."

"Thank you, Judge."

"When you've filled out the order, give it to my clerk. And be sure to contact my clerk before the deposition starts. If I'm available that day, I will be happy to rule by telephone on any objections. That'll be all. Next case."

As I took a blank order form over to the counsel's table, Barry stomped out of the courtroom, grumbling under his breath. I couldn't help but smile, even though one of the words he muttered sounded like *grunt* or *runt* but probably was a more pointed reference to me.

Chapter Five

It was close to six that night when I arrived at the downtown St. Louis Bread Company. Stanley and Jerry were at a table near the back. I ordered a hot tea and joined them at their table. Jerry was eating the second of his two turkey sandwiches and second bag of chips. He still had a large cinnamon roll on his tray, along with a large soda. Stanley was finishing a bowl of black bean soup. He also had a chocolate brownie and a glass of milk.

Stanley looked up at me, his eyes distorted behind the thick lenses of his black horn-rimmed glasses.

He set down his spoon. "Per your request, Ms. Gold, I have brought said evidence with me."

"Great. Let me see what you have."

Stanley's backpack was on the ground between his feet. He reached down, opened the backpack, pulled out a zip-lock plastic bag, and set it on the middle of the table. I stared at the bag. It contained two objects: a small tube of Blistex lip balm and a tan peg-like object about two inches long.

I pointed at the tan object. "What is that?"

"Exactly what it appears to be. The heel from a high heel."

I looked at the heel and then at the tube of lip balm and then at Stanley.

"This is your evidence?"

"It is, indeed."

"Evidence of what?"

"Of murder."

"Where did you find these?"

"On the concrete floor on the eighth level of the parking garage. Four spaces down from Ms. Bashir's reserved space."

I lifted the plastic bag and studied the contents in the light. "When?"

"The evening after her death. I went there on my break."

Jerry said, "I didn't know that."

"That is correct."

Jerry asked, "Were the police still up there?"

"Of course not. Her car was gone as well. I presume it was towed to a police lot."

I set the bag down. "What is the connection here with Sari's death?"

"Those items belonged to her."

"Explain the broken heel."

"She wore beige heels on the night of her death."

"And?"

"If she simply jumped off, she would not have broken her heel. Thus we have evidence of a struggle."

I studied the broken heel and then looked at Stanley. "What if she broke her heel climbing over the ledge?"

"That hypothesis is refuted by the Blistex."

"Explain."

"She had a cold sore during her last week."

"So?"

"Blistex is for cold sores."

"And?"

"Good grief, Ms. Gold. It's elementary."

"Then tell me."

He turned to Jerry. "Learned counsel inquires as to how the victim's Blistex ended up on the floor of the garage. Thoughts?"

Jerry frowned as he mulled it over. "It fell out of her purse?"

Stanley nodded. "You are correct."

I said, "Explain."

"Ms. Gold," Stanley said, exasperation in his voice, "the only reason the item fell out of her purse was because her purse was open at the time. Presumably, she was taking out her car keys."

"And that's why her Blistex fell out?"

"Egad, Ms. Gold. Visualize. Ms. Bashir is walking to her car, her purse open, she is rummaging around for her keys, she is attacked, she struggles, and in that struggle her heel breaks off and her Blistex falls out of the purse."

I stared at the Blistex.

Jerry said, "How can you be sure that's her heel?"

"I am."

Jerry took a long sip of his Coke. "I'm not so sure about that, Stanley."

"You are not me."

I said, "Have you mentioned any of this to the police?"

"I have not."

"Maybe you should."

Stanley stared at the plastic bag.

Jerry said, "I could go with you. My uncle was a cop."

"Good idea, Jerry," I said. "Stanley, you need to talk to the police. You need to show them your evidence, ask them your questions, and hear what they say."

Stanley picked up the plastic knife and fork. He leaned over the brownie and, with the concentration of a sushi chef, began cutting thin slices onto the plate.

I stood and looked down at Jerry. I gestured toward the front of the restaurant. "Can we talk a moment?"

Jerry seemed flustered but stood and followed me through the tables toward the entrance.

"I have to get home," I said, my voice low. "I don't know what to make of this. Maybe the police will. Can you take Stanley over to the police station after work? He needs to talk with the detectives who handled the case. Unless their hours have changed, the ones who worked her case should be there tonight, too. Stanley can show them his evidence and ask his questions—or have you ask for him."

Jerry's eyes widened. "Okay, Miss Gold."

"If there's really something there, the cops need to know it. And if not, Stanley needs to know it. Let's see what the detectives say. I'll call you tomorrow."

Chapter Six

"Your eulogy was beautiful," I said.

Malikah Bashir's eyes watered and she looked down at her lap. "Thank you, Miss Gold."

I slid the box of paper tissues across the desk toward her. "Here."

She nodded and took one.

We were in my office the morning after the memorial service. Malikah had called my assistant yesterday afternoon to see if she could come by this morning. She was Sari's first cousin. Their fathers were brothers.

I first met Malikah back when Sari was working for me during her third year of law school. Malikah was then in her senior year at the University of Michigan. She had come to St. Louis to visit her cousin and to interview for graduate school at Washington University, where she was now working on a master's degree in biomedical engineering. She was dark and slender, with shoulder-length black hair. She had on a loose-fitting gray cowl-necked sweater, khaki slacks, and brown penny loafers.

"My Uncle Ameer, Sari's father, asked me to talk to you, Miss Gold. He is very upset. We all are. He has trouble trying to understand his daughter's death. He has tried to talk with the police, with the men who investigated her death, but they have been difficult to talk to."

"How so?"

She shook her head. "I'm not sure. Maybe they are too busy. He is frustrated. He asked me to come meet with you. To see if he could hire you to talk to the police about his daughter's death, to find out about their investigation, to make sure there is no other explanation."

"Does he have a reason to doubt their conclusion?"

She shrugged. "I think he just wants someone here who knows the law, who can ask the police questions about Sari's death, who can help him understand what happened. I think he is just looking for some peace of mind."

I gave her a sad smile. "Understanding what happened may not bring your uncle any peace of mind."

"He probably knows that." She sighed, her eyes watering. "I think he feels he needs to do something, and this is the only thing he can think of."

She wiped her eyes with the tissue.

I leaned back in my chair. The suicide of a loved one is the hardest form of death for a family to accept. Ordinarily, I would have told Malikah to urge her uncle to seek understanding from a religious leader or a grief counselor, and not from a lawyer. But in less than an hour I would be picking up Stanley and Jerry at Stanley's house. The plan was for me to drive them to work while they filled me in on last night's meeting with the police detectives. Maybe I'd have some more information to pass along to Sari's father.

So I told Malikah I would do a little investigating and then talk with her uncle about what I found.

"Oh, Miss Gold, thank you so much. My uncle will be so grateful. He told me to tell you he will mail you a check for your legal fee. Please tell me what that amount will be."

"There'll be no fee, Malikah. I knew Sari. It would be my honor to help answer your uncle's questions. I'm hoping I will be able to give him some sense of closure, perhaps in a day or two."

In a day or two.

Looking back, I can't believe I actually said those words. I suppose I could have instead quoted from my favorite poem by my favorite poet, Seamus Heaney:

History says, Don't hope
On this side of the grave.

Except that passage continues:

But then, once in a lifetime
The longed-for tidal wave
Of justice can rise up,
And hope and history rhyme

So instead I gave her a hug and said good-bye.

Chapter Seven

"Are you shitting me?" Benny said. "You actually sent that whack-job to the cops with a Blistex tube and a broken high heel?"

"He's Stanley Plotkin, Benny. The guy is a genius. Literally. He's convinced she was murdered, and he claims the Blistex and the heel are evidence. I don't understand how his mind works or how those things are evidence of anything. But I'm also not a cop. I told Jerry to take him over to the station after work and talk to the detectives who investigated her death."

Benny chuckled. "I can't even imagine that scene. Like something out of a Monty Python routine."

We were having lunch at Whittemore House, the private faculty club at Washington University. I watched as the waitress and an assistant set down his lunch order, which included two sandwiches—crab cake on a bun, chicken salad on rye—plus a bacon-wrapped beef tenderloin and a side of French fries.

One of Benny's perks was a certain number of free meals with a guest each semester.

I raised my eyebrows. "Does all of that count as just one meal?"

"Very funny, Miss Quiche of the Day. Speaking of which, what the hell is that green crap in there? Parsley?"

"Spinach, and it's delicious."

"Fucking quiche." He shook his head. "Time to man up, Rachel."

I glanced around the dining room. With the exception of my lunch mate, the male faculty members of Washington University had apparently read the memo on how to dress like a male faculty member of Washington University. There was plenty of tweed, a fair number with suede elbow patches and, beneath those jackets, an assortment of turtlenecks and white shirts with bow ties. By contrast, Benny's ample girth today was clothed in a New York Rangers hockey jersey, baggy army pants, and red Chuck Taylor AllStar Hi Tops. Topping off that ensemble was a shaggy Jew-fro in need of a trim. If you want to get away with so scruffy a look at Whittemore House, you better reside in the academic stratosphere with Professor Benjamin Goldberg.

Despite his national reputation in the field of antitrust law, he remains my beloved Benny: fat, foul-mouthed, and ferociously loyal. And my best friend in the whole world. We met as junior associates in the Chicago offices of Abbott & Windsor. A few years later, we both escaped that LaSalle Street sweatshop— Benny to teach law at De Paul, me to go solo as Rachel Gold, Attorney at Law. Different reasons brought us to St. Louis. For me, it was a yearning to live closer to my mother after my father died. For Benny, it was an offer he couldn't refuse from the Washington University Law School.

"So," he said, "did he change their minds?"

I shook my head. "What Stanley viewed as evidence of murder they viewed as evidence of suicide."

"Such as?"

"Apparently, the two most common crimes in parking garages at night are robbery and rape. Neither happened to Sari. Her credit cards were still in her purse, along with eighty-three dollars in cash, all of which landed near her on the ground below. Her underwear was in place and there were no signs of sexual activity, forced or otherwise. According to the police, that showed she hadn't been killed by someone trying to rob or rape her. I talked to the detectives myself yesterday."

"What's Stanley say about that?"

"He claims those facts are equally consistent with a homicide motivated by something other than rape or robbery." I took a bite of my quiche. "There was no suicide note."

"Really?"

"The police couldn't find one, and they did a thorough search. No note in her apartment, in her office, on her computer, in her email, on her Facebook page, on her body, in her car. Nowhere."

"Is that significant?"

"Stanley thinks so, but the detectives told me that many people kill themselves without leaving a suicide note."

"So what about Stanley's evidence?"

"They confirmed that the heel on her left shoe was missing and that Stanley had found the missing heel. They're going to run the prints on the Blistex tube, but they said the results won't change their conclusion."

"Why not?"

"Their view is that things can fall out of an open purse, especially if she was in the process of climbing over the barrier. If you're about to kill yourself and a tube of lip balm falls out of your purse, why would you even care?"

"What's Stanley say?"

"In his scenario, she's walking to her car and looking in her purse for her keys when she's attacked. The tube falls out during the struggle and rolls under another car."

Benny shook his head. "I know you say this guy is smart, but does he really think a broken heel and a Blistex tube are proof of murder?"

"He views them as corroborating evidence."

"Corroborating what?"

"That she wasn't depressed or suicidal."

"And what's that based on?"

I sighed. "Her face."

"Her face?"

"Yes." I smiled. "To quote Stanley, 'I can assure you, Ms. Gold, that the orbicularis oris never lies.'"

"Who?"

"Not who. What. The orbicularis oris is apparently a facial muscle."

Benny stared at me. "A what?"

"I'm serious. Stanley is the idiot savant of facial muscles."

"What the hell is a facial muscle?"

"Normal people can tell whether someone is happy or sad or angry just by looking at their face. People with Stanley's autism problem can't. They can't read other people's emotions and moods. It causes all kinds of problems for them. According to his mom, a few years ago a doctor gave Stanley a chart of facial expressions. It's a chart created specifically for people with his problem. It shows a set of six or so basic facial expressions, and each one is labeled. So there's Happy and Sad and Angry and Scared. The goal is to help people like Stanley recognize the emotional states of people around them."

"Okay."

"The chart fascinated Stanley. He started doing research and learned all about FACS, which is an acronym for the Facial Action Coding System."

"What the hell is that?"

"From what I understand, FACS is a whole field of study. It identifies every muscle in your face and assigns an action code for each possible contraction or relaxation of one or more of those muscles. There are something like two dozen facial muscles and more than a hundred action codes, and hundreds of possible combinations. There's this famous FACS manual. It's more than five hundred pages long, and you can apparently use it to identify every possible emotion and mental state. For example, there are certain action codes for a genuine, involuntary smile, and other action codes for a fake one, like when a photographer tells you to smile."

"What's the purpose of all that?"

"Apparently, there are lots of purposes. Psychotherapists use the manual when they treat patients. The FBI uses it to train its interrogators so they can spot when someone is lying. Software companies use it to develop facial recognition systems. Even Hollywood uses it in their computer graphic animations to make their cartoon characters seem more realistic. Like the Na'vi in the movie *Avatar*. James Cameron is a big fan of FACS."

"And Stanley Plotkin uses it?"

I nodded. "He has a copy of the manual and studies it every day. Sometimes for hours, according to his mother."

"Does it work for him?"

"He's pretty observant, Benny. I'll give you an example. The night before last, Jerry and Stanley met with the two police detectives that handled Sari's death. I met with the same two yesterday. One of them is young and cocky—a red-headed guy named Rob Hendricks. You know the type. Top three buttons of his shirt open, thick gold chain underneath. The other detective—Harry Gibbs—is in his sixties, bald, bags under his eyes, low key, white short-sleeve shirt, and narrow black tie. I spent maybe thirty minutes with them yesterday. Afterward, I asked Stanley what he'd noticed about them. He told me that Hendricks was insecure and struggling with homosexual urges."

Benny laughed. "No shit?"

"I didn't ask him how he knew that stuff because I was more curious how he had concluded that Gibbs, the older one, was recently divorced and a recovering alcoholic. He told me that his first clue was when Hendricks made some crude joke about marital sex. He said Gibbs responded with a forced, voluntary smile. That indicated tension on the subject of marriage, which caused Stanley to study the ring finger on his left hand, where he detected what he said were superficial tissue scarring and skin color differentiation. He said that the scarring and color differentiation would have been caused by a ring that had been in place for years. From those two facts, he claimed you could infer that Detective Gibbs had been married and that the marriage had ended within the recent past. He said that the scarring and skin color would have been much harder to detect if the marriage had ended, say, five years ago."

"Jeez." Benny sat back in his chair. "And the alcoholism?"

"That was more observation than facial action codes. He told me that the whites of Detective Gibbs' eyes were a little yellow, which apparently is a sign of swelling of the liver, which he said is a symptom of alcoholism. That was confirmed, he claimed, by the redness of the detective's nose and cheeks, which were caused by broken capillaries. He said that's another symptom of alcoholism." I smiled and shrugged. "He's good at it, Benny."

"Damn, I'd like to meet this dude. Maybe take him along to a singles bar. Help me hone in on optimal targets of conversation."

"There's a vision."

"Hey, you're talking to a visionary."

"I'm telling you, Benny, Stanley's no fool. He's convinced that Sari was murdered." I shrugged. "I'm kind of leaning toward giving him the benefit of the doubt."

"Why?"

"He sees things that others don't. I spoke with Sari's father this morning. I didn't tell him about Stanley, but I promised him I'd do a little poking around, make sure there was no reason to doubt the official version of her death."

"But who would want to kill her?"

"I have no idea."

"Does Stanley?"

"Actually, he does."

"Who?"

"Someone in that law firm."

"No shit. Who?"

I shook my head. "He doesn't know. But he's convinced someone in the law firm killed her."

"What's the motive?"

"He doesn't know."

Benny finished off his second sandwich, took a big gulp of his iced tea, and sat back and stared at me. He shook his head.

"What?" I said.

"Listen to yourself. You've got some mailroom kook with a handbook on facial expressions and a tube of Blistex who claims that a confirmed suicide is really a homicide committed by someone in her firm for some unknown reason. You know what that sounds like?"

"Tell me."

"The start of the worst Nancy Drew mystery of all time."

I smiled. "I didn't know you were a Nancy Drew fan."

"Not exactly a fan. My sister had an entire bookshelf of them. I read a few when I got bored."

"I loved Nancy Drew," I said. "She was my hero in grade school."

"I dug her, too. Hot bod."

"Benny."

"Speaking of hot bods."

"Benny."

"Hey, I'm not the one at this table with the all-world tush. Not to say that mine isn't cute, albeit in need of a little manscaping. So tell me: which was your favorite Nancy Drew story?"

"Hmm." I leaned back in my chair, trying to remember. "One I really liked was when she goes to Scotland and ends up in that creepy old castle."

"Ah, yes, *The Clue of the Whistling Bagpipes*. Not a bad tale."

I stared at him. "I can't believe this, Benny."

"What?"

"How long have we known each other? Fifteen years? I never knew you read Nancy Drew mysteries."

"Girl, my hidden talents have charmed women around the globe. You have no idea. I have mad skills. To quote the great Walter Sobchak: 'You want a toe? I can get you a toe, believe me…Hell, I can get you a toe by three o'clock this afternoon—with nail polish.'"

"What are you talking about?"

He gave me a wink. "And trust me, when I say that this scenario of yours—you and that whacko and his tube of Blistex—when I say that sounds like the start of a bad Nancy Drew mystery, I know what I'm talking about."

I shrugged. "Don't forget, Benny, those mysteries always ended happily."

"Don't forget, Rachel, those mysteries were also works of fiction."

Chapter Eight

At ten o'clock that evening, Jerry Klunger and I walked into the main lobby of the Chouteau Tower. Tommy Flynn was seated in his usual spot at the security station in the front lobby. He had just shuffled the cards and was dealing a new game of solitaire when he saw the huge figure of Jerry Klunger approaching.

"Hello there, big guy."

"Evening, Mr. Flynn."

Tommy turned to me. "Ma'am."

I put my hand out. "Mr. Flynn, my name is Rachel Gold." We shook.

"Pleased to meet you, Miss Gold."

"Call me Rachel."

He grinned. "And you can call me Tommy."

He checked his wristwatch and leaned back to look up at Jerry. "Thought you boys got off at nine."

"We did, sir. I came back with Miss Gold. We were hoping to have a word with you."

"With me?" His eyes narrowed. "About what?"

Jerry looked around the empty lobby. "It's about Sari."

"She was a good gal." He shook his head sadly. "What about her?"

"Well." Jerry paused. "Stanley's got some doubts. I guess we all do. Miss Gold knew her, too."

"Doubts about what?"

Jerry took another glance around the lobby and leaned in closer. In almost a whisper, he said, "About how she died."

Tommy studied Jerry, who towered over the security desk, and then glanced at me. He checked his watch.

"Time for a smoke break. How 'bout you two keep me company?"

I followed Jerry and Tommy out of the building. Although our destination was a small plaza with a fountain just a block west of their building, to describe their walk as a stroll would mischaracterize both of their gaits. Tommy Flynn had the stiff, bowlegged stride of an arthritic man in need of two knee replacements. Jerry moved with the lumbering tread that had apparently earned him the nickname Sumo from the law firm's mailroom manager, Tony Manghini.

I was getting too old for these late-night rendezvous, I told myself. Fortunately, I'd been able to get home for dinner and had enough time to give my son Sam a bath, read him a book, and put him to bed before leaving the house to pick up Jerry. The babysitter tonight, as most nights, was my mother, who lives in the remodeled carriage house in back.

When we reached the plaza, Tommy took a seat on a bench facing the Chouteau Tower. Jerry and I sat on the bench opposite Tommy.

Tommy Flynn was the deliberate type, a man you don't try to rush. And since I was here to ask him a favor, I let him take his time. I watched as he lit a Camel cigarette with a brass lighter, inhaled the smoke deeply, held it a moment, and then blew it out in a thin stream that whirled and vanished in the night breeze.

"So," he said, "tell me about these doubts."

I glanced at Jerry. I'd explained to Jerry that he should try to take the lead, at least early on, since he was the one who had the relationship with Tommy Flynn.

Jerry said, "Stanley thinks Sari was murdered."

"What's he base that on?"

"He believes he found some evidence up in the garage, and he believes the police confirmed his evidence."

"Hold on, Jerry." Tommy turned to me. "Has anyone talked to the police?"

"Jerry and Stanley two nights ago," I said. "I followed up yesterday."

"Who?"

Jerry told him their names.

Tommy frowned. "Don't remember any Hendricks. Probably after my time. I know Harry Gibbs. You say he's a detective now, eh?"

Jerry said, "Yes, sir."

"*Detective* Harry Gibbs." Tommy chuckled. "Harry's a good man, but not exactly the sharpest knife in the drawer. So fill me in on your meeting, Jerry."

Jerry told him about the broken-off heel and the tube of Blistex and the information from the police report about Sari's wallet and her underwear and body.

Tommy flicked away the cigarette butt, pulled a new one out of the crumpled pack, and said, "Seems consistent with a suicide."

He lit the cigarette, exhaled the smoke through his nose in twin streams, and turned to me. "What's Stanley say?"

"He says it proves she was killed by someone who knew her."

"Who?"

"Someone in the law firm."

"Who?"

"He doesn't know," I said. "None of us do. That's why I wanted to talk to you."

Tommy's eyebrows rose. "You think I know?"

I smiled. "No. But I think you have access to information that might help move this forward and maybe even put Stanley's concerns to rest."

"Hold on. What else does Stanley have? Beside that heel and the Blistex?"

"He says she wasn't depressed."

"Really? Did they talk much?"

"No," I said.

Tommy frowned and took another drag on his cigarette. "Then how does he know she wasn't depressed?"

I gave him the short version of the FACS system.

When I finished, Jerry added, "Stanley has these pictures tacked up on the wall of his cubicle. They're kind of gross. Drawings of people's faces, but with the skin removed and all these arrows with the names of each muscle."

Tommy scratched his neck and nodded. "I remember those drawings. My last year on the force they had some FBI special agent give us a lecture on that FACS thing. Crazy stuff. Stanley's into that, eh?"

"Yes," I said, "and it seems to work for him."

Tommy raised his eyebrows. "How so?"

"You said you know Harry Gibbs?"

"Sure. We go way back."

"Jerry did all the talking during their meeting with the detectives, which lasted less than an hour. Stanley just observed. When it was over, he'd concluded that Gibbs was a recovering alcoholic who'd been recently divorced."

Tommy stared at me, lips pursed, and then he nodded. "Harry did have a drinking problem. That's how we met. Department made us both attend AA meetings at headquarters. Heard he got divorced last year. Stanley figured all that out, eh? What did he see in Sari?"

"That she wasn't depressed. She was agitated but not depressed."

Tommy squinted. "Pretty thin."

He flicked the cigarette butt away and checked his watch. "Gotta head back."

Tommy winced as he got to his feet.

As we started back down the sidewalk, he said, "So what's Stanley think I can do for you, Rachel?"

"I understand everyone in the firm parks in the garage. After seven at night, you have to use your keycard to access the walkway to the garage."

"That's correct."

"I assume there's a computer record for each night's keycard users, correct?"

"Yep."

"We'd like to see the records for whoever used their keycard the night she died. Especially between nine and eleven. That's the medical examiner's estimate for the time of death. She was wearing a wristwatch that shattered in the fall. The time on the watch was 10:03, which is probably the time she died."

"Between nine and eleven? It's probably just going to be people in that law firm. Only lawyers work that late."

"Correct."

Tommy stopped and turned toward me with a frown. "You understand these computer records aren't public documents."

"I do, and I could get a subpoena for them if I had to, but I'd prefer to keep this confidential."

"And why is that?"

"I knew Sari. Her father asked me to ask some questions about her death. The cops have concluded it was a suicide. Stanley believes otherwise. The cops have closed the matter, and they've pretty much dismissed Stanley's evidence. Was it a suicide? I don't know. I'm just trying to wrap up loose ends. One of those loose ends is the computer records of the cardkey users that night."

He rubbed his chin.

"You're asking a lot, young lady."

"I realize I am. Here's my card.

He held my card out toward the streetlight and studied it for a moment. Then he put it in his pants pocket

We started again toward his building, which was less than a block away. As we walked, I thought again about what Stanley had told me to say to Tommy. He hadn't told me why—just what. When we reached the entrance, Tommy turned to me.

"I'll think about your request, Rachel. No promises."

"I understand, Tommy. One more thing. It's what Stanley asked me to tell you. He told me to tell you that when you think about Sari Bashir you should also think about Mary Liz."

Tommy stared at me, his gaze growing distant. And then, without a word, he turned and entered the building.

Chapter Nine

We met the following afternoon at Kaldi's Coffee in the DeMun area. Just Tommy Flynn and me. He'd called that morning and left a message with my secretary that he'd be there at four-thirty.

He was at a small table in the back room when I arrived. I got an espresso and joined him. His shift started at six, and he was dressed for work—a nickel-gray long-sleeve shirt with epaulets, pleated-patch pockets with flaps, a security officer patch over the left pocket, black tie, black slacks, and thick-soled black shoes. With his shock of gray hair, bushy eyebrows, round face, and double chin, he reminded me of John Madden, the NFL color commentator and former football coach.

"Here you go," he said, handing me a two-page document. He had another copy on the table in front of him.

There were three handwritten columns of information. The first column was a list of twenty-nine names in what appeared to be chronological order—sixteen on the first page, thirteen on the second. The second column was titled "Time of Entry." The third column was labeled "Time of Exit."

"The walkway from the building to the garage locks at seven," Tommy said. "You need your cardkey to open that door after seven. Every time you swipe that card, the computer records it. I printed out the card-swipes for that night and put together this document. It shows all the folks who entered the walkway to the garage between seven and midnight that night."

According to the list, fourteen people entered the walkway to the garage between seven and eight p.m. I recognized the names of some of the lawyers from Warner & Olsen.

"These first fourteen, are they all lawyers, paralegals, and secretaries from Warner & Olsen?"

Tommy looked down at his copy.

"All but Melanie Farmer," he answered. "She's a young lawyer at Mead and London. Pretty gal with nice stems. Reminds me a little of Cyd Charisse."

Mead & London was a small personal-injury law firm in the building.

Each of the fourteen who entered the walkway between seven and eight had exited the garage within ten minutes of the time they entered. Same with the two—both lawyers at Warner & Olsen—who entered between eight and nine.

As for the last thirteen names, all listed on the second page of the document, there were entry times but no exit times.

"Why is that?" I asked.

Tommy said, "The gate at the garage exit slides down each night at nine. You don't need your cardkey after that. Instead, the gate is triggered by an electric eye. When a car approaches the exit, it passes the electric eye and the gate slides up. So there's no record for anyone who drives out of the garage after nine."

"But you still need your cardkey to drive into the garage after nine p.m.?"

"That's right. It's the only way you can get in after nine."

I studied the list. "So no one entered the garage after nine that evening."

"No one drove into the garage after nine. Actually, no one drove into the garage after seven. I checked."

I looked at the first seven entries on the second page—all names of persons who'd entered the walkway from the office to the garage between nine and eleven that night:

Name	Time of Entry to Walkway	Time of Exit
Sharon Faraday	9:12 pm	?
Susan O'Malley (8)	9:23 pm	?
Rob Brenner (7)	9:29 pm	?
Donald Warner (6)	9:35 pm	?
Sari Bashir (8)	9:48 pm	
Brian Teever (6)	9:52 pm	?
Bernetta Johnson	10:18 pm	?

"What are the numbers after some of the names?" I asked.

"All lawyers at Warner & Olson have reserved parking spaces. So do some of their administrative staff. Those numbers are the garage floors where their reserved space is located."

Thus, five of the seven people on the list, including Sari Bashir, were lawyers who parked in reserved parking spaces.

Tommy leaned across the table so that he was looking at the same page I was. "You can tell Stanley to eliminate Sharon and Bernetta from this list. I escort both of those nice ladies to their cars each night, and I always wait there until I see them drive down the exit ramp. Did the same that night."

The last six names on the list all entered the walkway after eleven that night, the last two were between midnight and one in the morning. All six were associates at Warner & Olsen.

He leaned back in his chair and gestured at the list. "There you have it, Miss Gold. Five lawyers entered the parking garage from the building between nine and ten that night. One of them died."

I stared at the names.

"So," he said, "what's your next move?"

I looked up. "I don't know."

He took a sip of his coffee and set it down on the table.

"I appreciate you meeting me here, ma'am."

"I appreciate you tracking down those names, Tommy."

"I've been doing some more thinking about Stanley's theory. It does seem far-fetched, but you can't dismiss it out of hand. He's a strange boy, for sure. A strange and troubled boy, but he's also one observant son of a bitch, pardon my French."

"He is."

"He told you to mention Mary Liz to me. Did he tell you who she was?"

"No."

"I've never told him about Mary Liz. Far as I know, I haven't talked about that poor girl for a long time."

"Tell me about her."

"She was the oldest of five McGuire daughters. Our next-door neighbors back then. Known her from the day her parents brought her home from the hospital. There'd been something special about Mary Liz from the get go. Maybe it was because she was the first. Or because she was so damn cute. Or because she'd been born just a month after Muriel's final miscarriage."

"Muriel was your wife?"

"A fine woman. She passed four years ago."

Mary Liz had been special, Tommy explained. He'd helped her father coach her soccer team in elementary school, Tommy had taken her fishing a few times over the years, and on Halloween nights when her parents had been too busy with younger sisters in diapers, he'd taken her trick-or-treating in the neighborhood.

"On her prom night," he said, "me and Muriel came over to take pictures before the kids headed out. I can remember marveling at how that little pigtailed, freckle-faced redhead had grown into such a lovely young woman."

The last time he saw her was on the morning her family drove her to Iowa to start her freshman year at Beloit. "I gave her a hug just before she got into the station wagon. She told me she'd see me again at Thanksgiving. As they pulled out of the driveway, she poked her head out the car window and said, 'I call the drumstick, Uncle Tommy.'"

He paused and wiped an eye with the back of his hand. After a moment, he continued.

"Those were her last words to me. Her funeral was closed casket, probably because she'd been dead for nearly two weeks when a pair of hikers came upon her body in the woods two miles from campus. According to the medical examiner, she'd been raped and sodomized before being stabbed to death. The McGuires sold their house the following spring and moved to Wisconsin." He looked up at me, eyes red. "Never caught her killer."

I waited.

He shook his head. "Never told Stanley none of that. Never even mentioned her name. I suppose he could have read it about in the papers. It was big news back when it happened. But that was twelve years ago."

"I read the articles this morning," I said. "They're in the newspaper's online archives."

"And?"

"One of the articles mentioned her home address. Do you still live next door to that house?"

He nodded.

I said, "The article on the funeral mentioned that you were one of the pallbearers and that you were a close family friend. It also mentioned that you were a St. Louis police officer."

"Anything else?"

"No."

He nodded. "If that boy can really read faces, maybe he saw something in mine that caused him to go back and find those articles. Like that stuff he figured out with old Harry Gibbs—the drinking and divorce and all."

"It's convinced him that Sari was murdered."

He pursed his lips as he mulled over something.

He gestured toward the list. "That list probably looks a lot like the list from any weeknight. But let's assume it contains four genuine homicide suspects. Persons of interest, we used to call them."

He took a sip of coffee and set the mug down.

"Let me cut to the chase," he said. "The police have closed the case. That means Stanley and Jerry can't expect help from them. That's big. They can't *make* anyone talk to them, they can't *make* anyone turn over evidence, and they sure as hell can't arrest anyone."

He paused to take another sip of his coffee.

"And then," he said, "there's the matter of the boys themselves. Jerry is a fine young lad with a good heart and good soul, but some of the tasks ahead are above that boy's pay grade. As for Stanley, well, this kind of investigation requires someone who can actually get folks to talk. When it comes to conversing, I think you'd agree that Stanley is not exactly Jay Leno."

I smiled. "Agreed."

Tommy said, "I admit those boys have me intrigued. But I don't add much value to any investigation. I'm not just an old fart with bad knees and arthritis, which anyone can see, but as for investigations, keep in mind I spent more than three decades on the force and never made detective grade. Now some of that may have been due to my drinking problems, which I have under control these days, and some of that may have been due to what one of my superiors described on my evaluation form as, quote, *authority issues*, unquote. To which I responded at the time, to his face, 'Captain, go fuck yourself,' which kind of set me back on the promotion ladder. Excuse my French, Miss—er, Rachel. My point here is that the addition of one retired cop named Tommy Flynn don't exactly transform that investigative crew into the A-Team."

He leaned back on his chair and gestured with open arms.

"There you have it," he said.

"Okay."

Tommy said, "All of which means one thing."

"What?"

"Them boys need a rabbi."

"Pardon?"

"Again, I go back to my days on the force. You wanted to get something done, you had to go get yourself an ally higher up. We used to call that fellow a rabbi, though I never figured out the resemblance to a Jewish preacher, but be that as it may, I'm assuming it's the same in a law firm. You got some heavy hitters on this list, and that means that even if them boys come up with a good idea for investigating, they're going to need a rabbi to sell it to the big dogs. You still following me?"

I smiled. "You think I'm the rabbi?"

He shrugged. "Seems to me you could be."

Part 2

Happy law firms are all alike; every unhappy law firm is unhappy in its own way.

Tony Manghini
Manager of Office Support Services
Warner & Olsen, LLP

Chapter Ten

Dick Neeler grinned and nodded. "I love it."

It had taken me three days to get to his office—three days of brainstorming and meetings and phone calls. Lots of phone calls. But here we were—Benny Goldberg as the spokesperson for Washington University's School of Law, me as the attorney for Sari Bashir's family, and Jerry Klunger as the designated representative of the law firm's staff.

Dick Neeler was a partner in the firm's intellectual property group. He and I had occasionally sparred over copyright disputes, although we'd always been courteous with each other. But more crucial for my purposes today, Neeler was on the Warner & Olsen marketing committee and, even better, chair of the firm's hiring committee, which meant he oversaw the firm's efforts to recruit new lawyers.

Law firms headquartered in St. Louis have learned that despite their national aspirations—Warner & Olsen's slogan: "Midwest Values, Global Reach"—their best hiring prospects are local. While, yes, the occasional Harvard or Stanford graduate might opt to return to St. Louis, usually for family reasons, it was far more efficient for St. Louis firms to focus their recruiting efforts on St. Louis law schools and the University of Missouri in Columbia. Thus it was best to appoint a hiring chair who could connect to those students.

Dick Neeler was the ideal choice. First, his persona was just right: he was a relentlessly affable and totally nonthreatening balding guy in his late thirties who had started his career at Warner & Olsen as a summer clerk and was absolutely convinced that there was no finer law firm on the planet. He reminded you of the rush chair at a college fraternity, which is actually what he had been, according to one of the framed photos on his wall. Just as important, Dick Neeler had the right academic pedigree for the job. He was a graduate of the Washington University School of Law, taught an advanced trademark seminar at St. Louis University, and was a fanatic Mizzou sports fan, having gone there as an undergrad. He was a past president of the Tiger Club of St. Louis and drove a custom gold-and-black Lexus with University of Missouri alumni license plates.

Neeler was, in short, the perfect tool for getting the law firm's higher-ups to approve the Sari Bashir tribute video proposal. Better yet, he was sufficiently clueless to serve as the figurehead for the project without ever suspecting any ulterior motive.

"This is super," Neeler said. "A beautiful homage to her and, frankly, a terrific opportunity for the firm. Great idea, Rachel."

I gestured toward Jerry Klunger, whose massive body was squeezed into the chair on my right. "Jerry is a big part of this."

"Nice work, big man," Neeler said, pronouncing it *big mon*, for some reason that he must have assumed sounded hip.

Jerry blushed. "Thank you, Mr. Neeler."

"And obviously," I said, nodding toward Benny, "the law school is on board."

"Professor," Neeler said, pointing his index finger at Benny and giving him a wink, "you da man."

Benny simply nodded, his expression neutral. To say I'd been nervous about bringing him to this meeting was an understatement. I'd tried to make Benny understand that his assessment of Neeler—"a total fucking douchebag"—was actually a good thing for us. But Benny has what charitably could be described as filter issues—issues that date back at least to his infamous deposition incident when we were both young associates at Chicago's Abbott & Windsor. He had gotten fed up with opposing counsel's constant objections. Finally, after yet another objection,

Benny got to his feet, leaned across the table, and informed his opponent *on the record*: "If you open that pie hole of yours one more time today, Norman, I am going to rip off your head and shit in your lungs." That portion of the deposition transcript became Exhibit A to the other side's motion for sanctions, and, ultimately, an urban legend of the Chicago Bar.

Neeler said, "Oh, boy, this really hits a home run with our diversity goals, too. A tribute for an Arab associate. Like, wowie wow wow, eh?"

"She was an American citizen," I said.

"Sure, but she was also Muslim. Allah and all that nutty stuff. It works. Believe me, it works like a charm. Allah akbar."

With his nodding and grinning and rocking back and forth, all Neeler needed was a yarmulke and *tallis* to pass for a crazed Orthodox Jew at prayer.

"So her father's already on board, eh?" Neeler asked.

"I spoke with him yesterday," I said. "He was touched by the idea. He wants to help. He said he would ask Sari's relatives to participate, too."

"That is totally awesome, Rachel. Totally!"

He leaned back in his chair, smiling. "If we can have this video ready before the hiring season next fall, think of the killer PR for the firm. And not just locally. We can have our marketing folks get that baby out to the legal press—*Above The Law*, *The Wall Street Journal Law Blog*, *The American Lawyer*. Grab ourselves some national coverage with this bad boy. Unbelievable."

I forced a smile. "Nice."

I had to wonder about the actual recruiting value of the video. Especially if Sari's death remained a suicide. What kind of message did that send? "Warner & Olsen—A Law Firm To Die For." Or maybe "Warner & Olsen—Til Death Do Us Part"?

In as deferential a voice as I could muster, I asked, "What do you recommend we do next, Dick?"

Neeler leaned forward and rubbed his hands together. "Your timing is perfect. Better than perfect. The executive committee meets the day after tomorrow."

He leaned back and pointed his thumbs at this chest. "Yours truly is on the agenda. I'm scheduled to make a presentation on next year's recruiting strategies. You've given me the featured item. I'll work up a budget, present it at the meeting, and by next week I'm hoping we'll have this sexy baby green-lighted. Oh, yeah." He leaned forward, eyes wide. "Lights, camera, action, dawg!"

Chapter Eleven

"Dawg?" Benny said.

I shrugged.

"A total fucking douchebag," he said.

"But he's our douchebag," I said. "If he can sell this project to the higher-ups, that's a big step forward."

"But just one step."

"I know."

"Still, the guy is a piece of work. And the name? Dick Neeler? Are you kidding me? Dick, meet my friend Jack Meoff. Are you any relation to Pat Maweiny?"

We entered the garage from the walkway—the same one Sari entered on her last night, the same one for which Tommy Flynn had generated the data for that night. This was mid-afternoon, though, and you didn't need a cardkey to enter.

At the garage exit down below, I handed the ticket to the attendant, who confirmed that it had been stamped by Warner & Olsen and raised the gate.

"So, Rabbi Gold, what's next?"

"Let's first see if Neeler can deliver. Then we can figure out the best way to proceed."

Neither Sari's father nor the dean of the law school knew the other reason behind the tribute video. As far as either man knew, the sole goal was to create a mini-documentary celebrating Sari's life and featuring interviews with friends, family, and colleagues. What they didn't know was that those colleagues would include the four lawyers from the firm who had entered the garage from the walkway after nine p.m. that night. Nor did they know that another goal of the tribute video was to capture those four lawyers on video answering certain specific questions prepared by Stanley Plotkin.

"So where do you stand?" Benny asked. "Are you a true believer?"

"I'm still an agnostic. I'm looking for closure more than anything else."

"Even if it turns out to be exactly what the cops concluded?"

"If the doubts are resolved, I'm okay. I like the idea of getting those four lawyers on video for Stanley to study."

I shrugged. "But if at the end of the process, at the conclusion of whatever might qualify as our investigation, I'll be happy if all we have is a beautiful tribute to Sari for her family and friends."

"Your video idea is brilliant," Benny said. "To quote that douchebag, 'better than perfect,' dawg. But I'm hoping for your sake the result confirms suicide. You start turning up some suspicious shit, girl, and you could find yourself in some deep shit."

"To quote you: 'one step at a time.'"

I turned onto the Forest Park Expressway.

"Speaking of pieces of work," Benny said, "your buddy Stanley Plotkin is one helluva piece of work."

"True."

I smiled at the memory of the meeting I'd convened that morning to introduce Benny to Stanley and Jerry. Although I set the meeting at Stanley's house in the hope that it would put him at ease, he stood throughout the meeting and stared at the bookcase until, near the end, Benny said, "Stanley, I understand you're a fan of facial actions, eh?"

Stanley leaned back from the book case, stretched his neck, and turned toward Benny.

"If by the term *fan*," he said in a loud nasal voice, "you have in mind an enthusiastic and raucous devotee, typically an emotionally fervent spectator at a sporting or cultural event, or an ardent and often obsessive admirer of a celebrity, such as that Kardashian woman with the enormous gluteus maximus, or a genre, such as science fiction, then no, Professor Goldberg, I am not a fan of the Facial Action Coding System. I am, however, intrigued by the system and what it reveals about human nature and emotions. I am an admirer, albeit not at the zealous level, of Paul Ekman and Wallace V. Friesen, who created the most comprehensive version of the coding system. The current version of their manual includes an additional author contributor, one Joseph C. Hager. Nathan Sanford, however, received no credit, and perhaps deserves none. Interesting, however, that his namesake received thirty electoral college votes in the 1834 election, losing out to John C. Calhoun, who received 182 votes."

To which Benny had replied, after a long pause, "Sorry I asked."

I took the Washington U exit to the law school and pulled up to the entrance

"You're coming to dinner, right?" I said.

"Your mom's making her stuffed cabbage, right?"

"Just for you, boychik."

"Oh, my God. Just thinking about it is giving me a chubby."

"Out of the car. You are truly disgusting. See you at six."

Chapter Twelve

Tonight it was Sam's latest favorite bedtime book, William Steig's *Sylvester and the Magic Pebble*. I'd read it to him each night for at least the last three weeks.

"...'Mr. Duncan put the magic pebble in an iron safe.'"

I paused and glanced over at Sam, who was staring at the page as he pressed his blankie against his cheek. The illustration showed Sylvester Duncan, a donkey, curled up on the couch, eyes closed, in the embrace of his mother and father.

"'Some day they might want to use it,'" I read, "'but really, for now, what more could they wish for? They all had all that they wanted.'"

I closed the book and reached over to turn off the lamp. I kissed my son on his forehead and then again on his nose.

"I love you, Sammy," I whispered.

"I love you, too, Mommy."

I turned toward Yadi, who was in his usual bedtime spot, curled up on the comforter at the foot of Sam's bed. Yadi jogged with me in the morning and walked with me before bedtime, but the rest of his life was devoted to Sam. He was our four-year-old collie-shepherd mix. He had one straight German shepherd ear, one floppy collie ear, and a sweet and gentle temperament unless you were a stranger approaching Sam or me, at which point he transformed into a truly intimidating junkyard attack guard.

"Good night, Yadi," I whispered.

He looked up, thumped his tail twice, and settled back down with a sigh.

I gave Sam a hug. "Sleep tight, little guy."

As I came down the stairs, I could hear Benny and my mother in the kitchen.

"So maybe he is a genius," Benny was saying. "But he's also totally wacky. A real nut job."

"He has problems," my mother said. "Such a sad situation. His two older brothers would make a mother proud. One is a doctor, the other a rabbi. Who could ask for more? And then there's poor Stanley. Barely got through high school because of all of his tsuris. But a smart boy, Benny, and not just with that Electoral College stuff. He knows classical music like the back of his hand. And zip codes? You have no idea. I'm telling you, he could teach that Alex Trebek a thing or two."

"Alex Trebek, eh? There's a universal standard. Jesus, Sarah, no one needs to know fucking zip codes. That's why Al Gore invented the Internet. I've met Stan the Man. He's meshuggah. Just because you play mahjong with his mother is no reason to let him anywhere near Rachel. Now he's got her in the middle of his craziness."

"What craziness?" I asked with a smile as I walked into the kitchen.

Benny rolled his eyes. "The evils of mahjong."

I joined them at the kitchen table, where Benny had already consumed almost an entire platter of my mother's kamishbroidt, a crunchy Yiddish cousin of the Italian *biscotti*.

My mother held up a teacup and saucer. "Some tea, doll baby?"

"Sure. Thanks."

She poured me a cup of tea.

I took a bite of a kamishbroidt. "Mmmm. Delicious."

It had been four years since Jonathan—my husband, Sam's father—died in a plane crash. My mother, God bless her, quit her job and moved in to help me raise Sam and my two step-daughters, Leah and Sarah. Eventually, my mother sold her condo and moved into our coach house in back. Leah is now a junior at Brandeis University, and Sarah is a freshman at Wisconsin. Although the two girls call me Rachel, all three of my kids call my mother Baba, which is Yiddish for grandmother. Their Baba is hard-headed and opinionated and sets high standards for her grandchildren. Don't ask the girls how many times their red-headed Bobba made them rewrite their college application essays. Though she can exasperate me like no other human on the face of the earth, we all adore her. Even me.

She plays bridge on Monday nights, mahjong on Tuesday, poker on Thursdays, and works out three days a week at the J, where she has her own fan club of suitors among the retirees who exercise there. The feisty Widow Gold the Elder has already turned down close to a dozen marriage proposals.

"So?" my mother said to me. "What's the next step?"

"We wait," I said.

"For what?"

"To see whether her law firm approves the video tribute."

"When will you know?"

I shrugged and looked at Benny. "A couple days?"

He nodded.

I smiled. "Meanwhile, tomorrow I dive back into the fish tank."

"The Barracuda?" Benny said.

"Yep."

"What?" my mother said. "You're suing a fish?"

"Worse," I said. "I'm suing a doctor. His lawyer's the fish."

"Actually," Benny said, "his lawyer's a schmuck."

"His name is Barry Kudar," I said. "His nickname is Barracuda."

"So what's tomorrow?" Benny asked.

"A deposition."

"Who?"

"The doctor."

"I thought you took his deposition already."

"I did. This is the follow-up."

"On what?"

"His financial records."

Benny smiled. "Ah, yes. The punitive damage claim."

I nodded.

"What doctor is this?" my mother asked.

"Jeffrey Mason," I said. "Heart surgeon and sexual harasser."

"Rachel represents the nurse he groped."

"Sofia Garcia," I said.

"Groped?" my mother said.

"Groped, propositioned, and harassed."

"This doctor. Not a Jew, I hope."

I smiled. "Not a Jew, Mom."

"Oh, thank God."

"I assume the doc is loaded," Benny said.

"My lips are sealed," I said. "The one thing the Barracuda got from the judge was a protective order to keep the doctor's finances confidential."

"Sexual harassment," my mother said. "In the operating room?"

"And elsewhere," I said.

"That's terrible. What does the hospital say?"

"They settled," Benny said. "Rachel sued them, too. Your daughter's one tough broad. The hospital paid up and got out."

"Well, you make sure that fish behaves tomorrow."

"I'll try, Mom."

Chapter Thirteen

I assumed it would happen early in the deposition, and it did. Just ten minutes in, right after my seventh question.

"Objection," Barry Kudar said. "I instruct my client not to answer."

I turned to the witness. "Are you going to follow your attorney's instructions, Doctor Mason?"

He gave me a smug look. "I most certainly am, counsel."

I pulled the telephone close enough to make sure it was on camera and then turned to the court reporter. "Let that record reflect that I am dialing the direct line of St. Louis Circuit Judge Henry Winfield."

I hit the speaker button and started dialing.

"What do you think you're doing?" Kudar demanded.

I paused and turned to him. "Exactly what the judge told me to do at the last court hearing, counsel. I called his chambers this morning to make sure he would be available if you instructed your client not to answer one of my questions."

I finished dialing the number.

"This is ridiculous."

"Be sure to tell that to the judge, Mr. Kudar. I am only doing what His Honor requested."

Dr. Mason looked from his lawyer to the telephone, which was now ringing, and back to his lawyer. For the first time that morning, he appeared to be unsure.

The judge's clerk answered the phone. "Judge Winfield's chambers."

"Good morning, Cecilia. This is Rachel Gold. I am taking the deposition of Doctor Mason. An issue has come up that the judge needs to resolve."

"Just a moment, Miss Gold."

Kudar stared at the phone, his eyes blinking. The vein in his temple was pulsing.

"Counsel?" the judge said.

"Good morning, Your Honor. This is Rachel Gold. I am calling because Mr. Kudar has just instructed his client not to answer one of my questions."

"Is that true, Mr. Kudar?"

"Uh, yes, Your Honor, I, uh—"

"Save it for later, counselor. Ms. Gold, can you have the court reporter read me the question?"

I turned to the court reporter.

"Your Honor," I said, "our court reporter is Ms. Virginia Hansen. Proceed, Ms. Hansen."

She cleared her throat. "Question: Your financial statement shows that most of your savings, close to six-point-five million dollars, are invested in an entity known as Structured Resolutions. Can you describe that entity? Response: Objection. I instruct the witness not to answer."

There was a long pause.

"Mr. Kudar," the judge said, "you instructed your client not to answer *that* question?"

"Correct, Your Honor."

"On what possible grounds, sir?"

"We have given Miss Gold my client's financial statement. Enough is enough. If she wants to know more about a particular investment, she should do her own investigation."

Another long pause.

"To be clear, Mr. Kudar. You do not contend that the question seeks information protected by the attorney-client privilege, correct?"

Kudar's turn to pause.

"That's true, Your Honor."

"And you do not contend that your client's answer would violate some confidentiality agreement with the investment entity, correct?"

"We do not, Your Honor."

"Your objection is ridiculous, Mr. Kudar, and your instruction is improper. Your objection is overruled, as is your instruction. From this point forward, Mr. Kudar, let the record reflect that every telephone call to me during this deposition that results in my overruling an objection of yours will cost you and your client five hundred dollars each. Is that understood, Mr. Kudar?"

"Yes, Your Honor."

"That'll be all. Ms. Gold, I do hope this is the last I hear from you today."

"I hope so as well, Your Honor."

The line went dead.

I turned to the court reporter. "Please read the witness my last question."

She did.

Dr. Mason shrugged. "Describe the entity? I believe it's a corporation."

"Do you own stock in it?"

"No. It sells a type of annuity. An annuity mutual fund, actually. That's what I own."

"So you own close to six-point-five million dollars in a fund of annuities issued by Structured Resolutions."

He leaned back, crossed his arms over his chest, and gave me a sneer. "I prefer to think of it as six-point-five million dollars of last laughs."

"Explain, please."

"As a plaintiff's lawyer, Miss Gold, you are no doubt familiar with the concept of a structured settlement."

I was. Most attorneys are. But this was too good to let pass, especially since this was a video deposition. I could only imagine the jury's reaction to the doctor's arrogant tone and

condescending appearance, both of which would be fully captured by the camera. This was exactly the Dr. Jeffrey Mason I
wanted the jurors to see. This was the Dr. Jeffrey Mason who
slid his hand down the back of my client's hospital scrub pants
and into her panties as they left the operating room, who told
my client that giving head was the best way to get ahead on
his team, who, apparently flaunting his knowledge of Mexican
slang, made several nasty suggestions about her *concha.* The same
Dr. Jeffrey Mason who dismissed these and other examples of
sexual harassment as harmless examples of his team-building
camaraderie.

"Just to be clear, Doctor," I said, "what is *your* understanding
of a structured settlement?"

"That's where a plaintiff and his ambulance-chasing lawyer
settle a case for a lump sum that gets paid out over time. Let's say
they agree to settle their case for two million, but the defendant
will pay that out over twenty years at one-hundred thousand a
year. That's a structured settlement: a big number, but paid out
over time. Usually, it gets paid out through an annuity."

"Does Structured Resolutions issue those annuities?"

Dr. Mason chuckled. "Oh, no. Much better."

"What do you mean?"

"Lots of those plaintiffs are like the dumb lottery winners—the
ones who discover that their 'million dollar jackpot' is actually
twenty annual payments of $50,000. They'd rather have a lump
sum now than have it dribbled out over all those years. Same
with these plaintiffs. They're not that savvy, and their lawyers are
plenty greedy, so they're willing to sell those structured settlements
at a deep discount to get the money now. Guess what? There's a
profitable after-market out there for the purchase of these settlements by investors looking to acquire a guaranteed future stream
of income at a good price. That's where Structured Resolutions
comes in. They buy these personal injury and medical malpractice
annuities and make them available to investors like me."

"You described your investment as six-point-five million
dollars of last laughs. Explain that, Doctor."

"Simple math. That six-point-five million is going to be worth almost double that over the next twenty years. I'm the one, and not those plaintiffs and their slimeball lawyers, who will get all the benefit of those settlements."

He grinned at the camera and chuckled. "That's what I call the last laugh."

Chapter Fourteen

"Rachel Gold?"

I looked up from my lunch.

"Len Olsen."

He gave me a warm smile as he reached out his hand. I set down my fork and we shook hands.

"Glad to finally meet you," I said.

"The pleasure is mine, Rachel." He gestured toward the empty seat next to mine. "May I join you?"

"Sure."

I was attending a lunchtime Continuing Legal Education program at the bar association offices. About forty attendees were spread around eight tables facing the podium, where the presenter—a trial attorney from Armstrong Teasdale—was getting his PowerPoint and other materials ready. I was seated at one of the rear tables, having arrived late. There were three of us at the table—and now, with Len Olsen, four.

As he took his seat a male server arrived carrying a plate with the event's lunch: a turkey sandwich on whole wheat, French fries, and coleslaw.

"Something to drink, sir?"

"Ice tea would be just fine. Thank you, son."

Olsen turned to me. "Rachel, I am so delighted to see you here. I wanted you to know how touched I was by that proposal of yours. A tribute to the late Ms. Bashir. It's a lovely idea." He placed his hand over his heart. "Truly."

I was experiencing that Len Olsen magic—that good ol' boy charm and soft drawl and heartfelt gaze that juries had been finding irresistible for decades. He was a handsome man in his early sixties with blues eyes that seemed to peer into your soul, but not in an intrusive way. I'd heard the same about Bill Clinton from a friend of mine who'd spent an evening with the former President. She told me he could charm your pants off. Literally. Same with Len Olsen, who'd been linked to a series of gorgeous women, most of them half his age.

Olsen had been profiled enough in local and national publications, including a recent piece in the *Wall Street Journal*, that his background was familiar, at least to the lawyers of St. Louis. He'd grown up on a farm in southeast Missouri, attended college on a football scholarship, enlisted in the Army after graduation, and spent three years in Vietnam, where he'd become a member of the elite Army Rangers. He'd earned a law degree at night while working days as an insurance adjuster in St. Louis. He began his career in the public defender's office representing indigent criminal defendants. Over his years in private practice, he'd become a preeminent trial lawyer specializing in complex litigation. Since my return to St. Louis ten years ago, he'd won multi-million-dollar verdicts for farmers, factory workers, and others against some of the largest corporations in America.

"Have you spoken with Dick Neeler today?" he asked.

"I had a phone message from him this morning," I said, "but I haven't called him back yet."

"He's calling with good news, Rachel." He placed his hand on my forearm and gave me a gentle squeeze. "The firm has approved your proposal."

"That's wonderful."

"It surely is." He took his hand away and smiled. "We'll have some work to do to get ready, of course, but we're eager to get started. We're committed to this, Rachel. Of course, we'll need to coordinate with you and her family and Wash U. I am sure Dick will be eager to talk to you about all of that. But for now, I just want say thank you, Rachel."

He paused and nodded slowly. "This is the right thing to do."
I smiled. "Her father will be so happy to hear this."

There was a deep *thwock* and a static *hiss* as the sound system turned on, and then a voice over the speakers, "Good afternoon, ladies and gentlemen, and welcome to our CLE today on expert witness depositions."

Ten minutes into the program, and before he had finished his sandwich, Olsen got a call on his cell phone. He took the phone out of his suit jacket, frowned at the number, and then answered with a whispered hello. He stood and quickly moved out of the room to continue the conversation.

He didn't return.

Chapter Fifteen

"How did you find out?" Neeler asked over the phone.

"Len Olsen."

"He called?"

"No. I ran into him at a CLE over lunch. He told me you had good news."

I was back in my office.

"He's sure right about that, Rachel. We got it approved. And frankly, Len Olsen played a big role."

"What do you mean?"

"Not everyone on the committee was thrilled with the idea."

"Tell me."

He paused. "This is hush-hush."

"My lips are sealed, Dick."

"There are five partners on the committee."

"Okay."

I reached across my desk and pulled over Tommy Flynn's list of lawyers who'd gone over the crosswalk after nine the night Sari died:

Name	Time of Entry into Walkway
Susan O'Malley (8)	9:23 pm
Rob Brenner (7)	9:29 pm
Donald Warner (6)	9:35 pm
Brian Teever (6)	9:52 pm

"Mr. Olsen chairs the meetings, so he only votes if there's a tie."

"Who else is on the committee?"

"Mr. Warner, of course. Then there's Brian Teever, Mark Reynolds, and Dorothy Read. Mark and Dorothy really liked the idea."

"But the other two didn't?"

"Especially Mr. Warner. He thought it was ghoulish."

"Ghoulish?"

"That's the word he used. He said that suicide was a sin and that it brought disgrace to her and to the law firm."

"Jeez."

"Actually, he did mention Jesus—but that's the way Mr. Warner is. He said the firm should move on. He said her death was a sad event but that we shouldn't blow it out of proportion. He said he thought the focus on her death could hurt the firm in the long run."

"And Teever?"

"Pretty much the same. He said we should let sleeping dogs lie and dead associates stay buried."

"He actually said that?"

"Yeah. He can be blunt. He said it was important for the people in our firm to move on, to get on with their lives and their careers."

"Wow."

"I know. But that's when Mr. Olsen stepped in. He said he thought the video tribute would be terrific way to transform a tragic situation into a profound testament. Those are the words he used, too. Profound testament."

"Nice."

"He said that Sari had been part of our firm, that her death was a tragedy we all shared. He said that a tribute video was a powerful way for the firm to come together to help her memory live on, to honor her to her family, to acknowledge the hardships of the practice of law. It didn't change any votes, though. So he cast the tiebreaker, and here we are."

"What's next?" I asked.

"We'll work out the logistics and the financial details on our end and then we'll be ready to roll. Hopefully in a week."

"I represent her family, Dick."

"I understand."

"Just to be clear, I have approval rights over the entire production. Nothing gets filmed and nothing gets included without my review. I will coordinate with Washington U, which wants a role in this as well. We won't slow things down, but we need to be part of the process from beginning to end. Understand?"

"Uh, okay."

"Not just you, Dick. Your firm needs to understand that."

"We do, Rachel."

"Good. This has great potential."

"I totally agree. As they say at Nike, let's 'Just do it.'"

Chapter Sixteen

"What the hell is a tribute video?"

I let Tommy Flynn answer.

"Your law firm," Tommy said, "is creating a video in her memory. From what Rachel tells me, folks are going to share their memories in filmed interviews. And not just people in your firm. Her father and her family, including that Arab gal who gave that nice eulogy at the service. Rachel here represents them. Some of those professors at the law school are going to take part, too."

Tony Manghini shrugged. "I haven't heard shit about this."

"It's just been approved," I said. "They're in the process of putting together an announcement."

Tony looked at me, then at Tommy, and back at me.

"And I am meeting with you two, why?"

I gave him the short version—Stanley's suspicions, the parking garage list of potential "persons of interest."

Tony listened as he sipped his second longneck Bud Select. It was late in the afternoon—after his quitting time, and just before Tommy's starting time. We were seated in a booth at the Hooters three blocks from the law firm's offices. Tommy Flynn had correctly assumed it was one place downtown where we were unlikely to encounter a lawyer from the firm—or from any firm. The noise and music helped insure that we were unlikely to be overheard, and the waitresses' outfits helped insure that we were unlikely to be noticed.

Tony Manghini's title at Warner & Olsen is Manager of Office Support Services, which puts him in charge of the mailroom, the copy center, office supplies, file maintenance and messenger services—and thus Stanley's and Jerry's boss. He apparently gave everyone under his supervision at least one, and often more, snide nicknames. Poor Jerry, not familiar with the works of Herman Melville, was mortified by one of his, apparently in the belief that Moby Dick referred to a part of his anatomy.

Tommy Flynn was here because of a link with Tony reaching back to Tommy's days on the police force and Tony's days as an instructor of English literature at one of the community colleges—a link Stanley had somehow intuited and that I had confirmed researching the local news archives online. It was a link that ended Tony's teaching career, put him through bankruptcy, and eventually brought him to Warner & Olsen.

Tony Manghini was in his late thirties, average height, somewhere between slender and skinny. He had on a silky black shirt, narrow yellow tie, dark gray dress pants, and expensive Italian shoes. He wore his dark hair slicked back and sported what could best be described as a 1970s porn star mustache.

He gave me a skeptical look. "So the tribute video is what? Just a pretext?"

"Not exactly" I said. "It's going to be real. Lots of folks will be interviewed. Maybe even you. When it's complete, the firm will have a copy, as will Sari's family and the law school. Dick Neeler hopes it'll go viral."

"Neeler." Tony shook his head. "What a tool."

"But," I said, "the video also is a way to get some of the lawyers at your firm on videotape for Stanley to review. That may lead somewhere, or it may lead nowhere. I'm kind of hoping the latter. But either way, the firm is going to produce the video."

Tony chuckled and shook his head. "Who's in charge of this crazy operation? Master Blaster?"

"The firm's in charge," I said.

"Or so they think."

I shrugged.

"Stanley Plotkin." Tony shook his head. "That boy's got something seriously wrong with him. You know about the zip codes and the electoral college votes?"

"And the facial-muscle actions."

"True that. You should see the charts he's got hanging in his cubicle. Human faces with the skin peeled off. Some weird shit."

Tony leaned back in the booth, took a sip of his beer, set the bottle on the table, and gave me a smile. "Okay, Counselor. Back to my question. Why me?"

I smiled. "Stanley."

"What does that mean?"

Tommy said, "He figured out our prior connection."

"How?"

Tommy shrugged. "I don't think he knows the details, like me being the first cop on the scene of the accident or getting called as a witness in the wrongful death case. But he told Rachel here that I should be the one to ask you because the circumstances of our acquaintance—how did he put it?— have given him insight into the origins of your sarcastic façade."

"Meaning?"

Tommy shrugged. "Meaning that if I were you, you might listen to Rachel."

Tony frowned and turned to me. "So what do you want?"

I said, "You're in charge of the firm's files. The gatekeeper. You get access to records that others can't, especially electronic records. Some of those records might be relevant here."

"Which ones?"

"I'm putting together a list."

He turned toward Tommy.

"Well?" Tony said.

"Well what?"

"Why should I sign on?"

Tommy shrugged. "Why not?"

"Why not?" Tony leaned back in his chair. "Are you shitting me, Tommy? What if one of those four lawyers actually did kill her?"

"Okay."

"Okay? *Okay?* Don't you understand?" He turned to me. "Lady, you got some big swinging dicks on that list of yours. This could get dangerous."

"Probably not for you," I said.

"Probably not?" He turned to Tommy. "As I was saying earlier, what do I need this shit for?"

"Some things aren't easy."

Tony stared at Tommy. "That's your answer?"

Tommy took a sip of his Coke and set it down. After a moment, he looked up at Tony and shrugged.

"And?" Tony said to him.

"And nothing."

"You think Stanley read something genuine in that girl's face?"

"He sure read yours and mine."

Tony was silent.

"A nice young gal died, Tony," Tommy said. "Maybe someone killed her. We need to figure that out."

Tony studied his bottle of beer, rotating it slowly in his hands.

"Hey," Tommy said, "life's messy. Maybe you shouldn't have been dating one of your students back then, but no one thinks you meant for her die. You were drunk, Tony. It was an accident."

Tony looked up. "So?"

"That's my point."

"Meaning?"

"What if someone *meant* for Sari to die? Threw her off the damn garage? Murdered the poor gal?" Tommy leaned back and shrugged. "You can't do nothing about a suicide but shake your head and feel bad. Same with a traffic accident death. But murder is different, Tony. You gotta do something about murder."

"Such as what?"

"Such as catching the killer."

"Jesus, Tommy." He turned to me. "This isn't Hollywood, Counselor."

"I know," I said. "We don't even know if there is a killer. We're only asking you to help us get access to some documents."

Tony finished off his beer, set the empty bottle on the table in front of him, and stared at it.

I waited.

He looked up at Tommy, a hint of a smile at the corners of his mouth. "You're crazy. The whole goddam lot of you."

Tommy grinned and reached across the table. "That's my boy."

"Fuck you, old man."

And then Tony turned to me.

"Get me your list, Counselor."

Chapter Seventeen

The announcement was far more dramatic than the typical interoffice email. With the help of its marketing gurus and the eager nudging of Dick Neeler, the law firm's two name partners participated in the creation of a three-minute video announcing the project.

The video was delivered via email to everyone at the firm, including those in the Kansas City, Memphis, and Tulsa offices. They copied me on the email and attachment, along with Benny and Malikah.

It was an impressive piece of work, opening with a series of still images of Sari Bashir while John Lennon's "Imagine" played in the background. Then it cut to a shot of Donald Warner and Len Olsen, seated side by side on a couch.

Warner went first. After mentioning how much he treasured his opportunity to work with Sari, he urged those who were asked to participate in the creation of the tribute to "treat the request not as a chore but as a special opportunity. Make time in your schedule to share with us your precious memories of Miss Bashir."

Then came Len Olsen, who started with a brief remembrance of working with Sari on a project and then shifted into full closing-argument mode.

He leaned in toward the camera. "We are truly one firm, a band of brothers and sisters that includes not just lawyers but our secretaries and paralegals and file room clerks and all of the other men and women who make this place so special. Each of you counts, and together you make this law firm count. We thank our partner Dick Neeler for heading up this project, we salute Jerry Klunger, one of our fine young mailroom clerks, who will pitch in with others to help move this wonderful vision closer to reality. We happily acknowledge our friends at Washington University School of Law, who will partner with us in the venture. And finally, and most important, with heavy hearts and with tears in our eyes, we turn toward Sari's family and make this pledge: We will make her memory a blessing to all of us."

The first three times I watched the video—back to back to back—I was alone in my office. The second and third time I focused on Donald Warner, feeling each time more doubtful about his role as a suspect. Maybe one of the other three had killed her—and I was willing to withhold judgment until the video interviews—but watching Donald Warner on the video made me dubious that Sari's death had been anything other than a suicide.

The fourth and fifth time I watched it that morning, I had company: Stanley, Jerry, and Benny. We'd actually scheduled the meeting in advance to talk about what documents and records to request from Tony Manghini. We met before Stanley and Jerry had to report to work. I cued up the video, which Jerry and Stanley had not yet seen. The first time, Jerry and Stanley watched in silence. Jerry blushed when Len Olsen mentioned his name. The second time took longer because of Stanley's commands to pause and rewind and pause at various points in the speeches of Warner and Olsen.

When we finished that second time, I closed the screen and turned to Stanley, who appeared to be studying the pattern of the throw rug beneath his chair.

"Well?" I said.

Stanley continued to study the rug tiles. "The speeches were ambiguous."

"How so?" I asked.

Stanley straightened and stared at me. "More than once during each speech the speaker's facial expression conflicted with the veracity of the assertion being made."

"Such as?" Benny asked.

"Mr. Warner expressed his sorrow at Sari's death, but his facial expression indicated embarrassment, not sorrow. At another point, he stated that he valued the time he worked with her, but his transitory facial expression suggested fear instead."

"What do you mean by that?" I asked.

"There are forty-six facial action units, or AUs," Stanley said, returning his gaze to the rug. "When Mr. Warner spoke of his time working with Sari, there was a moment—less than a second—when his face activated AUs one, two, four, five, twenty, twenty-four, and twenty-five. Specifically, the inner brow raiser, which is the Frontalis, Pars Medialis, the outer brow raiser, which is the Frontalis, Pars Lateralis—"

"—Whoa, captain," Benny said, holding up his hands, palms out. "I'll take your word for it. What about Olsen? Same thing?"

"Not precisely. When Mr. Olsen made reference to the long hours and great effort that Ms. Bashir devoted to one of his matters, there was a brief expression of disgust—mostly AU nine, which involves the Levator Labii Superioris and Alaeque Nasi. In short, a facial action expression inconsistent with the sentiment he was purporting to convey with his words."

"Okay," I said. "What do you make of those expressions?"

"I make nothing of them, Ms. Gold. I merely take note of them and, in response to your request, bring them to your attention. What makes them noteworthy for me is the inconsistency between the verbal expression and the facial expression. Whether they are noteworthy for you is for you to determine."

I turned to Benny, my face expressionless—or what I hoped was expressionless.

Benny shrugged. "For you to determine, Ms. Gold."

Chapter Eighteen

With Stanley's help, I prepared our initial document request for Tony Manghini. It turned out to be a more challenging task than I had expected. That was because the two richest sources of important documents—the ones on the hard drive on Sari's computer and the ones in the files in her office—didn't exist. The hard drive had been wiped clean before her computer was given to another attorney, and there were no paper files in her office because Warner & Olsen, like many of its counterparts, had "gone paperless." Thus the only documents available would be electronic ones stored on the firm's computer network.

For Sari Bashir, what I requested included her timesheets for the final month of her life, plus all documents she'd prepared and emails she'd saved to the network during her final three months.

For the four attorneys who'd entered the walkway after nine that final evening, I requested the last three months of their Outlook calendar appointments along with copies of their expense reports and long-distance telephone logs for that period. Although I wanted to see their emails as well, Tony explained that was too risky. Unlike Outlook calendar appointments—which were open for all to access because someone trying to schedule a meeting needed to be able to pick a date and time that all invitees could attend—any attempt to access an active email account would trigger a security breach warning to the firm's tech-support crew.

It took Tony a day to gather and print out all the materials, which he placed into a box labeled for delivery to the Husch Blackwell law firm in Clayton. He then added that box—which he'd conspicuously labeled "BOX #6"—to a set of five unnumbered boxes of documents already being delivered to that law firm in connection with a lawsuit. He assigned Jerry Klunger to oversee the delivery process. That afternoon, after calling me, Jerry Klunger stacked the boxes onto a loading cart, took them down the service elevator, loaded the other five boxes into a courier's van, and loaded BOX #6 into the back of my minivan. Later that afternoon, I dropped the box off at Stanley's house.

Two mornings later, Bea Plotkin greeted me at the door and showed me into the den, where Stanley was seated at the card table. There were four stacks of documents on the table and another stack in the box at his feet. He was studying what appeared to be a set of expense reports.

Bea Plotkin said, "Look who's here, Stanley."

He looked up from the documents, frowned, and looked down again.

"Are you sure I can't get you something to eat, Rachel?" she asked.

"Thanks, Bea, but I'm okay."

"How about some kamishbroidt? There's always room for kamishbroidt, even if it's not your mother's. I know Sarah makes luscious kamishbroidt."

I smiled. "Okay. I guess there's always room for your kamishbroidt."

"With a nice cup of Maxwell House? Good to the last drop, they say. Or would you prefer Sanka?"

"Maxwell House sounds good."

"With cream and sugar?"

"Just black."

"Stanley?" she said.

He looked up again from the documents. "While in theory I would like to agree with Ms. Gold, namely, that there is always room for your kamishbroidt, in reality that is not often the case in this household, given the sheer quantity of comestibles you insist that I consume, and that is especially so today in light of the immense breakfast you placed before me—" he paused to check his watch "—just eighty-seven minutes ago. As such, most of that food remains in my stomach and has not yet entered the small intestine. Thus there is not, at present, room in my digestive tract for your kamishbroidt."

"Maybe later, dear."

After Mrs. Plotkin left for the kitchen, I said to Stanley. "Find anything helpful?"

Stanley grunted. "There is sufficient data from which to construct certain hypotheses consistent with criminal activity."

"For all four?"

"To varying degrees, yes. Moreover, I have come across no material that would eliminate any of them."

I walked over to where he was seated. He was studying the expense reports for one of the attorneys—paging through the three-inch stack, one page at a time.

"I want to review these, too," I said. "I'll pick up the box this weekend."

"In addition," Stanley said, not looking up. "You should ask Mr. Flynn for printouts of the cardkey records for the garage walkway for the two week-period prior to Ms. Bashir's death."

"You mean the records for people leaving the building after seven at night?"

"Those would be the only records that exist. As you will recall, you do not need to use your cardkey before seven."

I smiled. "Yes, Stanley. And why do we want those records?"

"Patterns."

"What kind of patterns?"

Stanley looked up and then back down at the expense report in his hand. "We won't know what kind unless and until we find one."

"Rachel, dear."

I turned as Stanley's mom entered the den with a plate of kamishbroidt in one hand and a steaming mug of coffee in the other.

Chapter Nineteen

The three-minute video announcing the firm's tribute project had been created with high production values and a keen awareness of its likely broader audience. Within a day of its release inside the firm, word of its existence had shown up on various internet legal gossip sites, including the *Wall Street Journal* Law Blog and AboveTheLaw.com. By the end of the week, the video was on YouTube.

The following Monday, our project was the subject of a piece in the online version of the *National Law Journal*, which included a sidebar on the contrasts between the firm's two name partners—a contrast, the author noted, that went far beyond their physical appearance. The tall, gaunt Warner specialized in international corporate finance and tax. The handsome ex-quarterback Olsen specialized in lawsuits that garnered press coverage, including two that had landed him on *Larry King Live*. Donald Warner had worked in the Commerce Department during the first Bush Administration, was good friends with former U.S. Attorney General John Ashcroft, and had become a force within the Missouri Republican Party. By contrast, Len Olsen was an influential fundraiser for the Missouri Democratic Party, an occasional golf partner of Bill Clinton, and a guest at the Obama White House. Warner had married his high school sweetheart, was the father of six children, and was an active member of his church. Len Olsen, "thrice divorced, currently dates a St. Louis Rams cheerleader." The reporter even nailed the small contrasts: "While Warner's one grudging concession to casual Fridays is a blue Oxford shirt instead of the usual white one with his suit and tie, Olsen dons faded jeans and Nikes each Friday, and during the summer months sports a polo shirt."

I should have seen it coming. The first consequence of the media attention was the hiring of a professional videographer. I had assumed that the tribute would be a homemade project filmed with a video camera borrowed from someone at the firm. Instead, as Dick Neeler told me in an excited phone call, the executive committee had authorized the hiring of Sam Tilden, a videographer with Mound City Court Reporting. I knew Sam. Ironically enough, he'd been the videographer for my last deposition of Dr. Mason.

When I passed along the videographer news to Jerry and Stanley, Stanley's only comment was that Samuel Tilden lost by one Electoral College vote to Rutherford Hayes in the Presidential election of 1876.

The second unexpected development was Harry Hanratty. Again, I had assumed that someone at the firm—perhaps one of the trial lawyers with a polished delivery—would conduct the interviews and narrate the video. Instead, the firm hired Harry Hanratty, the longtime anchor for the Ten O'clock News on the local CBS affiliate. Although Hanratty had been retired for almost a decade, he was still known around town as the Walter Cronkite of St. Louis news. With his flushed cheeks, pug nose, toothy smile, and completely bald head, he was immediately recognizable at his favorite bars, restaurants, and nightspots, and he still got stopped in the aisles for handshakes and autographs at Cardinals, Rams, and Blues games.

Len Olsen was apparently the firm's connection to Hanratty. According to Dick Neeler, the two men were part of a group of well-connected fishing and hunting buddies who made a semi-annual trip to Jackson Hole.

Judging from Stanley's muted reaction, no Hanratty had ever garnered a single Electoral College vote. However, I was concerned by the unexpected injection of a professional journalist into the project—and especially one who had come of age during an era when investigative reporting was a component of local television news. I made a few phone calls, though, and discovered, to my relief, that the seventy-one-year-old Hanratty's top three interests in life were young women, single-malt Scotch, and blackjack, all three of which he pursued several nights a week at the area casinos.

Indeed, as was apparent during our first meeting with Hanratty in a conference room at Warner & Olsen—a meeting that included Dick Neeler, Sam Tilden, Len Olsen, Jerry Klunger, and myself—the Walter Cronkite of St. Louis had no interest in the subject of the tribute and no desire to do anything besides read a script prepared by others.

"Folks," he said in that familiar deep, gravelly voice, "I'm here to read words and collect my stake for the blackjack table. Took me half a century to figure out that the two greatest pleasures in life are old Glenfiddich and young ladies. Nice coincidence there, too. Both are at their peak in their twenties." He turned to me with a wink. "Present company excluded, Counselor. You are one fine specimen of a woman. My heavens. Anyway, as I was saying, I will keep my focus on those two great pleasures in life and leave you fine folks to worry about the rest."

Chapter Twenty

And so we did.

Although the executive committee had designated Dick Neeler as the producer of the video, he told me after the meeting with Hanratty that he would defer to me on most matters, including scheduling interviews and creating interview scripts for Hanratty, so long as he got the producer credit on the video.

That was good news. To the extent that I hoped to obtain any useful information in the interviews of the four attorney suspects, we needed to be able to include in their interview scripts certain questions that were important to our efforts but that might not seem directly related to that attorney's dealings with Sari.

I knew in advance that I couldn't be the onsite director for the interviews. After all, I had clients to counsel and cases to prepare. Fortunately, I was able to convince Neeler that Jerry Klunger could attend the filming in my absence. And as a precautionary backup measure, I called Sam Tilden the night before the first interview and told him to keep recording for several minutes after the conclusion of the interview. He didn't need to actually move the camera around, I told him. I just wanted to be able to hear any post-interview comments or conversations.

"Just in case," I explained, "we hear something that we might want to include in the video."

The first two interviews—conducted by remote with the subjects seated in a conference room in the Dykma Gosset law firm in Detroit—were of Sari's father and her aunt Rijja, who was the sister of Sari's deceased mother. Jerry sat in the Warner & Olsen conference room as Hanratty conducted the interviews over the air.

"Nice job, sir," the videographer Tilden said to Hanratty when the second interview ended and video feed from Detroit went dark.

As instructed, Tilden kept recording.

"Son of a bitch," Hanratty said. "Nobody told me I'd be interviewing ragheads. Missed our chance, boys. Could have asked them about the damn Taliban."

The next two interviews took place at Washington University, with Benny supervising. The first was Dean Hamilton, who essentially repeated his eulogy. It was moving footage, though, and would fit nicely within the video. The other interview was of Martha Eastman, a professor of environmental law who spoke poignantly of Sari's involvement with the school's environmental clinic and her commitment to that cause. I had tears in my eyes when that interview ended.

I had written the scripts for those first four interviews, which Stanley reviewed but made no edits. Stanley prepared the initial drafts of the final eleven scripts—which included nine attorneys, one secretary, and Jerry Klunger. I translated them into conversational English—not Stanley's strong suit—and added questions that actually had relevance to a tribute video.

Missing from the list of interviewees was Stanley Plotkin. I asked him if he wanted to be included.

"I share Mr. Olsen's opinion, Ms. Gold."

His words made me wince. Toward the end of our initial meeting with Hanratty, Len Olsen—who had attended primarily to introduce Hanratty—had called Neeler and me aside.

"Jerry will be a fine spokesperson for our mailroom staff," he said. "His empathy will come through in the interview."

He had smiled and nodded toward Jerry.

Then he leaned in and lowered his voice. "But we need to guard the tone of the video. Nothing jarring. I refer to Stanley. If he insists on an interview, so be it, but I urge you not to include him in the final cut."

I had assumed that Stanley would not want to be interviewed and had asked him only to be polite. But Stanley's response made me realize that Jerry must have overheard what Olsen said to Neeler and me. That would have upset Jerry, and Stanley would have detected that emotion. He must have pried the information out of Jerry.

"I don't care what Olsen said," I told Stanley. "You knew Sari. If you'd like to be interviewed on camera, we'll do it."

Stanley didn't respond.

◇◇◇

The first of the firm interviewees was Brenda Muskie, Sari's sixty-two-year-old secretary. Brenda broke down several times during the interview as she described Sari's good manners, respect, and work ethic.

"She worked so hard," Brenda said, dabbing her cheek with a handkerchief. "I would come in some mornings and could tell from the pile of papers on my desk that the poor dear had been there until midnight. She would apologize for all the work she gave me, but I told her again and again that I was honored to be able to help." Her lips quivered. "Oh, my goodness, she was such a gentle soul."

After Brenda left the room, Hanratty said, "We nailed that one, boys. Won't be a dry eye in the house."

The second law firm interview was Rebecca Hamel, a second-year associate that Sari had mentored. She, too, spoke beautifully of Sari's graciousness and commitment, of the long lunch hours they had spent together as Sari coached her in the basics of life in a big law firm.

The physical contrast between Sari and Rebecca added an unspoken element of poignancy to Rebecca's description of their close relationship. Sari was the elegant Middle East princess—slender, olive skin, dark eyes, strong nose, black hair. Rebecca was the Midwest state fair beauty queen—tall, blond, leggy, piercing blue eyes. But not the cheerleader version. There was nothing giggly or effusive about Rebecca Hamel. Like Sari, she had a reserved air, but while Sari's was deferential, Rebecca's was cool and controlled. This was one woman you didn't want to mess with. That became clear when the camera went dark and Hanratty metamorphosed into the old lecher in a singles bar, even asking Rebecca what her sign was. He dropped the names of a few local VIPs he knew and then tried to get her phone number. I could hear the steel in her voice as she declined his request.

I smiled. *My kind of woman.*

After she left, Hanratty chuckled. "That is one fine piece of ass."

There was a *Snap!* sound.

"Christ Almighty," Hanratty said, "what the hell happened to your shirt, big guy?"

"Uh," a flustered Jerry said, "my pen broke."

"Damn, son," Hanratty said, "you got ink all over the front of your shirt."

"Yes, sir."

I would later learn that Jerry had snapped his pen in anger after Hanratty's piece-of-ass observation.

Harnratty said, "So is that a wrap for today?"

"Yes, sir," Jerry said. "We start tomorrow at one o'clock."

"Another pretty gal, I hope?"

"No, sir."

"Who's up next?"

"Mr. Teever," Jerry said.

"Teether?"

"Teever, sir. Mr. Brian Teever."

"Who's he?"

"A partner, sir."

"Trial lawyer?"

"No, sir. He is in Trusts and Estates."

"Did he draft her will?"

"No, sir. I think Miss Bashir worked with him on estate planning matters."

"Okay. See you tomorrow, big guy. You, too, Sammy."

After I turned off the TV, I made a note to follow up with Rebecca.

Chapter Twenty-one

Benny picked up Jerry and Stanley on his way to my office that Saturday. They arrived at quarter to ten. My son Sam's religious school class at the synagogue ran from 9:30 until 11, so we had enough time before I needed to pick him up.

The four of us gathered in my conference room to watch the uncut video of the Brian Teever interview, which had been filmed the prior day. I loaded the DVD into the system, pointing the remote toward the screen, and turned to Stanley.

"Ready?"

He stared at the screen. "Proceed."

I pressed PLAY.

The blank screen flickered and resolved into a shot of Brian Teever from the waist up. He was seated on a leather couch in his office. Behind him on the wall were framed diplomas and certificates and photographs of Teever posed with various noteworthies. Per my instructions, Sam Tilden had started filming before the official start of the interview. Teever was fiddling with the tiny clip-on microphone, which he was trying to fasten to the lapel on the suit jacket. Off camera, Harry Hanratty sounded as if he were talking to someone on his cell phone.

Tony Manghini had described Brian Teever as Central Casting's answer to a call for a Big Law senior partner. The description fit: the silver hair, the strong chin, the golf course tan, the gray pinstriped Brooks Brothers suit, the navy-and-red repp tie, the gold cufflinks.

Teever got the clip-on mike fastened and looked up toward the camera with a slight frown. After a moment, he cleared his throat, a hint of impatience in his expression. Hanratty seemed to get the hint, because he abruptly ended his cell phone conversation.

"Okey-dokey," Hanratty said offscreen. "Let's get this show rolling. Sam, how we doing?"

"All I need is a sound check," said the offscreen voice of the videographer.

"That's your cue, Brian," Hanratty said.

Teever's focus moved slightly to the right, indicating that Hanratty was seated next to the videographer.

"Give ol' Sam here a testing-one-two-three. He needs to make sure you're coming in loud and clear."

Teever straightened his tie and cleared his throat. "Testing, one, two, three."

"That's good," the videographer said offscreen.

"Brian," Hanratty said, offscreen, "we're going start this in just a minute or two. The goal here is to give the viewer a little sense of your feel for Miss Bashir." Hanratty chuckled. "Not literally, of course."

Teever didn't smile.

But I did. With the exception of the most senior of partners in the firm, apparently no one called Teever by his first name. From what I'd gleaned, at the law firm he was strictly Mister Teever. While the same was apparently true of Donald Warner, the reasons were far different. As I learned during my days as a junior associate at Abbott & Windsor in Chicago, there were certain older men you addressed as Mister out of a blend of admiration and respect. And while Donald Warner would not likely ever generate the same level of affection that you may have had for, say, your favorite high school teacher, you called him Mister Warner for some of the same reasons you called your teacher Mister Lubeck. It just felt more natural. By contrast, you called Brian Teever Mister Teever because his demeanor conveyed a sense of his lofty status within in the law firm hierarchy. You'd no more call him by his first name than you would the Queen of England.

Teever certainly had the pedigree. He'd prepped at St. Louis Country Day School and earned his bachelor's and law degrees at Yale, where he'd allegedly been a member of the Skull and Bones Society with classmate George W. Bush. His legal specialty was trusts and estates, and his client list included the landed gentry of St. Louis, many of whom were members of St. Louis Country Club, where Teever had served an unprecedented two terms as president and now chaired the mysterious admissions committee. Supposedly, he'd brushed aside a new client inquiry from a representative of August Busch—either the III or the IV—because he deemed the brewery family too loutish. His only concession to the firm's Casual Fridays—where even many of the younger partners wore chinos—was a navy blazer. And thus I had to grin as Hanratty addressed Teever like they were old drinking buds from the American Legion Hall.

"Feel free to stop me, Brian," Hanratty was saying, "if you have a question or want to re-shoot one of your answers or whatever else comes to mind. This interview may last twenty minutes, but it's just raw footage. The edited version will be less than five, and you'll have the final say on your portion of the video. What do you say, Brian? Shall we get this puppy rolling?"

Through gritted teeth, Teever said, "Fine."

There was a pause, and then Hanratty morphed from drinking bud to portentous offscreen narrator:

"Brian Teever. Senior partner at Warner & Olsen. Former chair of the American Bar Association's Trust and Estate Law Section. An attorney known for his ability to recognize legal talent amongst younger attorneys. Mr. Teever, tell us about Sari Basher."

Teever nodded thoughtfully, lips pursed. "She was a fine young attorney. Diligent, hardworking, reliable."

"Was her career goal to become a trusts and estates attorney?"

Teever smiled slightly and shook his head. "No. Ms. Bashir had her sights set on corporate law. That was her passion. But, frankly, that actually made her achievements more impressive. She brought the same level of attention and dedication and client concern to the practice of trusts and estate law as she did to corporate law. That is the mark of a fine young attorney with good potential."

"I understand Miss Bashir worked on a large estate planning matter for you during her final weeks."

"She did." Teever turned toward the camera. "It was a complex situation involving numerous subtle issues and several moving parts. Ms. Bashir did an excellent job."

"Tell us more."

Teever turned slightly toward Hanratty and frowned. "What do you mean?"

"Give us a little background. Tell us about your relationship with Claire Hudson."

A pause. Teever's eyes narrowed.

"Pardon?" he said.

"Claire Hudson. And her husband Dave. According to Sari's timesheets, she spent nearly forty hours working on that matter during her final two weeks. Something to do with an outfit called Structured Resolutions. Does that help ring a bell?"

Teever stared at Hanratty, lips pursed. "We can't talk about that here."

"Really? Why not?"

"Because it is a confidential matter protected by the attorney-client privilege." He nodded at the camera. "Do not include this in the video."

"No problema, Brian. We'll deep-six that footage and move on."

"Do you have any grasp of the attorney-client privilege, sir? I am not going to sit here in front of a camera and disclose confidential details of the estate plans of my clients. If you want to ask me general questions about Ms. Bashir, proceed. But no details about any client. None. Do you understand?"

"Got it, big guy. Read you loud and clear."

Teever shook his head. "I have a busy day. You have what you need from me. This interview is over."

"Brian, Brian, hang on. I didn't mean to offend you. How about a few more questions? I'll make them softballs."

But Teever had already removed his microphone and dropped it onto the couch as he stood.

"I need to get back to work," he said, his voice muffled as he stepped offscreen. "Pack up your equipment and get out of my office. Now."

After a few moments of silence, the screen went blank.

Chapter Twenty-two

Benny broke the silence with a chuckle. "Now that is what I call genuine cluster fuck."

A moment of silence, and then Stanley spoke. "If by the term 'cluster fuck,' Mr. Goldberg, you are referring to the military slang nomenclature for a confusing or chaotic situation caused by a failure of communication, often involving an excessive amount of personnel attempting to accomplish a given task, then you are mistaken, sir. What you witnessed was not a cluster fuck. What you witnessed was confirmation of Mr. Teever's motive for killing Sari Bashir."

"Is that so?" Benny said. "Please enlighten us, Mr. Holmes."

"To recap: based on Mr. Teever's time of departure on the evening of Ms. Bashir's death, he is a suspect. In order to proceed—namely, to evaluate the likelihood of his role as the murderer—we must first identify his motive for killing her."

"Aren't you assuming too much?" Benny asked.

"The assumption is purely arguendo, sir. We assume that he is the killer purely for the purpose of determining whether he had sufficient motive to commit the homicide. The existence of a compelling motive is essential to the analysis. One does not hurl a young woman off the eighth floor of a parking garage without a motive unless one is insane—and our four suspects exhibit no reliable indicia of psychosis. Thus if Mr. Teever did not have a discernable motive, we can eliminate him from our list of suspects and focus our attentions on the other three. If, however, we conclude that he did have a sufficient motive, then we proceed accordingly."

"And that interview convinced you that Teever had a motive?" Benny asked.

"That is correct, sir. Or at least a potentially sufficient motive."

"What was his motive?"

"You saw it for yourself, sir. That videotape confirms that Mr. Teever was engaged in a clandestine, professionally unethical, and presumably undisclosed sexual relationship with a client of the firm."

A pause.

"Oh?" Benny said. "And who was he banging?"

"Claire Hudson. She is, as confirmed in the video, a client of the firm and the spouse of another client of the firm, both of whom Mr. Teever is currently representing in the preparation of their wills, trusts, and other estate plan documents."

"You're telling me you deduced all of that from this video-tape?" Benny said.

"I am merely stating that this videotape confirms prior suspicions."

"And what were those prior suspicions based on?"

"Evidence, sir. Evidence."

"What evidence, Stanley?"

Stanley stood and walked toward the side wall. He stopped a few feet from the wall and began stretching his neck.

I turned to Benny. "Among the documents we obtained are Teever's expense reports for the last three months. Actually, the expense reports for all four of the lawyers. It was Stanley's idea."

"And what did they show?" Benny asked.

"The other three lawyers had physical receipts for each charge," I said. "If they took someone out to lunch, their expense report for that lunch would include a copy of the lunch bill. But Teever didn't seem to save his receipts, so each month his secretary would turn in a single comprehensive expense report that would include a copy of his American Express bill for that month. She would circle and number each of the charges that were business expenses, and then would attach some pages giving the details for each of those expenses."

"And?" Benny said.

I turned to Jerry. "Do you have copies?"

"Yes, ma'am." Jerry rummaged through his folder of documents. "Here is the one for the last month."

He removed a photocopy of the four-page American Express bill and fanned the pages out on the table so that Benny and I could see them. Stanley was still over in the corner facing the wall. Jerry removed a three-page typewritten document that was stapled in the upper right corner and set that document on the table in front of him.

"Give them an example of an annotated charge," Stanley commanded.

Jerry leaned over the first page of the American Express bill and ran an enormous forefinger down the column of merchants.

"Here's one," he said. "Tony's Restaurant. Do you see the number three here?"

Benny leaned forward to look where Jerry was pointing. There was a handwritten numeral 3 in the margin to the right of the final column, which showed a charge for $278.00.

"Here's the explanation for number three," Jerry said, turning to the second page of the three-page document. "Dinner with Harold Townsend," he read, "Senior Vice President, American Pipe Corporation. Charge: Client Entertainment."

Benny picked up the four pages of the American Express bill and studied them one by one.

"So he claimed fourteen of these charges as business expenses?"

"Yes, sir."

"Lot of other charges on this bill besides those fourteen."

"Yes, sir."

"Groceries, drug store, cleaners, Starbucks—personal stuff."

"Yes, sir."

"Even his barber's here." Benny looked up at me. "Christ, sixty dollars for a fucking haircut? Who's cuts his hair? Vidal Sassoon?"

"That is impossible," Stanley announced, turning from the wall to face Benny. "Mr. Sassoon died on May ninth of 2012. That was a Wednesday."

"A Wednesday, eh?" Shaking his head in amusement, Benny looked down at the American Express statement. "So what did you spot here, Jerry?"

"Well, sir, I didn't really spot anything. This was for Stanley. He was curious about this hotel charge on page three."

Benny found it. $247.43 for the Marriott Hotel in downtown St. Louis on the third Wednesday of that month.

I said, "That was two weeks before Sari's death."

"So what's the issue there?"

"Stanley," I said, "can you explain it to Benny?"

Stanley turned toward Jerry. "Her timesheets."

"Oh, right," Jerry said.

Jerry pulled a set of documents—about thirty pages' worth—out of the folder. They were held together by a binder clip on the top. About a dozen little colored flags were affixed to the right sides of the pages.

Jerry said, "Stanley saw some entries that might have been related to the hotel charge."

"What kind of relation?" Benny asked.

Stanley announced, "Ms. Bashir worked on an estate-planning matter for Mr. Teever. The clients are David and Claire Hudson. On the same date that Mr. Teever incurred the hotel charge, Ms. Bashir billed seven-point-five hours to the Hudson estate-planning matter, along with approximately eight hours to other matters. The following day she billed another eight-point-two hours to the Hudson matter, plus nearly nine hours to other matters."

"So," I said to Benny, "it was possible that Teever had obtained a room for her so that she wouldn't have to drive home late at night."

"Possible," Stanley announced, "but unlikely."

"Why unlikely?" Benny asked.

After a moment of silence, Stanley said, "Because on the first Wednesday of that month Mr. Teever incurred the identical charge—$247.43—at the same hotel but, according to Ms. Bashir's timesheets, she did no work on the Hudson matter any day that week. Moreover, Mr. Teever incurred three such hotel charges the prior month, all in the same amount, and none of those five hotel charges was submitted to the firm for reimbursement. In short, they were personal charges."

"Okay," Benny said. "So?"

"Jerry made inquiries."

Benny looked at Jerry. "What kind of inquiries?"

Jerry cleared his throat. "It was Miss Gold's idea. I called the Marriott and pretended to be an assistant to Mr. Teever. I explained that he'd misplaced the receipt for that particular stay and that I needed a replacement receipt. I told them that I would be happy to drop by to pick it up. They agreed to print off a duplicate for me."

"And?" Tony said.

"Here it is." Jerry removed a sheet of paper from the folder and set it on the table between Benny and me.

As Benny leaned over to study it, Stanley said, "You will note three charges. One for the room, one for room service, and one for parking. Ms. Gold had Jerry call back to ask for the specifics of the room service charge and the parking charge."

"And?" Benny said to Jerry.

"The room service charge was for a bottle of champagne and a cheese and fruit plate. The parking charge was for three hours."

"Thus it appeared from the charges," Stanley said, "that the purpose of the hotel room was not for a night's rest but for an illicit assignation during the middle of the day."

Benny said, "Why a nooner?"

Stanley stretched his neck. "If by the term 'nooner' you are referring to an assignation that takes place during business hours, the first clue is the parking charge. One car, three hours. The offices of Warner & Olsen are less than four blocks from the Marriott. Thus it is highly unlikely that Mr. Teever would have driven there. Instead, it is far more likely that Mr. Teever's companion drove to the hotel, parked her car there, and had the charge billed to the room. Further confirmation is contained in Mr. Teever's American Express bill, which includes two charges that evening—one from Starbucks, one from Straubs grocery store. The Starbucks and the Straubs on his statement are both located within walking distance of his residence in the Central West End. Indeed, charges from those two establishments appear frequently on his credit card bills. Thus it would appear that Mr. Teever concluded his three-hour sojourn at the Marriott prior to his departure from the law firm at the end of the day, all of which supports the inference that this transaction took place *during* the day, and involved a companion who drove to the hotel and who participated in the consumption of the alcoholic beverage and the array of dairy and fruit products that comprised the room service order. Given that the Hudson estate-planning matter is the only client matter associated with Mr. Teever on which Ms. Bashir worked, the search for a motive pointed toward a possible illicit sexual tryst with either the husband or the wife. Because Mr. Teever exhibits no indicia of either a homosexual or bisexual predilections and because Mr. Hudson's office is approximately five blocks from the Marriott, it seemed unlikely that Mr. Hudson would have driven his car to the hotel to engage in a furtive homosexual liaison with Mr. Teever. Thus I focused on Mrs. Hudson. Confirmation that she was Mr. Teever's hotel companion that day, and presumably other such days, occurred when Mr. Hanratty asked Mr. Teever to describe his relationship with Claire Hudson."

"Ah, yes." Benny grinned. "That question seemed to come out left field."

Stanley stared at him.

"Actually, Mr. Goldberg," he finally said, "that particular question came out of the script I prepared for the interview."

"It sure pissed him off," Benny said.

"Actually," Stanley said, "Mr. Teever's facial actions in response to that question momentarily registered guilt and then fear."

"How?" Benny asked.

"Mr. Teever initially looked down and away, which is a reliable indicator of guilt or shame. As for fear, when he looked up at the camera his lower facial muscles, and specifically, his Risorius, known as the lip stretcher, and his Labii, known as the lip depressor, were activated. According to the dictionary, panic means a sudden strong feeling of fear that prevents reasonable thought or action. Guilt is defined as remorseful awareness of having done something wrong. Juxtapose them and you have compelling evidence that Mr. Teever is involved in an illicit sexual relationship with a client who also happens to be the spouse of another client."

Silence for a moment.

"Okay," Benny said. "So he's banging his client's wife. Got it. How does that fact get Sari killed?"

Stanley said, "That fact alone does not provide sufficient motive for Ms. Bashir's murder. But for our purposes here, that fact creates a plausible first event in a chain of events that could result in her murder. The second event, which we cannot yet establish, is that Ms. Bashir discovered the existence of that illicit relationship. If that occurred, and if Mr. Teever believed that she might disclose that fact to others, he would have had sufficient motive."

"How so?" Benny asked.

"Mr. Teever is on the Missouri Bar's Board of Governors and is the chair of the Professionalism Committee. These are highly prestigious positions within the legal profession, and Mr. Teever is an individual whose entire persona conveys great concern with the preservation and expansion of his prestige within the legal profession. Moreover, his positions with the Missouri Bar provide him with oversight duties in the enforcement of the Missouri Rules of Professional Conduct. His conduct with Mrs. Hudson violates several provisions of the Rules of Professional Conduct and, if exposed, could result in his disbarment and thus his disgrace and concomitant loss of prestige. For example, Rule 4-1.8, which is entitled Conflict Of Interest: Prohibited Transactions, expressly states in subsection j that, quote, 'a lawyer shall not have sexual relations with a client unless a consensual sexual relation-ship existed between them when the client-lawyer relationship commenced,' closed quote. In this case, even assuming that the sexual relationship existed prior to the commencement of the client-lawyer relationship, the existence of that relationship at the time he also represented her husband violates at least two other Rules of Professional Conduct. In short, if Ms. Bashir had discovered this misconduct, she would have a professional obligation to report him to the chief disciplinary counsel of the Missouri Bar. The likely repercussions from that would have given someone in Mr. Teever's position sufficient reason to silence her permanently."

Benny leaned back in his chair, crossed his arms over his chest, and turned to me. "Son of a bitch."

Chapter Twenty-three

Next up were Susan O'Malley and Rob Brenner. Susan was a senior associate in the bankruptcy group. She'd joined the firm the same year as Sari Bashir. Rob was a junior partner in the litigation department. Harry Hanratty knocked off both interviews Monday morning. As per our arrangements, the videographer left a copy of the DVD for Jerry, which he and Stanley viewed during their afternoon break, and then Jerry arranged for a messenger to deliver it to my office, where I watched it before going home.

O'Malley's image appeared on the screen as she took a seat behind her desk. Although Susan O'Malley, like Rebecca Hamel, had blond hair and blue eyes, the similarities ended there. Rebecca could have passed for a model for L.L. Bean or REI, while Susan had the hulking aura of an ex-jock, which she was. She had rowed all four years on the Georgetown University varsity crew team—her freshman and sophomore years in the number five position, known in rowing jargon as the Power House, and her last two years in the number six position, known as the Meat Wagon. She still had that Meat Wagon look—all six-feet and two hundred pounds of her. She wore her hair in a short bob and had on a pair of tinted rimless eyeglasses.

Harry Hanratty leaned into the picture to shake her hand. Although his back was to the camera, you could almost feel him wince.

His initial questions led her through the basics—her background, her years at the firm, her area of specialization. And then he moved on to the subject of the interview.

"I understand that you and Miss Bashir were part of the same entering class your first year here."

"That's correct."

"You started off in the bankruptcy department?"

"I did. I'm still there."

"Miss Bashir was over in the corporate department?"

"Yes, although all associates get occasional projects from outside their department."

"But you started in different departments, right?"

"We did."

"So let me ask you, Miss O'Malley, how would you describe your relationship with Miss Bashir?"

During the two-second pause between the question and her response—as Stanley Plotkin would later point out—Susan O'Malley's facial muscles underwent a combination of actions signifying anger and jealousy, a pair of emotions out of synch with her bland answer, "We got along fine."

Later in the interview, according to Stanley, her facial muscles formed the same combination of actions at the end of a series of seemingly innocuous questions, all scripted by Stanley, that culminated as follows:

"Did you two socialize outside of work?" Hanratty asked.

"Not really."

"What about at firm functions?"

A puzzled frown. "What do you mean?"

"For example, at the firm's annual party last September?"

Pause.

"I don't recall seeing Sari that evening. However, I am sure there were firm functions we both attended."

◇◇◇

Rob Brenner was up next. I'd asked Tony Manghini to brief me on several of the attorneys. According to Tony, Brenner was a rising star among the firm's junior partners. Just thirty-five, he already had a client base that generated annual legal fees in excess of a million dollars, mostly in defense of consumer class-action claims against financial institutions. That was Brenner's litigation specialty, which probably explained why I'd rarely come across him in my practice. Although we happened to be in one pending class action where we represented different defendants—I was local counsel for a Florida bank whose lead attorney was a law school classmate of mine in a Tampa firm—the case was in its early stages, and I had had little contact with Brenner.

If you looked up Brenner's bio on the firm's website, you'd be struck by the handsome face staring back at you—dark-haired, square-jawed, piercing eyes. If you came across him in the hallway, however, you'd be struck by his height—or, rather, lack thereof. The photograph conjured up a tall leading man. The reality was five seven, according to Manghini, who referred to him, behind his back, as the Little Corporal.

To describe Brenner as intense was like describing Death Valley as warm. The term didn't capture the essence of the man. By the time Brenner arrived at the office each morning at seven—Bluetooth earpiece in place, third Starbucks venti black coffee in hand—he'd already done a full circuit on the weight machines, run six miles, made several calls, and sent numerous emails from his iPhone.

Not surprisingly, the same qualities that made Brenner valuable to the partners made him despised by the junior associates and support staff. If you were unlucky enough to be a young associate assigned to one of Brenner's cases, you knew that you'd better be in your office and at attention by his seven o'clock arrival. And you also knew that you'd better have your cell phone with you at all times after hours, including on your nightstand, set on vibrate, while you slept. From what Manghini had gleaned in conversations with associates, a typical Brenner assignment would arrive in your email inbox late on a Friday afternoon or early on a Saturday morning, and always with a deadline of Monday morning, even though Brenner might not get around to reviewing it until the end of that week, which is when he would send out the follow-up assignment.

He was even more demanding and disrespectful with the support staff, Manghini told me. No secretary assigned to him had lasted longer than six months. He'd reduced almost every female staff member to tears at least once, and had so rattled a young copy center clerk over some collating glitches that the poor guy actually wet his pants.

Thus I was not surprised that Brenner did the video interview with a frown on his face, the Bluetooth device fastened to his ear, and a mechanical pencil in his hand. He tapped the pencil on the desktop throughout the interview, which created enough of a distraction for the viewer that the video was essentially worthless for any use beyond Stanley's review.

Brenner's manner during the interview could charitably be described as brusque. He allowed that Sari Bashir appeared to be a qualified young associate, emphasized that he had no experience working with her and thus no view as to the quality of her legal work.

"But you did know her, correct?"

Tap, tap, tap.

"Correct."

Tap, tap.

"And you were fond of her?"

Tap, tap, tap.

"Fond?"

Tap.

"How would you describe your relationship with Ms. Bashir?"

Tap, tap, tap, tap.

"Relationship?"

"Did it change over time?"

Tap, tap, tap.

"Did what change over time?"

Tap.

"Your relationship with Ms. Bashir?"

Tap, tap, tap, tap.

"This interview is over."

"Hey, I didn't mean to get you upset, pal."

Tap.

"I am not upset. I am not your pal. I am, however, busy. Please leave."

Tap, tap.

And then he stood and walked off screen.

"Jesus," Hanratty said offscreen, "what an asshole. We had ourselves a real pair today, eh, Sam? First that bull dyke and then this little shithead."

The screen went blank.

I copied and emailed the video to Benny before leaving the office. He called me later that night.

"What the fuck is up with Brenner?" Benny said. "He is one nasty little prick."

"Agreed."

"Is he married?"

"Divorced," I said, "about two years ago, according to court records online."

"So what's the deal? Was he banging her?"

"Sari?" I said. "They had some sort of relationship. Or maybe just a sexual encounter. According to Stanley, the relationship ended or the encounter occurred about a month before she died. Whatever, it was not pleasant."

"She dump him?"

"Don't know."

"What's Stanley say?"

"He says the questions about his relationship with Sari generated angry facial actions."

"Well, duh. I could see that."

"Me, too—at least sort of."

"Hmmm," Benny said. "You think Plotkin's skills are rubbing off on me?"

"I'll get worried when you start citing electoral college votes."

"So when's the big swinging dick going on?"

"If you mean Donald Warner, tomorrow at ten."

"You going?"

"I have a front row seat."

"Can't wait to hear about it."

Chapter Twenty-four

Donald Warner's video interview was scheduled for 9:30 that morning. I arrived at 9:10 and was escorted to his corner office on the fifteenth floor. His secretary told me that he was in a meeting down on fourteen but would be there by 9:30.

"Mr. Warner is always on time," she said.

I could hear Hanratty's raspy voice from down the hall in the break room. He was apparently flirting with two secretaries, who were giggling over something he said.

Sam Tilden was in Warner's office setting up the video camera on the tripod. He had it aimed toward Warner's desk, which was a mahogany George Washington desk with brass handles and stationary boxes on either end.

I had to smile at the sight of the brown paper bag resting on the corner of the desk. The legendary brown paper bag. It was a part of the Donald Warner lore that the media loved to repeat. Except for the occasional client luncheon, Warner apparently can be found at noon most days seated at his desk with the contents of his brown paper bag neatly arranged before him on a paper napkin: a peanut-butter-and-jelly sandwich on white bread, a plastic sandwich bag filled with Pepperidge Farm Goldfish crackers, a Red Delicious apple, and a small bottle of apple juice.

That brown paper bag had become an emblem of the man who seemed the epitome of the conservative Midwest Republican, and thus the subject of much speculation as the next Senatorial election season approached. After the debacle of the last election, where the Missouri Republican candidate self-destructed over an idiotic comment about women, rape, and pregnancy, the GOP was looking for someone with solid conservative credentials *and* the discipline to stay on message. The pundits agreed that Donald Warner satisfied those criteria. This was not a man to ad lib. Indeed, he relied on detailed handwritten notes for even the most casual of meetings and presentations.

Mounted above the credenza was a family portrait made-to-order for a political candidate. Seated on the loveseat were Warner and his wife, a plump, attractive brunette in her late fifties. He wore a dark suit and tie, and she wore a sky blue dress and pearls. Standing behind them were their three children. In the middle was Donald, Jr., in his mid-twenties and tall as his father. To his left stood Melissa, in her early twenties, and to his right stood Kelly, in their late teens. Curled up on the rug in front of Warner was Scout, the family's golden retriever.

I stood to look at the framed pictures along his office wall, all of which were consistent with his persona. They included photographs of Warner standing beside various state and national Republican figures, including two former Presidents, Senator Roy Blount, and former Senator John Danforth. And there was the mandatory GOP gun shot: a photo of Warner and former Vice-President Dick Cheney, both in hunting gear and holding rifles. There were also photographs of him at various local charitable and community functions, including one, shovel in hand, at the groundbreaking ceremony for the expansion of the St. Louis Art Museum, where he was the president of the Museum's board of trustees.

I paused before the photo of Warner and former United States Attorney General John Ashcroft, which appeared to have been taken at the Department of Justice in Washington, D.C. They were both members of Assemblies of God churches—a conservative evangelical denomination that had inspired Benny to ask me yesterday, "Do you know why Donald Warner and his wife won't have sex standing up?" The answer: "Because someone might think they were dancing."

"Good morning."

I turned to see Donald Warner enter his office.

He gave me a pleasant smile. "Hello, Miss Gold."

We shook hands. He was taller than I had fully realized—probably about six-foot six.

I said, "Good to see you, Mr. Warner."

"Please," he said with a chuckle. "Call me Donald."

"And you can call me Rachel."

"Fair enough." He turned toward the videographer. "Mr. Tilden, correct?"

"Yes, sir."

"Good to see, young man. Where is our Mr. Hanratty?"

"Down the hall, sir," Sam said. "I'll get him."

After Tilden left, Warner gestured toward one of the chairs facing his desk. "Please have a seat, Rachel."

I did.

Warner settled into the highback leather chair behind his desk. His face was long, almost gaunt, with prominent cheekbones and ears. In his black suit, white shirt, and gray-and-black striped tie, he seemed a mix between a well-mannered undertaker and Ichabod Crane.

"So tell me, Rachel," he said, "how is our shoot going so far?"

"We have some beautiful footage from members of your firm."

"I'm glad to hear that."

His glance rose above my head. "Ah."

He stood and came around the desk. "Hello, Harry."

They shook hands and exchanged greetings.

Hanratty turned to videographer. "We all set, Sam?"

"We are. Here's the script."

"Excellent." Hanratty flipped through the pages and then looked up at Warner. "Donald, you're good right where you are. Make your self comfortable. And just let us know—uh, what's that line from *Sunset Boulevard*?"

Warner smiled. "I'm ready for my close-up, Mr. DeMille."

Hanratty laughed. "You nailed it, Donny. Sam? Let's roll."

"We're taping," Sam said.

Hanratty cleared his throat and shifted into his Voice of God mode.

"We are speaking with Mr. Donald A. Warner. He is, of course, the Warner of Warner & Olsen and one of the most respected citizens of our fine city. Thank you for speaking with us today, Mr. Warner."

Warner gazed into the camera. "It is an honor for me. Miss Sari Bashir was a treasured member of our law firm. I had the great pleasure of working with her."

"So I understand. Please tell us about that."

Warner glanced down at his notes.

"Miss Bashir was a member of our mergers-and-acquisition team on an international transaction last year. She handled the due diligence, which in even the best of transactions can be somewhat tedious. Long hours, thousands of documents to review, small print, arcane terms. It was a grueling assignment, but Miss Bashir never complained, never let the tasks overwhelm her, and did a stellar job from start to finish."

"That's a wonderful tribute, Mr. Warner."

Warner smiled. "She more than earned it."

Hanratty flipped to the next page of the script. I knew what was coming. I tried to keep my face blank as Hanratty resumed.

"Rumor has it, Mr. Warner, that you were initially opposed to this tribute video."

Warner seemed genuinely taken aback by the question. He paused, seeming to gather his thoughts and his words.

"Sari Bashir's death," he said quietly, "was a tragic event for this law firm and for me personally. The loss of a young person is always painful, and a loss by suicide is especially so. I suppose it was through that pain that I first viewed the idea of this tribute. I feared it might be gloomy and morbid."

He paused again. With a sad smile, he said, "I was wrong. There is, I have learned, a wise Jewish expression when one speaks of the dead. That expression is, 'May her memory be a blessing.' I hope that's what this tribute video will accomplish."

Even Hanratty seemed moved by that answer. Nearly a minute passed before he turned to the next page.

"We're almost through. Sam will edit this down and get rid of my segues here. Anyway, back to the script."

Pause.

"In addition to her mergers-and-acquisition work, I understand Ms. Bashir did some work for you on some political issues."

Warner seemed puzzled. "Political issues?"

"Campaign finance regulations, if I'm not mistaken."

Warner paused. "Not for me. For a client."

Hanratty chuckled. "One of your supporters, I hope."

Warner frowned. "Harry, this is a confidential matter. Move on to another topic." He glanced over at Sam. "You need to edit this out. This is a sensitive area for clients."

"Okay," Sam said.

He turned to Hanratty. "Anything else?"

"One last topic. And one of your favorites, I think. I understand you are a big fan of the St. Louis Symphony."

Warner smiled. "I am indeed. My wife and I have had season tickets for more than two decades."

"Were you aware that Sari Bashir was a big fan of classical music?"

Warner raised his eyebrows and smiled. "I did not realize that. Lovely."

"You may have just answered my next question."

"What was that?"

"I was wondering whether you ever ran into her at one of the concerts."

"No, I never did. What a shame."

"What about other places?"

"Pardon?"

"After hours. Senior partner, junior associate. Did you have a surprise encounter with Sari Bashir outside the office?"

Warner frowned. After a moment, he said, "Not that I recall."

Chapter Twenty-five

As I headed back down the hallway toward the main reception area, a female voice called, "Miss Gold?"

I turned. An attractive redhead in a gray skirt and white blouse was approaching. She looked to be in her late twenties or early thirties.

She smiled. "I'm Laura. Mr. Olsen's secretary. He was wondering if you'd have a few minutes to talk after Mr. Warner's interview."

I glanced at my wristwatch. "Okay."

"Wonderful. This way, Miss Gold."

I followed her back around the corner to another corner office. This one had a plaque outside the door that read Len Olsen. Interesting. The plaque outside Donald Warner's office read Mr. Warner.

Laura tapped lightly on the doorjamb. "Mr. Olsen?"

Len Olsen looked up from his computer and smiled at me. "Ah, Rachel. Thanks so much."

He got to his feet and came around the desk to greet me. This was Friday, and thus casual day at the firm. Olsen had on a crisp white shirt with the sleeves rolled to the elbows, faded Levis, a khaki braided-cotton belt, and brown Sperry Top-Siders. We shook hands.

"Have a seat." He gestured toward the L-shaped leather couch in the corner of his office. "Make yourself comfortable. Would you like something to drink. Coffee? Tea? A soda?"

"No, thanks. I'm fine."

I looked around the office as I took a seat. Len Olsen's office was a contrast to Donald Warner's, beginning with the chrome-and-glass-top desk and a decidedly different set of framed celebrity photographs on the "Me wall." I saw shots of Len Olsen with Democratic politicos (President Bill Clinton, Missouri Governor Jay Nixon, Missouri Senator Claire McCaskill), sports figures (Ozzie Smith, Kurt Warner, Tony LaRussa)), and media personalities (Len Olsen in mid-interview with Larry King, with Chris Wallace, and with Anderson Cooper).

There was a framed display of Olsen's yellow-and-black Army Ranger badge and a photo of him posed in front of a small Cessna jet at what appeared to be, from the sign in the background, the Valley Park airport in southwest St. Louis County. As I recalled from a recent *St. Louis Magazine* profile of him, Olsen was a pilot, having learned that skill during his military service. The law firm owned the plane, which Olsen used to fly his litigation team to the rural county seats around the Midwest and South where many of his cases were tried.

On his desk were two framed photographs, both featuring Olsen and a beautiful young blonde, presumably his current girlfriend. One shot was taken at a fancy charity ball: Olsen was in a tuxedo, and she was in a formal black gown. In the other photo, they were posed on a white sandy beach, both dressed in what could be called resort wear casual: a blue-and-gold Hawaiian-print short-sleeve shirt and khaki shorts for him, a striking white crochet mini-sundress and sunglasses for her. As I recalled from that magazine profile, in addition to his swanky condominium in midtown, he owned another one in Vail and a beach house in Mozambique, which is where this dazzling beach shot must have been taken.

But the most striking feature of his office was the pair of large framed posters from the 1938 Warner Bros. film, *The Adventures of Robin Hood*. They hung side by side on the opposite wall. One featured a smiling Errol Flynn in a feathered green cap above the banner: The Best-Loved Bandit of All Time! The other featured

Flynn and Claude Rains (as Prince John) in a swordfight on a staircase.

According to that magazine profile, many viewed Olsen's love of that movie as both a tribute to an actor to whom he bore a striking resemblance, and a good-natured reference to Olsen's specialty. He'd built a career of taking from the rich and giving to the poor. Specifically, he'd won multi-million-dollar verdicts for farmers, mineworkers, and others against some of the largest corporations in America. He'd used some of that money to help fund the Sherwood Forest Trust, which provided food, clothing, and medical supplies to impoverished families in the Bootheel in southeast Missouri, the rural area where Olsen had grown up.

"Laura, dear," Olsen said, "you can close the door now."

He took a seat facing me on the other side of the couch.

"So," he said, his smile fading, "how was Donald?"

"He did well. There will be two or three nice sound bytes that will make it into the video."

"Excellent. I'm relieved, Rachel. I don't know whether anyone told you, but Donald was not enthusiastic about this tribute video."

"So I've heard. He even talked about that during the filming."

Olsen raised his eyebrows. "Really?"

"I don't think it will get into the video, but he did explain his concerns."

"I suppose we're an odd pair, Donald and I. Republican and Democrat, corporate lawyer and plaintiff's lawyer, glass-half-empty guy and glass-half-full guy." He shrugged. "Probably what keeps this place hopping, eh?"

I smiled. "Maybe so."

"So how is the project going?"

"Quite well. There are only a few more interviews of people at this firm and then, as they say, it's a wrap."

"When am I up?"

"I think you're scheduled for next Tuesday. That's the final day."

"Good." He leaned forward, giving me a full dose of those baby blues. "We can't thank you enough, Rachel. This will be a special gift to the family and to our firm."

Not sure whether he was ending the conversation and getting ready to put the moves on me, I smiled, stood and reached out my hand.

"I'm glad you feel that way, Len. I hope the film will live up to your expectations."

He stood.

"I'm sure it will, Rachel."

We shook hands and I left.

Chapter Twenty-six

I sang the last notes of "Swing Low, Sweet Chariot" then leaned over and kissed Sam on his nose.

"I love you, Smooch," I said.

He smiled. "I love you, Mommy."

Sam's smile never failed to brighten my day and remind me of the magic of life. Of course, he also happened to be the cutest little boy on the planet, at least in my totally objective opinion. He had his father's dark features, my curly brown hair and green eyes, and the gentle disposition of his namesake, my dear late father Seymour, whose Hebrew name was Schmul (Samuel).

"I can't wait for tomorrow," I said.

I was one of the parent volunteers on his school's field trip to the zoo.

His smile broadened. "Me, too."

I wrinkled my nose. "But no snakes this time, okay?"

"They won't hurt you, Mommy."

"They give me the creeps. Yuck."

That made him laugh. "Oh, Mommy."

I gave him a hug. "Have a good sleep, cutie."

I stood and scratched Yadi's head, which made his tail flop.

I paused at the bedroom door and blew Sam a kiss. "Good night, Smooch."

As I came downstairs, I could hear Benny and my mom at the kitchen table in the midst of what sounded, bizarrely enough, like a theological discussion.

"Of course it's crazy," Benny was saying. "But there's nothing in Mormonism that's any crazier than any other religion, including ours."

"Ours? That's a shanda, Benny. Why would you say such a thing?"

"Why? Where should I start? How 'bout Noah's Ark? That's certainly credible. Or maybe Lot's wife turning into a block of salt? I'm all for well-seasoned food, Sarah, but that's an even bigger size that you can get at Sam's Club. And Jonah and the whale? Jacques Cousteau is spinning in his grave."

"Those are allegories. No one believes they really happened."

"Allegories? Try to sell that to an Orthodox Jew. That stuff is the word of God to him."

"But an angel named Moroni? Burying gold tablets in upper state New York? That's meshuggah, Benny."

"Check out the Book of Exodus. Angel Moroni? How about a badass angel zooming around Egypt killing all the first-born kids? And our boy Moses? Turning his rod into a snake and parting the Red Sea? That trick puts David Copperfield to shame."

"Enough, Rebbe Goldberg," I said. "Time for dessert. Mom, Benny brought us a box of donuts from your favorite place."

My mother's eyes widened. "World's Fair Donuts?"

Benny shrugged. "Of course."

My mother placed her hand over her heart. "God bless you, Benny. Such a mensch."

I kissed my mother on top of her head. "I'll make us tea."

Sarah Gold is one of a kind—the most determined and exasperating woman I know. Life trained her well. She came to America from Lithuania at the age of three, having escaped with her mother and baby sister after the Nazis killed her father, the rest of his family, and whatever semblance of religious faith my mother might ever have had. Fate remained cruel. My mother—a woman who reveres books and learning—was forced to drop out of high school and go to work as a waitress when her mother (after whom I'm named) was diagnosed with terminal liver cancer. My grandmother Rachel died six months later, leaving her two daughters, Sarah and Becky, orphans at the ages of seventeen and fifteen. Two years later, my mother married Seymour Gold, a gentle, shy, devoutly Jewish bookkeeper ten years her senior. My sweet father was totally smitten by his beautiful, spirited wife and remained so until his death from a heart attack a decade ago on the morning after Thanksgiving.

She is now the Widow Gold the Elder. I am the Younger.

By the time I poured our tea, Benny was finishing his third donut, a chocolate long john.

"So," he said, reaching for his fourth, a glazed one, "how's the non-crime investigation going?"

"Slowly."

"Let's recap. You have three suspects with something to hide, right?"

"Maybe four."

"What are they hiding?" my mother asked.

Benny said, "First, we have Mr. Nooner, aka Brian Teever.

"Nooner?" my mother said.

"As in shtupping over the lunch hour at a downtown hotel," Benny said.

My mother shrugged. "I can think of worse things."

"Please, Mom."

"Here's worse, Sarah. Shtupping your client's wife over the lunch hour."

"Oy."

"Oy is right."

"Technically," I said, "she was a client, too."

I turned to my mom. "Teever was doing their estate plan."

"And doing David Hudson's wife," Benny said.

"Who is David Hudson?" my mother asked.

"A big shot in town," I said. "He's the CEO of Laclede Bio-Chem and sits on a bunch of boards, including the United Way. You don't want to get on the wrong side of David Hudson."

"Still," Benny said, "even if we assume that Sari found out about Teever's affair, that doesn't seem like much of motive to kill her. Even if she planned to rat him out."

"But it would compromise him. He'd have to worry about her husband. And as Stanley pointed out, Teever is vulnerable. He serves on the Missouri Bar's Board of Governors. His oversight duties include enforcement of the Missouri Rules of Professional Conduct, which his affair certainly violates."

"Nevertheless," Benny said, "murder?"

My mother said, "You have two other suspects?"

"Stan the Man does," Benny said. "I've seen the videos. One is a gal who could play defensive end for the Packers and the other is a midget with an attitude."

My mother frowned and turned to me.

"Two attorneys, Mom. Susan O'Malley and Rob Brenner. She's kind of big, and he's kind of short."

"And they're suspects?" she asked.

I shrugged. "Persons of interest."

"And?"

"We don't have much. According to Stanley, who watched the tapes of their interviews, both of them had some prior relationship with Sari. Based on his reading of their faces, he says there was a sexual aspect to each encounter and they both ended badly."

"So they might be jealous?" my mother said.

"Or spurned."

"Spurned?" she said. "And that makes them suspects?"

"Maybe." I shrugged. "The police have a term for it. Crimes of passion. It's at the root of a lot of killings."

My mother took a sip of her tea and mulled it over. "How do you get more information?"

"I'm not sure. Maybe documents. Stanley figured out a lot from looking at Teever's expense account records. More than I would have"

Benny said, "You said maybe a fourth suspect? Is that Donald Warner?"

I nodded. "I was at his interview today."

"And?"

"He seemed genuine. He admitted he was initially opposed to the idea of the video and explained why."

"But?"

"I had Stanley watch the tape, but even I could tell two questions rattled him."

"Which ones?" my mother asked.

"The first was my idea, the second Stanley's."

"What was yours?" Benny asked.

"We had Tony Manghini download all of the Word documents Sari created in the past few months. She did a legal memo for Warner about three months ago that was a follow-up to a prior one on campaign finance issues. The prior one focused on Super PACs."

"What's a Super PAC?" my mother asked.

"A big force in elections these days," I said. "They're a special type of political committee. One of the big ones is American Crossroads. They spent over a hundred million dollars in the last election. Sari's prior memo went over all the reporting and recordkeeping requirements under the Federal Election Commission regs."

"And her update?" Benny asked.

"That one focused on 501(c)(4) organizations. According to her memo, they used to be mainly social policy outfits like the Sierra Club or the National Rifle Association. But there are lots of new ones that get involved in election campaigns. Big money, too."

"What's the difference between the two?" my mother asked.

"The 501(c)(4)s aren't subject to the federal election laws and they don't have to disclose their donors. That's a big deal. They can spend money in an election but no one knows who's funding them."

"What did her memo cover?" Benny asked.

"They're regulated by the Internal Revenue Service. Section 501(c)(4) is actually a section of the Internal Revenue Code. Thus they have to comply with all the IRS regulations. Sari's memo flagged the key issues there."

"Does Warner have a 501(c)(4)?" Benny asked.

"Don't know. He claimed Sari's memo was for a client."

"Who?"

"He said it was confidential, but according to Sari's memo it was for something called Missouri's New Moral Majority."

"Who are they?"

I shrugged. "No idea. I did one of those business name searches on the Missouri Secretary of State's website. All I came up with were two old non-profits with Moral Majority in their names, but both had forfeited their charters more than twenty years ago."

Benny said, "So what did Stanley say about Warner's reaction?"

"He said his facial expression showed a mixture of guilt and shame."

"Really?" Benny raised his eyebrows. "That sounds like Warner has some political connection to that 501(c)(4)."

"Maybe. But guilt and shame? Seems a little extreme."

"Not if the guy really is Mister Squeaky Clean. He might feel a little guilty if he's hoping to get some future campaign dough out of that outfit."

"You said Stanley had a question, too," my mother said.

"He did. An odd one. Donald Warner is a big shot with the St. Louis Symphony. Apparently, Sari loved classical music and went often. Stanley's script had Hanratty ask Warner whether he'd ever run into Sari at the symphony."

"And?" Benny said.

"The answer was no. But then Stanley had a follow-up question about whether Warner had ever run into Sari after hours anywhere else."

"And?"

I frowned. "Stanley might be making me facial-action crazy, but Warner hesitated before saying no. Stanley said the emotion he showed was primarily confusion."

I reached into the donut box and pulled out my favorite World's Fair Donut, a buttermilk cake one.

I saluted Benny. "Thanks."

He grinned. "I got you two of those."

I took a bite. "Yum."

"Meanwhile," Benny said, "if I may quote Roy Scheider from *Jaws*, you're going to need a bigger boat."

I took a sip of tea. "Meaning?"

"Meaning no matter how brilliant Stanley is, you're going need someone else in that firm. Someone who can do more than read facial expressions."

"I agree."

"And?"

"I'm meeting with her tomorrow."

Chapter Twenty-seven

"All most people saw was Muslim and Christian, light and dark, tall and short." Rebecca Hamel shrugged. "We had more in common than most folks realized."

"Such as?" I asked.

"We were both the first kids in our families to go to college. Both of our dads are blue-collar guys who work with cars."

"Really?"

"Sari's dad works the assembly line at the Ford Motor plant in Dearborn. My dad fixes cars in his own garage down on Gravois."

Rebecca Hamel and I were having lunch in a back booth at Atomic Cowboy, a hipster restaurant in the Grove, and thus off the lunchtime radar for Warner & Olsen lawyers. I wanted to make sure Rebecca would be comfortable.

I'd been intrigued by her from the moment I watched her interview. Despite her fair hair and fashion model features, there was nothing perky about her. She had a cool aura with a hint of grit.

More important, though, was her relationship with Sari. Although they met when the firm assigned Sari to serve as Rebecca's associate mentor for Rebecca's first year at the firm, it was obvious from the video interview that their relationship had grown far deeper over the year and a half before Sari died. Despite Stanley's uncanny ability to spot inconsistencies and other clues in his review of the video of our suspects, it was clear to me that we'd need more than just someone reading facial actions to figure out whether Sari's death was indeed a suicide.

Rebecca leaned back in the booth and shook her head, her eyes distant.

"What?" I asked.

"We weren't twins, Sari and me. I go deer-hunting each fall with my dad. Been doing that since junior high. He started taking me about a year after my mom died. He taught me everything from cleaning a rifle to field dressing a kill. I invited Sari to join us this year."

"And?"

She smiled. "Sari was horrified. Never held a rifle in her life. Couldn't imagine shooting anything. She was a vegetarian."

Rebecca's smile faded. "Deer season opened that Friday at dawn. Sari died Thursday night."

The waiter arrived with our food—hamburger and fries for Rebecca, grilled fish tacos for me.

After the waiter left, I asked, "Did you notice any change in her mood those last few days?"

Rebecca pondered the question. "She broke our rule the last day."

"What rule?"

"No emails."

"What do you mean?"

"Sari and I made that rule. We couldn't believe how many emails we'd get each day from people on our own floors. This one litigation partner—his office is two doors down from mine. I get at least five emails a day from him, sometimes long ones. He could save time by walking twenty feet down the hall and talking to me. Same on Sari's floor, which is mostly corporate. So we made our rule. If you don't have time to come see the other person to talk about something, then you have to call them on the phone. But no emails. Ever."

"I like that rule. So what happened?"

"That last day. Thursday. We were supposed to have lunch."

"And?"

"Around ten that morning my computer beeps. Means I have a new email. I checked. It was from Sari. First ever."

"What did it say?"

"Real short. 'Can't do lunch. Need to reschedule.' Something like that."

"What did you do?"

"I stared at the message. Should have picked up the phone." She shrugged. "But I sent her a short reply. Something like, 'No prob—can reschedule.' I ended it with something like, 'You okay?'"

"Did she respond?"

Rebecca shook her head. "I had to leave early that day. Get my rifle ready, pack my gear. On opening day of the whitetail season my dad picks me up at around two in the morning. It's about a two-hour drive down to this property one of my dad's buddies owns. They served together in Vietnam. He's a Homeland Security agent now. Anyway, I left early that day—or at least early by law firm standards. Probably around five-thirty. But first I went up to Sari's floor. I'd been bothered by that email. I wanted to check on her."

"Was she there?"

Rebecca nodded and pursed her lips. "It was odd."

"How so?"

"She was standing at the window, back to the door, just staring out and twisting a handful of her hair. I can remember trying to figure out what she was looking at. Her window faced north. Beyond her I could see a towboat pushing a line of barges up the Mississippi. I called her name. She spun around, eyes wide. But then she lowered them and sat down. I asked her what was going on."

"And?"

Rebecca shook her head. "All she said was, 'Not now.' 'When?' I asked. 'Later,' she said. I told her I'd be back in two days and we'd talk." Rebecca paused. "She was dead by then."

Her eyes watered as she took a bite of the hamburger and chewed.

We ate in silence for a while.

"I've done a lot of thinking," she said.

"About her death?"

Rebecca nodded. "I did some research. There are about a dozen warning signs for suicides. Sari had none of the obvious ones."

"Such as?"

"Threatening to kill yourself. Suddenly doing risky things. Talking about death in odd situations."

"But?"

"There are other possible indicators. Withdrawing from friends or family, having feelings of depression."

She looked down at the half-eaten hamburger. "I wonder if I'd paid more attention, if I hadn't been so focused on that hunting trip, maybe I could have done something."

This seemed the right moment. "Maybe there was nothing anyone could have done."

"Maybe." Rebecca looked up. "Maybe not."

"Maybe she didn't commit suicide."

Rebecca narrowed her eyes. "What does that mean?"

"Let me explain."

Part 3

It is a truth universally acknowledged that a single lawyer in possession of a good book of business must be in want of an equity partnership.

Tony Manghini
Manager of Office Support Services
Warner & Olsen, LLP

Chapter Twenty-eight

"And?"

He shrugged. "It's probably no big deal."

"Pinky," I said, "what's with the shrug?"

He pursed his lips and tugged at the skin on his neck as he stared up at the ceiling.

He lowered his eyes. "I'm probably too much of a skeptic."

"You're a CPA, Pinky. Being a skeptic is a good thing."

"Please tell that to Naomi." He gestured toward the framed photograph of his wife on his desk. "Know what her nickname for me is? Mr. Party Pooper, that's what." He sighed. "Sixteen years of marriage and that's my nickname."

Pinky was Pincus Zuckerman, a principal in the accounting firm of Grossberg, Bernstein, Feldman & Zuckerman—or, as Benny referred to them, Jews "R" Us. I'd known Pinky since my junior year of high school. We'd been paired, to the great good fortune of my GPA, as lab partners in Chemistry. We may have seemed an unlikely pair back then—he was a short, pudgy, nearsighted self-described nerd, and I was a cheerleader and varsity field hockey player. But we became good pals that year, much to the astonishment of our respective circles of friends.

While some might try to attribute my affection for Pinky to an odd affinity for overweight brilliant Jewish boys, he and Benny Goldberg were about as opposite as two overweight brilliant Jewish boys could be. Benny was fat in the muscular way an offensive lineman in football is fat. Indeed, he'd played offensive tackle on his high school football team. Pinky Zuckerman was fat in the soft, mushy way the Stay Puft Marshmallow Man was fat. Benny had an unruly head of curly black hair—the classic Jewfro—whereas Pinky had finally given up on the comb-over and was now bald except for a wreath of hair on the back and sides of his head. And finally, of course, Benny was the most vulgar person I have ever known, while Pinky had never—NEVER—uttered a curse word in my presence.

Pinky had been my accountant since I moved back to St. Louis and opened my law office. He did my law firm's books and my personal taxes. He'd also served as an expert witness for me in two trials involving an accounting of profits. The juries adored him, and the court of appeals upheld his opinion both times.

I'd consulted him on the personal financial records of Dr. Jeffrey Mason, the defendant in my sexual harassment lawsuit on behalf of Sofia Garcia. We were scheduled for a court-ordered mediation in about two weeks, and I assumed that the mediator would pressure my client to settle for mid six figures, which was far less than I thought we could get at trial. But it's one thing to hit the jackpot in court, and it can be quite another to try to collect on that jackpot. Because Mason had more than six million dollars invested in something called Structured Resolutions, I wanted to get Pinky's assessment of the doctor's liquid assets before we went into the mediation.

"So what made you skeptical?" I asked. "Structured Resolutions?"

He nodded.

I said, "I never even knew that those kinds of businesses existed."

"Oh, they're more common than you think. There are some big players in the structured settlement business. Companies like Peachtree Settlement Funding and J.G. Wentworth and Liberty. They buy structured settlements from plaintiffs who want the money now instead of spread out over time. That's how they advertise: get cash for your structured settlement payments now. Some guy settles his medical malpractice claim for a million dollars, but under a structured settlement he actually gets fifty grand a year for twenty years. If he wants to cash in and take a huge discount, he can go to one of these outfits."

"So they're legit?"

"Most of them."

"And Structured Resolutions?"

He shook his head. "I don't know."

"What do you mean?"

"I can't find anything on them. These outfits typically have a website. It's how they attract plaintiffs looking to cash in, and it's also how some of them attract investors. Most are registered in the state where they are incorporated, and if you dig hard enough you can find some financial information. I even found information on a few of them on Dunn & Bradstreet. But not that doctor's outfit. No website, no financial information, no state of incorporation. They appear to be an offshore entity."

"Is that bad?"

"Not necessarily. They'd hardly be the first company to set up headquarters outside the country, usually to avoid taxes or regulations. But without reliable financial information on them, I can't tell you whether you could access that money."

"What about those statements I gave you? The ones they had to turn over to me. Mason seems to be earning a pretty decent return on his investment."

"Seems to be." Pinky shrugged. "The company is outperforming the big players in the industry. But those statements are fairly opaque, Rachel. General, conclusory, not much detail. It appears that the doctor owns an interest in a fund composed of annuities. Sort of like a mutual fund, I guess. In other words, Structured Resolutions might not be the actual annuity company but more like a mutual fund comprised of annuities—or interests in annuities of other companies. Again, I'm not saying there's anything wrong with that outfit. Heck, the numbers are impressive."

"How so?"

"That doctor's statements go back six years. They show he has been earning a consistent seven percent on his investment all six years. It looks like you need to make a ten-year commitment on each new investment."

"What do you mean?"

"Over those six years he's bought in three different times, each for more than a million dollars, once for almost three million. But each time you buy in, it's almost like buying an annuity. If you try to cash out before ten years, you get hit with big penalties. Of course, when your ten years are up, you can always renew. It's probably to everyone's advantage. The investor gets to lock in a rate and avoid taxes, and the company gets to minimize the fluctuations of its funds. Like I say, that's probably what's going on."

"But just probably?"

He shrugged. "I'm just saying I'm a skeptic, Rachel. Here's another example. There's a reference in the statements to audited financials. The auditors are a CPA firm. An outfit called Durlester Minogue. I'd never heard of them. I Googled them and came up with a phone number and a P.O. box in Pontiac, Michigan, which is near Detroit. I called the number a few times. No one ever answered."

"It just rang?"

"Yep. No voice mail." He signed. "You do this stuff long enough and sometimes a warning light starts blinking."

"It's blinking here?"

He nodded. "But some things do check out. Those statements have what they describe in a footnote as a representative sampling of the annuities in the settlements of the underlying lawsuits. There are more than a dozen lawsuits listed. They're all over the country. I had one of my associates do a docket search for the cases. Sure enough, they're all real, and they all settled. So that part is good. The rest, though, makes me nervous. But that's me, and you know me, Rachel. If I were your client and needed to count on money from that Structured Resolution account, I'd feel a lot safer getting it by way of a settlement, even if it's for less than I might get from a jury. You know the old saying: 'Pigs get fat, hogs get slaughtered.'"

Chapter Twenty-nine

This time Rebecca Hamel and I met in my office. If someone had really killed Sari Bashir, and if that someone was really one of the four lawyers, then more than one public meeting with Rebecca might be too risky for her—and, I suppose, for me. For added safety, since the calendar on her computer could be accessed by others at the law firm, I told her to be sure to enter an out-of-office meeting that would be difficult for someone at the firm to independently verify. That's exactly what she did. According to her calendar, she had an eight a.m. appointment for an oil change at Hamel Auto Repair. The Hamel was Bob, her father.

At our first meeting two days ago over lunch at Atomic Cowboy, I told her about Stanley's belief that Sari had been murdered and explained how we'd come up with a list of suspects consisting of the four attorneys from her law firm who'd entered the walkway to the garage that night, namely, Susan O'Malley, Rob Brenner, Donald Warner, and Brian Teever. I'd asked her to go back through her memories and documents to see what, if anything, she could recall about Sari's dealings with any of those four attorneys. We agreed to meet at my office this morning to go over whatever she was able to recall.

Rob Brenner, as Stanley had already deduced from the video, had made an unsuccessful pass at Sari. It occurred about six weeks before her death. According to what Sari had told Rebecca, Brenner had given her a legal research task in connection with an upcoming hearing on a summary judgment motion. Claiming, perhaps accurately, that his schedule for that week was booked solid during the days, he arranged for them to meet to discuss her research results over dinner at a restaurant downtown. He had two drinks before dinner and almost an entire bottle of wine during the meal. Sari, a Muslim, didn't drink. They spent maybe ten minutes talking about her research before Brenner shifted into seduction mode. On the way out of the restaurant he put his arm around her waist and slid it down her hip as he suggested that she might like to drop by his condo for a nightcap. When she politely declined, he became belligerent and made a few vague threats about her future at the firm. Sari had been shaken by the experience. After a couple sleepless nights, she'd confided in Rebecca, who was furious and urged Sari to file a complaint, but Sari refused. As far as Rebecca knew, Brenner had avoided all contact with Sari after that.

"And Susan O'Malley?" I asked.

Rebecca gave me a sad smile. "Poor Sari."

"Really?"

She nodded. "Every September the firm puts on this social event for the lawyers. We jokingly call it the Senior Prom. It's always held at a ballroom in some fancy hotel. This year it was at the Ritz in Clayton. Because there tends to be lots of drinking, the firm picks up the tab for anyone who wants to spend the night at the hotel. Susan likes to drink, and she always books a room. Seems she had the hots for Sari. I'm not sure what happened, but she apparently groped Sari in the bathroom or the hallway and tried to get her to go upstairs to her hotel room. Sari freaked out and left the party and went home. I found all this out when I asked her the following Monday why she'd disappeared."

"Any repercussions?"

Rebecca shrugged. "If there were, Sari never told me."

"How about Donald Warner?"

"I know Sari worked on some corporate deal with him—some sort of acquisition, I think." She shook her head. "I don't remember her saying anything about him, good or bad."

"Did she ever mention running into him somewhere after work?"

"I don't think so."

"How about research she did on election law issues?"

Rebecca frowned, trying to remember. "Election law issues."

"Anything?"

"She worked on something. I think it was for Mr. Warner. She mentioned it."

"Do you remember what she said?"

Rebecca thought about it and shook her head. "Nothing specific."

"Finally, how about Brian Teever?"

"She worked on one estate plan with him. The clients were a wealthy couple."

"The Hudsons?"

"Maybe. I can't remember their names. Sari spent time with the wife."

"Why?"

"The couple had some really valuable things at their house. Paintings, jewelry, stuff like that. Part of Sari's assignment for the estate plan was to identify each item of personal property for some schedule or list or something like that for the will or maybe the trust."

"Was the wife's name Claire?"

"Yep. That's it. Claire."

"Do you remember what else Sari told you? About the art or the jewelry or anything else?"

"She told me they had these two paintings that were each worth over a million dollars. They were by modern artists. I hadn't heard of them." Rebecca leaned back in the chair, trying to remember. "One other thing. She told me that she was bothered by one of their investments."

"Which one?"

Rebecca shrugged. "I don't remember. She said they had millions of dollars in it but she couldn't find any public information on the company."

"What did she do?"

"I know she told that woman—Claire—to ask her husband about it. She said something to Mr. Teever, too. That's why I remember."

"What do you mean?"

"I had lunch with her the day she told Mr. Teever. She told him that morning."

"And?"

"She was upset. He'd given her a real lecture. She thought she was doing her job, being vigilant and all, but Mr. Teever told her she was way out-of-bounds. He told her she should never talk directly to a client about something like that, that she should only tell him and let him decide whether it merited the attention of the client. He told her to finish up her list of the clients' personal property as soon as possible and that she should cease all further work on that matter. He told her not to contact the wife again. Ever. She left his office in tears."

"Wow."

"Yeah. Mr. Teever can be like that. That's what I told her. None of the associates like working for him."

"So she backed off?"

Rebecca frowned. "Maybe, maybe not. Sari never said anything to me after that, but she could be persistent, especially if something bothered her."

Chapter Thirty

"Mozambique," Benny said. "Is that in the Caribbean?"

The four of us—Benny, Stanley Plotkin, Jerry Klunger and I—had just finished watching the video of Len Olsen's interview. Stanley appeared to be troubled by some aspects of the interview, but so far had only stated that Olsen's praise of Sari was insincere. The interview had taken place in Olsen's office, and the two framed photographs of him and his girlfriend were in the background, which led to my mention of his two vacation homes—the one in Vail and the other in Mozambique.

I shrugged. "I'm not sure."

Stanley announced, "The Republic of Mozambique is situated in southeast Africa. The capital city is Maputo, known as Lourenco Marques before its independence from Portugal. It is bordered by the Indian Ocean to the east, which is the ocean visible in the background of that photograph of Mr. Olsen and his female companion. For those requiring a more precise description of the location, Tanzania is along the northern border, Malawi and Zambia are along the northwest, Zimbabwe is to the west, and South Africa and Swaziland are to the southwest."

"Swaziland?" Benny asked. "Did you just make that up, Stan?"

"I did not, Professor Goldberg. The nation and its people are named after the country's nineteenth-century king Mswati the Second."

Benny chuckled. "The man is a walking Wikipedia. What else can you tell me about Mozambique?"

"The official language is Portuguese. The country has no extradition treaty with the United States. It became independent from Portugal on June 25, 1975. It has a tropical climate with two seasons—a wet season from October to March and a dry season from April to September. Is there any additional information you require?"

"I'm good, dude. King Mswati the Second, eh? Nice."

I filled them in on my meeting with Rebecca Hamel. Her description of Sari Bashir's concern over the mysterious large investment in the portfolio of assets of Claire and David Hudson, clients of Brian Teever, triggered a reaction from Stanley, who turned to Jerry.

"Tomorrow you need to request that Mr. Manghini retrieve a copy of the Hudson estate plan from the client safe."

Jerry's eyes widened. "Do you think he will?"

"You should inform him that you are making that request at the behest of Ms. Gold. Mr. Manghini will comply with any request from Ms. Gold."

"What if he asks me why Miss Gold wants a copy of that file?"

"He will not do that."

"Why not?"

"Because he will assume that you do not know why she has made that request. For a combination of reasons, including the priapic, he will comply with Ms. Gold's requests."

"What is the client safe?" Benny asked.

Jerry said, "It's where the firm stores important client documents."

"Such as," Stanley said, "original executed trust and estate instruments. The documentation for the high net-worth individuals that Mr. Teever represents often includes detailed financial statements of the sort that Ms. Bashir was apparently compiling or reviewing for the Hudsons."

Benny grinned at me. "Priapic, eh?"

I rolled my eyes.

Chapter Thirty-one

"A Pious?" Benny shook his head. "That figures."

I sighed. "A Prius, Benny."

"Not in my experience."

"Oh?"

"Science has shown a statistically significant correlation between Prius owners and sanctimonious upper-middle-class douchebags."

"I have a friend who drives a Prius."

"We're talking statistical significance, woman. One friend does not refute basic math, and basic math proves that most Prius owners are self-righteous douchebags. It's one of the fundamental statistical truths of car ownership."

"There is more than one?"

"Of course. We have the Subaru Outback, or as it's more commonly known in the industry, the Lesbaru. And then there is the Smart Car aka the Ultimate Buzz Kill."

"Enlighten me."

"According to the most recent scientific data, the correlation between bachelors who own Smart Cars and bachelors who get laid is nearly zero."

"Is that so? Who exactly keeps track of this scientific data?"

"Excellent question, Ms. Gold. Unfortunately, disclosure of that information is beyond your security clearance."

"Ah, yes, available only to subscribers of *Benny Goldberg Magazine*."

"Mock me if you choose, fair lady, but answer this one question: have you ever had sex with a man who owned a Smart Car?"

"Next question."

"How about this one, Miss Marple? What exactly are we doing here parked outside the offices of Warner & Olsen at 9:30 at night?"

"I told you. We're trying to investigate a pattern."

"Tell me again."

"I asked Tommy Flynn to print out the last few months of cardkey information for weekday nights. Since we already had the record of who entered the walkway the night Sari died, I wanted to see if there was any pattern."

"And the only hit you got was Donald Warner?"

"Yes—or at least the most direct hit. There were lots of other nights when one or more of those lawyers left the office late—sometimes even after midnight. As did other lawyers at the firm. And there were some nights when all four of them stayed late and left within an hour or so of each other, although that seemed kind of random. But from our list of suspects, none had consistent Thursday departure times except for Warner. On the night she died, he entered the walkway around 9:30. The records show that he leaves the office around that same time about three Thursdays a month."

"Which proves?"

"Nothing. But it makes me curious. There's no record of when he left the office on most other nights, which means he left before seven o'clock, since you don't need your access card for the walkway until after seven. The records show he occasionally left after seven, but never later than nine."

"And thus?"

"And thus I have no idea. That's why I wanted to see where he goes on Thursday nights. If he just drives home, then it probably means he has some sort of regularly scheduled conference call or meeting that night. Maybe for one of his boards. If so, maybe I could dump him from the list."

"Speaking of dumps…"

I gave him a look.

"No, I'm good. But do you remember our nighttime stakeout a few years ago? We were at that self-storage operation out by the airport?"

I thought back. "Vaguely."

"Then you may also recall that while we were sitting there in your car waiting for something to happen I provided you with some enlightened commentary on an important gap in world literature."

"You mean your demented rant on why no one in a novel ever makes a poop?"

"A 'poop'? Did you just say 'poop'? Good grief, Rachel. That is proof of the detrimental side effects of raising a child. But back to my commentary. It was a thoughtful and, if I may say, a profound discourse on the noteworthy absence of a certain bodily function from the novel. Great characters in world literature eat and sleep and eat some more and occasionally fuck but they never ever take a shit. Huck and Jim on that raft for weeks, Captain Ahab on his ship, Jay Gatsby in his mansion, and even Tarzan in the fucking jungle, for God's sake. Nary a dump."

I sighed. "Yes, Benny, I do recall that rant."

"Well, my dear, I must amend it."

"Oh?"

"I finally dragged myself through that James Joyce piece of shit—no pun intended."

"*Finnegans Wake?*"

"Of course not. No one has ever read that book. Anyone who claims they have is full of shit. Again, no pun intended."

"*Ulysses?*"

"Exactly."

"You read it?"

Benny shrugged. "Sort of."

"What does that mean?"

"To quote the great Lord Arthur Balfour, 'He has only half learned the art of reading who has not added to it the more refined art of skipping and skimming.' Try to read *Ulysses*. You'll see what I mean."

"So what caused you to amend your prior diatribe?"

"A massive dump. In Chapter Two. Probably the biggest one in the history of world literature. And guess what? It's by a member of the tribe."

"A yid?"

"You got it. Leopold Bloom. You'd be proud of him. And then, near the end of the book, Leo and that other guy—that pretentious putz from *Portrait of the Artist as a Young Man*—they stand side by side under the night sky and take huge pisses together."

"That is an endorsement worthy of a dust jacket blurb."

"Good point. Maybe I'll contact the publisher. You never know—wait—"

He squinted through the windshield and pointed toward the parking garage exit. "That him?"

The exit barrier arm was rising. A silver Prius with Missouri license plates passed through the gate and onto the one-way street.

"Yep."

I waited until he was slowing at the red light at the end of the block before starting my engine. The Prius turned right at the corner, heading south. I followed, staying a block behind it.

When he reached the Highway 40 overpass, Warner drove past the west entrance ramp on the right and turned left onto the east ramp.

"Where's he live?" Benny asked.

"Out in West County."

"Interesting."

We followed him onto the Poplar Street Bridge heading east over the Mississippi River, passing the Welcome to Illinois sign halfway across. Although I was not exactly versed in the art of tailing someone, Donald Warner was no challenge. His cautious and conservative demeanor matched his driving style. He stayed in the right lane and kept his speed a few miles below the speed limit, which made him easy to follow. He took the Route 3 exit and headed south.

Benny said, "Jeez, you think he's going to a strip joint?"

There were several strip clubs in what St. Louisians refer to as the East Side, and a few of those clubs were along Route 3.

I stayed further back now, since the traffic was lighter on this undivided highway. We passed the turn-off for PTs Cabaret, probably the best known of the East Side strip clubs. About two miles further south, Warner's left-turn blinker came on. I slowed as he turned left onto a paved road. I turned onto the same road, but his car was out of sight by then. I started down the darkened road accelerating slightly.

"There," Benny said, pointing to the right.

There was a side road. About fifty yards down it opened on the right into a large parking lot.

"Did you see his car?" I asked.

"I saw taillights. I think it was his car."

As we pulled onto the parking lot I could see Donald Warner walking toward the building. His tall, lanky body was unmistakable.

"That's odd," I said.

"What?"

I pointed. "He's wearing sunglasses and a baseball hat."

He lowered the brim of the hat as he opened the door and entered.

"Well, well, well," Benny said.

"What?"

"Look where we are."

He was pointing up at the neon sign above the entrance. The sign read Steamhouse Saloon and featured a brightly lit illustration of a man, arms crossed over his bare chest, wearing nothing but a cowboy hat, a bandana around his neck, cowboy boots, and tight cut-off jeans that revealed enough beneath the denim to confirm, even from three parking rows back, that he wasn't Jewish.

Benny said, "Something tells me that Donald Warner did not drive over here tonight to attend a meeting of the Republican Party."

"Wow," I said.

"Let's check it out."

"I don't know, Benny. I don't want him to see me."

"We can at least poke our heads in there. I'll go in front to make sure he's not by the door."

We parked, and I followed Benny across the parking lot. The building was a nondescript windowless one-story structure about the width of…well…a nightclub. You could hear the pounding bass of the dance music as we approached the door.

A sign by the door read:

NOTICE: WHAT HAPPENS IN THE STEAMHOUSE
STAYS IN THE STEAMHOUSE
NO CAMERAS OR CELL PHONES ALLOWED
LEAVE THEM IN YOUR CAR OR CHECK THEM INSIDE

I turned to Benny.

"In the car," he said.

I returned to the car to store our phones and then we entered the building. The bald, tattooed bouncer greeted us inside the narrow foyer, which was screened off from the rest of the place by a heavy black curtain. Seemingly unfazed by me, he took our ten-dollar cover charges, looked in my purse, had us walk through a metal detector, and gestured us toward the curtain.

Benny went first. Pulling back the curtain, he peered around and turned back to me with a grin. "I hope you're a fan of thongs."

Red thongs were the theme of the Steamhouse Saloon, along with white cowboy hats and black cowboy boots. Those three items comprised the entire uniform of all of the waiters and bartenders.

The room was large—at least the size of a basketball court. A bar ran the length of the side wall and was manned by three good-looking and impressively endowed young men, each dressed in the saloon's uniform. All three had hairless chests, plenty of tattoos, and cute tushes.

There were three dancers, one each on round elevated plat-forms at the end of a catwalk. The three catwalks, joined at the small stage on the back wall, angled out into the crowd, with groups of men seated around each platform. As with the other staff, the dancers wore nothing but the uniform. Waiters moved among the crowd with serving trays held over their heads, oddly effeminate as they sashayed along in their boots and thongs.

The clientele ran the gamut from college-age to senior citizen and from blue jeans to suits and ties. I scanned the room, standing on my tiptoes, just in time to see Donald Warner disappear through the large Western-style swinging doors at the far end of the room.

The music was almost painfully loud. I had to point and shout to Benny about Warner. He nodded. With hand signals, he told me to wait by the bar and he'd be back in a few minutes.

I ordered a Schlafly Pale Ale on draft. My bartender—gorgeous but obviously not Jewish—set down my drink and gave me a friendly smile.

"Cheers, honey," he said.

I raised my glass. "Cheers."

Benny passed through the swinging doors at the far end of the room. I sipped my beer and watched the dancer on the table nearest me. His principal dance move was a bend-over-and-shake-your booty maneuver known, I believe, as "twerking"—a move that delighted the customers seated on chairs around the platform. Perhaps I was jaded, but the vibe of the Steamhouse Saloon was as depressing to me as the vibe at the heterosexual version of these strip clubs.

I was still nursing my beer and leaning back against the bar when Benny reemerged, pushing through the swinging doors on the far end of the room. He walked briskly across the floor, caught my eye, and nodded toward the exit. I followed him out of the building and onto the parking lot.

"Well?" I said.

"Let's get in your car first."

We did.

"So tell me," I said.

"Donald Warner definitely has a secret life over here."

"What's behind those doors?"

"A locker room, three saunas, and about twenty private—" and here he paused and made air quotation marks with the index and middle fingers of each hand "—massage therapy rooms. I got there just in time to see an older man and this young blond guy disappear into one of those rooms. They both were wearing nothing but towels around their waists."

"Okay."

"I poked my head into one of the empty rooms. There's a table that I suppose could pass for a massage table, although it's maybe knee-high instead of waist high. There're towels stacked on the counter along with several tubes of K-Y Jelly, a basket of condoms, and a few contraptions I'd never seen before."

I leaned back in my car seat and exhaled slowly. "Thursday nights."

"Yeah."

"Was Warner in one of those rooms?"

"Probably. I couldn't tell for sure. There were maybe five of those little rooms occupied. I wasn't going to knock on the doors. There was another door at the far end—a big metal door—with a sign that read Private. I tried the handle. Locked. It had one of those finger-pad combination locks above the handle. I suppose he could have been back there."

My initial reaction was that Warner's conduct was too risky for someone with political ambitions, but then I thought of all those family-values politicians and anti-gay preachers who'd been caught, literally, in compromising positions.

As if reading my mind, Benny said, "Remember, the presence of a dick automatically deducts seventy-five points from every man's IQ."

"So it would seem."

I started the engine and turned to Benny. "Even if we assume Sari discovered his secret, is that reason enough to kill her?"

"Unless she followed him over here, how would she even find out?"

"I watched his interview. That question Stanley included about Warner running into Sari after hours. He seemed more confused than rattled by the question. Maybe he has a secret boyfriend. Maybe she came across the two of them somewhere else."

"And what? Tried to blackmail him?"

I shrugged. "Something's off." I put the car into gear. "We're missing something here."

"What?"

I sighed. "I don't know."

Chapter Thirty-two

They were my version of Tinker to Evers to Chance. Tony Manghini made a copy of the Hudson estate plan and gave it to Jerry who gave it to Stanley, who took it home to his mother, who gave it to my mother, who gave it to me.

One of the estate documents—Appendix B to both living trusts—was a list of marital assets. In addition to jewelry, furniture, and the two valuable paintings Sari had mentioned to Rebecca (one by Mark Rothko, the other by Francis Bacon, each valued in the high-six figures), the list included a spreadsheet of investments. There were recognizable individual stocks—Apple, General Electric, Google—and a trio of mutual funds from Vanguard. But there was also an 8.76 million-dollar entry for an investment in Structured Resolutions—the same company that had appeared on the financial statement of Dr. Jeffrey Mason, the defendant in my sexual harassment lawsuit, the same one that Pinky Zuckerman had tried without success to evaluate.

Thus my next issue: who to confront? David Hudson, CEO of Laclede BioChem? Claire Hudson, wife of David Hudson and lover of Brian Teever? Or Brian Teever?

I settled on Claire, which then posed the issue of where and how to approach her. One option was the lobby of the Marriott Hotel after one of her assignations with Teever, but that seemed a strategy better suited for a private eye in a detective novel. Sam Spade I'm not.

And even if she were still doing nooners with Brian Teever and even if I could figure out from Teever's expense reports when such future nooners would likely occur, I had no idea whether she exited the hotel in the company of Teever (which would make an approach too risky) or whether she even passed through the lobby on her way out of the hotel or simply rode the elevator down to the garage level.

A Google search supplied a possible solution. It revealed that Claire Hudson served on the board of the Woman's Exchange. Headquartered in the posh suburb of Ladue, the Woman's Exchange is a charitable enterprise dating back more than a century and devoted to the sale of handmade goods created by impoverished women and men. Even so, the wealthy female patrons of the Woman's Exchange know it less for its good deeds than for its Tearoom. On any given weekday at noon, the Tearoom is filled with that special breed of women known as the Ladies Who Lunch, many of whom order the Tearoom's Famous Salad Bowl, a concoction about as Old School as the patrons: chopped iceberg lettuce, chicken, ham, bacon, hardboiled eggs and Swiss cheese tossed in a thick Mayfair dressing.

That Claire was on the board significantly increased the odds that I could find her at the Tearoom on one of her non-nooner lunch hours. The next morning I called the Tearoom at ten-thirty, told the hostess that I was supposed to meet Claire Hudson for lunch but confessed that I couldn't remember whether our date was for today or tomorrow. She checked her reservation book and told me that Mrs. Hudson had reservations for four that day at 12:30. I thanked her and hung up without telling her my name.

I arrived at 1:15. Having studied the photograph of the board of directors on the organization's website, I was able to spot Claire Hudson at a table along the far wall with three other women I didn't recognize. I told the Tearoom hostess that I was there to see Mrs. Hudson but would wait for her in the Children's Boutique.

"And your name?"

"I'm Rachel."

"Okay, Miss…"

"Just tell her Rachel."

Although I'd dined in the Tearoom only once, I'd been a patron of the organization's Children's Boutique for years. I've purchased several adorable handmade outfits for my young cousins and the children of friends.

Twenty minutes later, as I was looking through the handmade children's toys, I heard someone clear her throat. I turned. Claire Hudson stood in the doorway, giving me a puzzled look. She was in her forties. Average height, fifteen pounds overweight, red hair cut in a bob and parted on the right, blue eyes, round face. Her appearance was more pleasant than beautiful, her aura more high school Home Ec teacher than sultry adulterer.

"Are you Rachel?"

"I am." I put down the toy and walked toward her. "Thank you for meeting with me."

She frowned. "Do I know you?"

"No."

"What do you want?"

"Let's step outside. I'll explain."

She crossed her arms over her chest. "First tell me what you want."

"Just to ask you a few questions. This won't take long."

"How did you know I was here?"

Time to ramp it up a bit.

"I had two choices for the lunch hour," I said. "This one seemed the better option for both of us."

"What was the other option?"

"The Marriott Hotel downtown."

She took a step back, her eyes widening. "What?"

"I'm not here to talk about that part of your life, Claire. It's none of my business. But another part is. That is why I am here. What I need to ask you won't take more than a few minutes. We can get it done quietly and privately in my car in the parking lot or we can do it publicly with a subpoena. I assume you'd prefer the quiet option."

"What is it you want?"

"I'll explain. But not here in the hallway." I gestured toward the front door. "We can sit in my car. It's right out there."

I walked over to the door and turned back to her. "Let's go, Claire."

It was at least half bluff—if she refused, what could I do?— but it worked. She followed me to my car. I opened the passenger side and she got in. I came around to the driver's side and joined her on the front seat.

"Thank you, Claire."

She stared out the windshield in silence.

"You remember Sari Bashir?" I said. "The associate who helped Brian Teever with the estate plan for you and your husband? The one who committed suicide?"

"Yes."

"You knew her."

She nodded. "A sweet girl."

"And apparently concerned about one of your investments."

Claire turned to me with a frown. "How did you know that?"

I offered a friendly smile. "It's my job."

"What exactly is your job?"

"That's not important now. Let's get back to Sari. She was worried about one of your investments."

Claire nodded, staring out the windshield.

"Specifically," I said, "she was worried about all the money you had tied up in an outfit called Structured Resolutions."

She turned back to me, squinting slightly. "She was."

"Back when she raised the issue, did you know anything about Structured Resolutions?"

She thought it over. "Not really."

"Did you know it was in your investment portfolio?"

"Maybe. Probably not."

"You told Brian Teever about her concerns?"

"I did."

"And?"

"He told me not to worry."

"Anything else?"

"Just that a young associate had no business prying into the financial affairs of a client, that he would take her off the matter, that I wouldn't have to deal with her anymore."

"But did he tell you anything else about the investment?"

"No."

"What about your husband?"

"What about him?"

"Did you ask your husband about that investment?"

She stared at me. After a moment, she said, "Yes."

"When?"

"After my conversation with Brian."

"And?"

She smiled. "He told me it was pure gold. The best thing in our portfolio. He told me not to worry. He said we'd been getting great returns five years in a row, that it beat the market every year."

"Did he tell what it was?"

"What do you mean?"

"What kind of company it was?"

She frowned. "Something about buying settlements from personal injury lawyers. I didn't fully understand the details. Annuities, I think. Anyway, he told me there was nothing to worry about."

"Did he tell you how he found out about the company?"

"At the club."

"Which one?"

"St. Louis Country Club."

St. Louis Country Club is the oldest and most exclusive of the St. Louis country clubs.

"Who told him about it?" I asked.

"He'd heard stories about it."

"What kind of stories?"

"Just what a good investment it was. And how difficult it was get your money in."

"Who told him?"

"Probably one of his golf buddies. Or someone else out there. We're not the only St. Louis Country Club members with money in that outfit."

"You say it's hard to invest in Structured Resolutions?"

"According to David, you need someone with the right connections."

"Did your husband have someone?"

"Brian."

"Brian Teever?"

She nodded.

I thought that over.

"Is he a member of St. Louis Country Club?"

"Oh, definitely. His family has been in that club going back at least to his grandfather."

"So he sold your husband the investment?"

"No, but he told David he thought he could get him a chance to invest. That was a big deal."

"Why?"

Claire shrugged. "Apparently, you can't just put your money into Structured Resolutions. It's like a closed fund or something. You have to have a contact, some insider who can get you access. Brian had that contact."

"Do you know who the contact was?"

She shook her head.

"Could it have been Brian himself?"

"I don't know. I really don't."

I paused, going back over her answers, trying to see if there were any gaps. "After you had that conversation with Brian Teever, the one about him taking Sari off your matter, did you ever hear from her after that?"

Claire paused, her lips pursed, and then she nodded. "I did. She called me."

"When?"

"A couple days later."

"What did she say?"

"She said she was sorry, that she didn't mean to overstep her bounds, but that she'd been concerned about that one invest-ment in our portfolio. I told she didn't need to apologize, that I appreciated her concern for us. I told her that Brian—that Mr. Teever had assured me everything was okay, that I had nothing to worry about."

"And?"

Claire shrugged. "And that was pretty much it, I think. She said that was good to hear—about what Mr. Teever said and all. She said she still had one or two more issues to run down but that she wouldn't bother me about them unless there was a reason. I said it wouldn't bother me, that I really appreciated her concerns for us, even if those issues turned out to be no big deal."

"Did you ever hear from her after that?"

"No." She sighed. "The next thing I heard was about her death. So sad."

Chapter Thirty-three

"Barry." I sighed and leaned back in my chair.

I was on the phone with Barry Kudar, aka the Barracuda. I'd called him after returning to the office from my meeting at the Woman's Exchange with Claire Hudson.

"What?" he demanded.

I said, "We can do this the easy way or we can do this the hard way."

"I don't see why we have to do it either way."

"Barry, I couldn't care less how you see it."

"What's that supposed to mean?"

"Do you really want to get hauled back before Judge Winfield one more time in this case? Does your client want to pay more sanctions? Do you?"

No response.

"Well?" I said.

"I don't understand, Rachel. You have all of my client's financial documents, and you took his deposition on those documents. What more do you want?"

"To fill the gap."

"What gap?"

"In his financial records. We have a mediation coming up. We're not participating in that mediation until your client fills in the gap."

"What are you talking about?"

"Structured Resolutions."

"Huh?"

"Look at your client's financial statements, Barry. He has six-and-a-half million dollars in Structured Resolutions. It's his biggest investment. By far."

"So?"

"I have a question for him about that investment. Just one question. We can haul him in here for another deposition or you can ask him yourself and call me with the answer."

No response.

"Your choice, Barry. As I said, we can do this the easy way or we can do this the hard way."

"What's the question?"

"Structured Resolutions is a private fund. You can't just call your broker and invest in it. Apparently, you need a connection to get access to the fund."

"How do you know that?"

"That doesn't concern you, Barry."

"Maybe it does."

"It doesn't. Back to my question. Because Structured Resolutions is a private fund, Dr. Mason needed a connection to get access to it. That's my question. Who was his connection?"

"That's it?"

"At least for now. But I need the answer. It's almost three o'clock. Get back to me today."

I hung up without waiting for a response.

I had a stack of phone calls to return, an inbox filled with unanswered emails, and a demand letter to write—and I needed to get all of that done so that I could get home in time to prepare dinner for Sam and me. Tonight was my mother's bridge club meeting.

I'd forgotten about the Barracuda until my cell phone rang on the drive home. The caller ID showed it was Kudar's law firm.

"Yes?" I said.

"Brian Teever."

"Okay."

"Is that it?"

"For now."

This time he hung up first.

Chapter Thirty-four

Ameer Bashir, Sari's father, came in from Detroit for the formal premiere of "Homage to Sari," the tribute video. The showing took place at ten-thirty that morning in the auditorium of the St. Louis Public Library's main branch. Warner & Olsen arranged for buses to shuttle the firm's lawyers and staff to the library. About a hundred and fifty people attended, including Sari's father, her cousin Malikah, and me. Benny had hoped to attend but was teaching a class that morning. I took a seat off to the side so that I had a clear view of Brian Teever, who was seated in the second row center. I spotted Stanley Plotkin. He was standing alongside a row of seats near the back. I recalled his obsession with odd numbers. Jerry Klunger was seated at the end of the row where Stanley stood.

Donald Warner and Len Olsen each made brief introductory remarks—Warner stiff, reading from notes, Olsen at ease and speaking off-the-cuff, acknowledging Sari's father and her cousin from the stage. Olsen explained that the movie was being streamed to conference rooms in the firm's other offices and that it would soon be available online at the firm's website.

I watched Teever throughout both speeches. If there were any telltale facial actions, I missed them. Toward the end of Warner's talk Teever bowed his head to check his cell phone, presumably for emails. He put it away a minute or so into Olsen's talk.

The film itself, about twenty minutes in length, was beautifully made, professionally edited, and emotionally balanced—respectful, affectionate, and genuinely moving without any overly mawkish elements. Harry Hanratty served as the film's narrator but never appeared on screen. His interview questions had been edited out so that the viewer only saw the seemingly unprompted reminiscences of the lawyers, professors, and others who had known Sari. Although most of the images of Sari were from photographs taken over the past few years, there was an adorable video clip of her on a grade school field trip to the Detroit Zoo that had me wiping tears from my eyes.

Although the tentative plans had been for Sari's father to say a few words to the audience after the screening, he was too choked up to speak, so Len Olsen concluded the event on a solemn and respectful note and the audience quietly filed out of the auditorium.

I'd driven Malikah and Ameer to the event. I drove Malikah back to her apartment near Washington University, where she said a tearful good-bye to her uncle, and then I drove Ameer Bashir to the airport, where he had a flight back to Detroit.

On the drive, I brought him up to speed on my investigation, which had not turned up much, and what little it had turned up didn't seem particularly incriminating.

"I'll keep poking around, Mr. Bashir. I still have a few leads."

"Thank you so much, Miss Gold."

I took the airport exit off the highway.

"There is one issue," I said, "that you might be able to help me with."

"Please tell me."

"We're trying to track down an accounting firm in the Detroit area. I don't know whether it's important, but I'd like to close the loop."

"In Detroit you say?"

"Actually, Pontiac."

"Is it Durlester Minogue?"

I slowed the car and turned to him. "How did you know?"

He sighed. "Sari asked me."

I pulled the car over to the road shoulder.

"When?"

"About a week before she died."

"Did she tell you why?"

"No. She just said she was working on a matter and was trying to track down the firm. She said no one answered their telephone and that she only had a post office box for an address."

"Were you able to find them?"

"No. I have a friend who works for the Housing Commission in Pontiac. I called him. He looked into it and called me back."

"And?"

Ameer Bashir shook his head. "No such company in Pontiac. He even talked to the Post Office. Durlester Minogue once rented that P.O. box but not for the last two years."

"Who has it now?"

"A collection agency."

I shifted the car back into Drive. "So no Durlester Minogue in Pontiac?"

"I could not find one. Not in Pontiac, not in Detroit. Do you know why she wanted me to find them, Miss Gold?"

I shook my head. "Not yet. But I will find out. I promise."

Chapter Thirty-five

"Geneva Estates?" Benny said.

"That's the address. For both of them."

"What is it?"

"Some sort of retirement community."

We were in my car heading west on Interstate 44 just outside St. Louis. I'd met Benny for lunch at Mission Taco in the Loop. When he found out where I was headed after lunch, he insisted on coming with me.

"Which one is Henderson?" Benny asked.

"For the accounting firm."

"The one in Pontiac, Michigan?"

"Yep."

I had searched the State of Michigan's government websites for some record—any record—of the Durlester Minogue accounting firm. All I found was a listing for a resident agent named Bruce Hohlcamp. A Google search turned up his obituary three years ago in the *Detroit Free Press*. He had died at the age of seventy-two.

But the resident agent listing on the State of Michigan website showed that the accounting firm was actually a Missouri limited liability company. I did a business name search on the Missouri Secretary of State's website and came up with Martin Henderson as the registered agent for Durlester Minogue LLC.

"Henderson is the successor?" Benny said.

"He is. According to the online records, he's been the registered agent for two years. Before him, there was a guy named Howard Proctor. Oddly enough, same address."

"Geneva Estates?" Benny said.

I nodded.

"Wonder what happened to him," Benny said.

"So did I. I found his *Post-Dispatch* obit. Heart attack. He was eighty-three."

"CPA?"

"No. According to the obituary, he was a retired professor at Fontbonne. Philosophy. A widower. No kids."

I took the next exit and headed south.

Benny said. "And the other guy?"

"Stanley Boudreau. According to the Missouri Secretary of State website, he's the registered agent for Structured Resolutions."

"That's the offshore outfit?"

"Right. I guess they need a Missouri registered agent to do business here."

"Is Boudreau another *alter kocker*?" Benny asked, using the Yiddish term for old geezer.

"Probably. It's an assisted-living complex. I don't think anyone in there is below seventy." I put on my turn signal. "Here we are."

I pulled into the parking lot. Geneva Estates was a large, two-story red-brick building with a portico in front. We parked on the lot and headed toward the entrance. As we approached, the doors swung open and Len Olsen emerged, talking on his cell phone. He was in full lawyer attire—navy blue suit, crisp white shirt, red-and-gold striped tie. His eyes widened when he recognized me.

"Got to hang up, Pete," he said. "Call you back in five."

He put the phone in his suit jacket pocket and gave me a warm smile.

"My goodness, Rachel Gold. How are you, dear?"

"I'm good, Len. This is my friend Benny. Benny, Len Olsen."

They shook hands.

Len squinted and pointed an index finger at Benny. "Professor, right? Wash U Law?"

"Guilty as charged."

Len chuckled. "Caught you on *Hardball* with Chris Matthews a couple weeks ago. You held your own."

"Thanks."

"Is Geneva Estates a client?" I asked Len.

"Oh, no." Len shook his head and chuckled. "Purely personal. My mother lives here. I moved her up to St. Louis about ten years ago. After my father passed."

"Does she like it?" I asked.

He shrugged and smiled. "Some days. She misses her home and her neighborhood. But my sister and I both live up here now. Having her near us makes more sense. What about you, Rachel? What are you doing all the way out here in the middle of the day?"

Before I could think of a response, Benny said, "My fault. I dragged her along after lunch. My great aunt lives here. Aunt Boopsie. Rachel's a good sport. She agreed to come with me."

"Boopsie?" Len said.

"That's what we call her. Her husband was Big Man. Boopsie and Big Man. Quite a pair." Benny checked his watch. "We got to get in there, Rachel. My antitrust class starts in forty-five minutes."

"Goodbye, Len," I said.

"So long, Rachel. Nice to meet you, Benny."

"Same here."

When we stepped inside the building, I pulled Benny close and whispered, "You're a genius."

"Like I told you, woman, I got mad skills."

"Boopsie?"

"Best I could do on the fly. We needed a name he couldn't check me on. And since she's supposed to be my great aunt, her last name could be anything."

We approached the receptionist. Beyond her to the right was a TV lounge, to the left a brightly lit dining area. It was past lunch time, and there were only three elderly women around a table in the dining area. In the TV lounge there were two older men watching CNN on a large wall-mounted flat-screen TV.

The gray-haired woman at the front desk gave us a perky smile. "Can I help you folks?"

"I hope so," I said. "We're in from out of town and were hoping to see Martin Henderson. He's an old family friend."

She gave us a big smile. "Why, certainly. If you'll sign in, I can take you over to the Memory Care wing. That's where Martin is these days."

I opened the guest sign-in book and paused, trying to decide how to sign us in. Benny and I had once posed as a married couple named Nick and Nora Charles. That was Benny's idea. Clever at the time, but too risky now, especially since Len Olsen had seen us. I looked up the list of sign-ins on the page. Four rows up was Len Olsen. He'd signed in at 12:20 and had written "Lucille Olsen" in the column titled Resident Visited. I glanced up at the receptionist, who was typing something on her computer. I wrote in "B. Goldberg & Friend" in barely legible script, and under Resident Visited I scribbled in Boopsie. I closed the book and straightened up.

The receptionist stood and turned to me with a big smile. "This way."

We followed her down a short hallway to a locked door. She punched a code into the keyboard, waited for the beep, and opened the door.

"Have a good time," she said.

Benny and I stepped inside and she closed the door behind us.

There was a nurse's station to our left, a dining room ahead, and another TV lounge to the right. About a dozen elderly men and women, mostly women, were seated in the TV lounge watching a soap opera—or at least facing the TV. About half of them were asleep.

A woman in a nurse's outfit approached with a big smile. "Hello. Who are we here to see?"

"Martin Henderson," I said. "He was a friend of the family, and we promised to see him when we were in St. Louis."

She smiled. "How nice."

She gestured toward the dining area. "There's a little lounge beyond the tables. See the couches? Make yourselves comfortable and we'll bring Martin over."

Five minutes later a heavy-set black man in a blue orderly's outfit escorted an elderly white man toward us. The white man looked to be in his eighties. He was frail and moved with a slow, deliberate shuffle, taking tiny steps as he stared at the floor.

"Here we are, Martin," the orderly said in a cheerful voice. "Some friends of yours have to come to visit. Can you say hi?"

Martin Henderson slowly raised his eyes and looked at me and then Benny. His face was expressionless, his mouth sagging open.

The orderly helped him get seated and then backed up. "Call if you need help," he said to me. And then he bowed and stepped away.

"Hello, Mr. Henderson," I said in a friendly voice.

Henderson turned slowly toward me, his eyes blank. He said nothing.

"We came here to talk to you about Durlester Minogue."

No response.

"Do you know anything about the company?"

He stared at me, expressionless. In a hoarse voice, he said, "She doesn't have the tickets."

"What tickets?"

After a moment, "She doesn't have the tickets."

"Do you have the tickets?" I said.

He stared at me and then turned slowly toward Benny. "No mustard," he said.

"No mustard?" Benny said. "Bummer, eh?"

He just stared, his head tilted slightly, mouth open, a rivulet of drool sliding down his chin and then trickling onto his pants.

On the way out of the Memory Care unit, as the nurse punched the code into the keypad, I asked, "Is Stanley Boudreau in here or over in the assisted living wing?"

There was a beep and the nurse opened the door. "Stanley is here with us," she said. "He's asleep now. His days and nights are turned around. He's up most of the night and sleeps during the days."

"Is that unusual?" I asked.

She gave me a sad smile. "Unfortunately, it's not unusual with our dementia patients. Many of them have their days and nights turned around."

Chapter Thirty-six

We all have our secrets.

Even Paul Rogers, who is one of the classiest people I know. In his late sixties now, Paul remains one of the top municipal lawyers in Missouri. A former chair of the American Bar Association's Committee on Land Use Planning, Paul sits on the boards of several St. Louis companies and non-profit organizations. The press coverage of most local charity galas includes a photo of Paul in a tuxedo standing next to his graceful wife Marie.

But Paul's secret is his passion for Woofies. While those from outside St. Louis might be wondering what bizarre sexual kink goes by that name, most of us natives would simply nod in pleasant surprise. That's because most of us would expect to find Paul Rogers at noon seated at a prime power-lunch booth in an upscale restaurant in Clayton or downtown. Instead, he and I always met at his favorite lunchtime spot: Woofies, a genuine Chicago-style hot dog shack in Overland, a near suburb.

I smiled as I watched the former president of the Bar Association of Metropolitan St. Louis study the menu on the wall and then order his usual: a Big Daddy with extra grilled onions, chili cheese fries, and a lemonade. I opted for pure Chicago—a Woofie dog with mustard, neon-green relish, and sport peppers, an order of fries, and a Coke.

Paul grinned in anticipation as he watched them pile the grilled onions onto his quarter-pound dog. Today was obviously not a court day because he was dressed in what I call his Mister Rogers outfit, right down to the cardigan sweater and blue sneakers.

We took our trays of food over to a pair of stools along the side wall counter just beneath framed signed photographs of Stan Musial and Chuck Berry.

Paul lifted his hot dog with both hands and glanced over at me with a big grin. "Oh, what a treat."

As is typical for any two people who've spent time in Chicago, we had debated who served the best hot dogs in that town. My pick was Wiener Circle on North Clark in the Lincoln Park area. Paul's was Fluky's in Rogers Park—in part for the quality of their hot dogs and in part for sentimental reasons, since Woofie's founder, the late Charlie Eisner, had apprenticed at Fluky's.

We ate our hot dogs in silence, showing proper respect for Vienna Beef. When Paul finished, he wiped his mouth with a paper napkin, took a sip of his lemonade, and turned to me.

"I confess, Rachel, I'd never ever heard of that outfit before."

"But some of your fellow club members had?"

"Oh, yes."

In my struggle to make sense out of Structured Resolutions— and in the hopes of finding a potential source other than Brian Teever—I decided to see whether the St. Louis Country Club pattern existed anywhere else. I had friends who were members of the two Jewish country clubs in town, and I asked them to make discreet inquires about Structured Resolutions among the members. Bellerive Country Club is the other exclusive local country club for WASPs, and I knew that Paul Rogers was a longtime member. I'd asked him to make inquiries there and promised to buy him lunch as a reward.

My two Jewish friends reported back that no one at either club had heard of Structured Resolutions. Apparently, Paul had different news from Bellerive.

"What did you hear?" I asked.

"The investors love it. They've earned solid returns year in and year out, regardless of what the stock markets are doing."

"Are there a lot of investors at Bellerive?"

"Doesn't sound like it. I spoke to three who'd put money in it. Lots of money. Seven figures for two of them. I can't tell you who they are, of course, but I can tell you that you would recognize their names."

"Did they tell you how they were able to invest in the company?"

"That part is fascinating," Paul said. "It's difficult to get in. Apparently, it's closed to the general public. If you want to invest, you need a contact person. That's what all three told me."

"What does the contact person do?"

"Make the inside connection, I gather. He can try to convince the company to allow in another investor. There is some sort of waiting list, but your contact person might be able to move you up to the head of the line."

"Did they tell you who their contact person was?"

Paul nodded.

"Was it the same contact person each time?"

"Yes, it was."

"Brian Teever?" I asked.

Paul frowned. "No one mentioned him."

"Who was it?"

Paul lowered his voice. "This is confidential, Rachel."

"I understand."

"You can never connect me with this information, or it will get back to the three gentlemen I mentioned."

"You have my word, Paul"

He nodded. "Rob Brenner."

I was surprised. "Do you know Rob?"

"I do. I've occasionally played golf in a foursome with him."

"At Bellerive?"

"Yes."

"Is he a member?"

"He is."

I absorbed the information, not sure what to make of it.

"Rob is a relative newcomer," Paul said.

"To the club?"

"Oh, no. His father Ken served a term as president of the club. A good fellow. Corporate lawyer. Had his own firm in Clayton. Passed away a few years ago. No, I was referring to this investment vehicle. Structured Resolutions. According to my sources, Rob has been the point person for the last year or so. Bill Dayton was his predecessor. Literally, I suppose."

"What do you mean?"

"Bill is deceased. He died about two years ago. Actually, he was killed."

"How?"

"A hunting accident. Bill Dayton was a big-time hunter. Went antelope hunting in Montana, elk hunting in Wyoming, and deer hunting here in Missouri. That's where he got shot."

"Who shot him?"

"No one knows. They did an investigation but never turned up any suspects. Happens more often than you might think, Rachel. I read somewhere that almost a hundred people die in hunting accidents each year. Poor Bill was one of them that year."

Chapter Thirty-seven

I paused at the bedroom door. "Goodnight, Sam. I love you."

"I love you, Mommy."

I blew him a kiss, he blew one back, and I pulled the door halfway shut.

I came down the stairs and stepped into the dining room, where my motley crew had gathered. When I'd gone upstairs with Sam to give him a bath and put him to bed, the "crew" had been just my mother, me, and Benny, who'd joined us for dinner. Now the crew included Stanley Plotkin, Jerry Klunger, Rebecca Hamel, and Malikah Bashir. I'd wanted Stanley and Jerry there because Stanley got the whole thing started, and wherever Stanley went Jerry needed to follow. Rebecca was there because she was the associate at Warner & Olsen who'd been the closest with Sari and thus knew things about her that none of the rest of us knew. Because Rebecca—like most big firm associates—worked late, she was able to give Stanley and Jerry a ride to my house. And finally there was Malikah. She needed to here on behalf of her Uncle Ameer, Sari's father. I wanted to keep Mr. Bashir in the loop, although I was still unsure of what that loop was.

While I'd been upstairs, the crew had been overseen by my mother, who had baked enough rugelach to feed them for a month. Rugelach, and especially my mother's version, was one of Benny's favorites—a cream cheese pastry rolled around currants and toasted walnuts and topped with cinnamon sugar. There were three platters piled with rugelach and a pitcher of iced tea and a pot of hot tea. Benny had opted for a bottle of Schlafly American IPA. He'd brought a six-pack to dinner.

My arrival brought the crowd to seven—an odd number, and thus Stanley stood and stepped back toward the wall. Jerry looked at me with a sheepish smile and shrugged.

I poured myself a cup of hot tea, ate a rugelach, and started in on my status report. As for Structured Resolutions, I explained, everything about the company seemed fishy except for the St. Louis investors, who composed a Who's Who of the city's elite. Among other suspicious elements, Structured Resolutions was an offshore entity with somewhat opaque financials and a Missouri registered agent who was an elderly man with Alzheimer's disease. The financials were "audited" by a nonexistent accounting firm in Pontiac, Michigan, whose resident agent in Michigan was dead and whose registered agent in Missouri had dementia and lived in the same memory care facility as the registered agent for Structured Resolutions.

"But what looks really shady to me," I said to the group, "apparently doesn't seem to be bother people far savvier than me. As far as I can tell, all of the investors—or at least the ones in Missouri—are high net-worth individuals who are members of either the St. Louis Country Club or Bellerive Country Club. As exclusive as those country clubs may be, Structured Resolutions seems even more exclusive. If you want to invest your money in the company, you need to know an insider who can get you access. As far as we can tell, there are two insiders, and they're both at Warner & Olsen. Brian Teever is the insider at St. Louis Country Club, and Rob Brenner is his counterpart at Bellerive."

Stanley announced, "This is a Missouri-centered operation."

"Why do you say that?" Rebecca asked.

"Elementary, Ms. Hamel," Stanley replied. "Jerry Klunger conducted a fifty-state search of business records this afternoon. There are no registered agents outside of Missouri. As Ms. Gold can confirm, a financial institution with operations inside a state is required to appoint a registered agent in that state. While the appointment may be a mere formality, failure to do so can trigger immediate and unwanted attention from state regulators. Thus the absence of such agents in the other forty-nine states would provide reasonable grounds to conclude that Structured Resolutions is not active in those states."

Benny tilted his bottle toward Stanley. "Dude's got a point."

"Good work, Jerry," I said. "That helps narrows the focus."

Jerry blushed and lowered his head.

"From what Rebecca has told me," I said, "and what I learned from Claire Hudson—"

"Who is that?" Malikah asked.

"She and her husband David are clients of the law firm. Actually, she is, or was, having an affair with Brian Teever, who was doing their estate plan. Their investments include millions of dollars in Structured Resolutions. Anyway, we've learned that something about that investment bothered Sari, but when she started making inquiries, she got in trouble with Brian Teever. As I mentioned, we've learned that Teever was the insider at St. Louis Country Club that got the Hudsons into Structured Resolutions."

"And what does all this mean?" Malikah asked.

I shrugged. "We don't know. That's part of why I wanted to get us all in the same room. One option is to figure out a way to approach Brian Teever or Rob Brenner."

"Another option," Stanley announced, "is to approach Beth Dayton."

I stared at Stanley, who was staring at the philodendron plant in the corner of the living room.

"Who is Beth Dayton?" I asked.

"Jerry," Stanley commanded.

Jerry cleared his throat. "You mentioned to Stanley that there was a man named Bill Dayton who used to do what Mr. Brenner does now."

"Right." I turned to the others. "Bill Dayton was the insider at Bellerive Country Club, but he died a couple years ago in a hunting accident."

I paused.

"Beth Dayton," I repeated, turning to Jerry. "She's Bill Dayton's widow?"

Jerry nodded.

"How did you find that out?"

"Stanley told me to do an online search for Mr. Dayton's obituary. It listed Beth Dayton as his widow. Stanley had me do a search for her current residence."

"And Stanley thinks I should talk to her?" I said.

Jerry shrugged. "I think so."

I turned to Stanley. "Why?"

"Consider the facts, Ms. Gold," he said. "Your spouse of thirty-one years is shot and killed in the woods. The shooter is never identified. That is noteworthy. According to the International Hunter Education Association, during the past year one-thousand and fifty-seven people in the United States and Canada were shot during the hunting season. Of that total, one hundred and three expired from their gunshot wounds. The shooter was identified in all but two of those fatalities. The statistics for the prior two years are similar. Thus the unidentified shooter in such a fatality is the outlier. As for Ms. Dayton, that lack of identification results in a lack of closure. I defer to your cognitive, emotive, and deductive abilities as to whether a lack of closure is of significance here."

Chapter Thirty-eight

There was a knock on the door.

"Come on in," Benny called. He looked over and gave me a wink.

The door swung open. Rob Brenner stood in the doorway.

"You must be Rob," Benny said, standing up to greet him.

"I am."

Brenner stepped into the office, glancing over at me with barely disguised surprise.

Benny came around his desk, hand extended. They shook hands.

"Good to meet you, Professor."

"Same here. Do you know Rachel Gold?"

I stood. "Hello, Rob."

We shook hands.

He said, "Good to see you, Rachel."

Benny gestured toward the two chairs facing his desk. "Have a seat."

We were in Benny's office at the law school. The meeting, the location, and the cover story were all Benny's idea. My role was as the lawyer for the would-be investor, an unnamed but important donor to the law school who had expressed an interest in investing some of his own money—and his potential ten million-dollar endowment to the law school—in Structured Resolutions.

Brenner listened as Benny explained it all. They were a true study in contrasts. Trim and coiffed, dressed in a gray pinstriped suit, crisp white Oxford shirt, gold monogrammed cufflinks, and red-and-navy striped tie, Rob could have stepped out of a "Dress for Success" piece in *GQ*. Chubby and unshorn, dressed in a yellow-and-brown bowling shirt with Medina Sod on the back, baggy cargo pants, and red Converse Chuck Taylors, Benny could have stepped out of the bowling lane in *The Big Lebowski*.

Benny ended his spiel with an emphasis on the confidential nature of the meeting. No one at the law school other than the dean and the head of development knew about the meeting, and Brenner could not have any contact with them or anyone else at the law school about the subject matter of the meeting.

Brenner frowned when Benny finished. "I don't understand."

"You don't understand what?" Benny said.

"Why me?"

"Two reasons, Rob. One, you're a graduate of this law school, as was your father, who was, according to our development office, a generous contributor to the annual fund. Thus I assume you have ties to this law school. Correct?"

Brenner nodded, still frowning. "And the other reason?"

"Just as you have ties to this law school, I understand you have ties to Structured Resolutions."

"What do you mean by ties?"

Benny chuckled. "Oh, I think you know exactly what I mean, Robby. Now our donor is not a member of your country club. He's actually a member of the Laclede Club. A prominent member, I might add. I would hope that his membership in that club wouldn't matter, especially given the opportunity our donor represents for both the law school and your company."

Benny and I had picked the Laclede Club for two reasons: it was the third of the exclusive country clubs for gentiles and its members included three extremely wealthy graduates of the Washington University School of Law. None were actually practicing attorneys. One was the CEO of a successful corporation, one managed his family's foundation, and the third headed an investment banking firm. Each had a net worth well in excess of $50 million.

"Who is this donor?"

Benny shrugged with his hands out, palms up. "Ah, I'm afraid I can't disclose that."

"Why not?"

Benny turned to me. "Rachel, would you care to explain?"

I turned to Brenner. "The donor wishes to remain anonymous up until the announcement of the endowment."

Brenner said, "Doesn't he understand that he's going to have to disclose his identity if he plans on investing his money?"

"He does," I said. "But just not yet."

"So what's the next step, Rob?" Benny said.

"The next step?"

"Investing the money," Benny said. "We're talking tens of millions of dollars."

"How did he find out about Structured Resolutions?" Brenner asked.

"Apparently," Benny said, "he knows some other investors. They spoke highly of the company. One of his acquaintances— a member of Bellerive Country Club—told him you were the man to see."

"Which acquaintance?" Brenner asked.

Benny turned toward me.

"That's confidential," I said.

Brenner leaned back in his chair and tugged at the skin on his neck as he thought it over.

He turned to me. "So what's the next step?"

I smiled. "You tell me, Rob. You're the one with the inside contacts. I'm just the go-between."

He nodded, lips pursed. "I'll need a few days."

"Don't wait too long," Benny said. "Our donor is anxious to get moving. If he can't do the deal with your outfit, he moves on to Plan B. If that outfit of yours is looking for a big investor, we just brought them Godzilla."

Brenner nodded again, clearly mulling it over.

"You pull this off," Benny said, "and you're going to have one grateful law school dean. This is all hush-hush, but I understand there's going to be an opening next fall on the National Council. Deliver here, big guy, and you just might be the right man to fill that opening."

Benny had played that card well.

Although Brenner tried to keep a poker face, I didn't need Stanley Plotkin to interpret Brenner's reaction to the possibility of a spot on the National Council, which is an advisory board of distinguished Wash U law school alumni. It includes judges, general counsels of Fortune 500 companies, and law firm partners from around the nation. Brenner was one of the most unabashedly ambitious people I knew. To hobnob with fellow members of the National Council had to be one of his fantasies.

"Here," I said, handing Brenner one of my business cards. "Give me a call. As the professor mentioned, the sooner the better."

After Brenner left, Benny leaned back in his chair and lifted his feet up onto the desk. "We set the trap. Let's see if that arrogant little weasel takes the bait."

"Taking the bait." I sighed and shook my head. "I wish I knew what that meant here."

"Huh?"

"Benny, I have no idea what's really going on behind the curtain here. I need a plan. This all feels too improvised."

"That's okay," Benny said. "Think of yourself as the John Coltrane of this investigation."

"I'd rather be the Sherlock Holmes."

"Hey, I'd rather be Eli Manning or Ron Jeremy, but you gotta play the cards you're dealt."

Chapter Thirty-nine

We met in the living room of Beth Dayton's residence, a two-bedroom condo on the twenty-first floor of The Plaza in Clayton. The view from the floor-to-ceiling picture windows included the Ritz-Carlton in the foreground, the Art Museum atop Art Hill in the middle distance, and the Gateway Arch downtown.

I had called Beth Dayton, Bill's widow, to ask if I could meet with her. *About what?*, she had asked. I'd explained that I had some questions about her late husband's involvement with a certain investment vehicle.

"Structured Resolutions?" she'd asked.

"Actually, yes."

"Good. How about at my place tomorrow morning at ten? I'll have them send up coffee and Danish."

And she did.

We were seated across from one another—Beth on the couch, me on the loveseat, and between us an elegant walnut and glass coffee table on which sat a pot of coffee and a plate of sweet rolls.

"What do you know about Structured Resolutions?" I asked.

She shook her head. "Not much. It's some sort of company that people invest their money with—or in. Something to do with annuities, I think."

"When did your late husband get involved with it?"

"About eight years ago, right after his business went south."

"South?"

She gave me a sad smile. "Downhill. Into the sewer. Well,

almost. He was in the real estate development business. Mostly apartment complexes, some commercial properties. Dayton & Son. He was the son. His father, Ben, founded the company right after World War Two."

"Is Ben still alive?"

"Oh, no. He died almost twenty years ago."

Beth Dayton had a sturdy aura. She was in her late sixties, her silver hair cut in a short bob. She had strong features, dark blue eyes, and teeth that seemed unnaturally white. She was wearing a tan collared shirtdress, matching flats, a string of pearls, and pearl earrings. She had on her wedding band and engagement ring.

From a distance, Beth had striking features, but up close you could see the damage from too much sun over too many years, especially on her face and neck—liver spots, wrinkles, discolored skin patches.

I took a sip of coffee and set the cup on the saucer.

"What happened to the business?" I asked.

"Same as what happened to a lot of developers back when the market collapsed."

"That must have been hard. For both of you."

"Especially Bill," she said, her eyes going distant. "He'd been an active member of this community for decades, Rachel. He was proud of his role in so many organizations—the Veiled Prophet Ball, the Boy Scouts, the library, United Way. His business problems threatened all of that. Even worse, he had to lay off employees, including some who'd been with him for decades. And then the bank began foreclosure proceedings on our home."

She shook her head. "It was a dark time for us—especially Bill."

"And you say that's when he got involved with Structured Resolutions?"

She nodded.

I said, "How exactly did that happen?"

"His lawyers."

"What do you mean?"

"Bill's company had used the Warner & Olsen law firm for years. Len Olsen handled a couple lawsuits for him, Donald

Warner was the corporate lawyer, and Brian Teever did our trusts and wills. There were others, too. I can't remember all their names. Anyway, when the bank started foreclosure proceedings, Bill brought in the law firm to defend us."

"Do you remember who?"

She frowned. "Not really. He was closest with Len and Donald, so he would probably have called one of them first."

"Who actually handled the matter?"

"I recall a big blonde. Tough-looking gal."

"Susan O'Malley."

"Susan," she repeated. "I think that was her name. She worked on the matter with a fellow named Brenner. Rob, I believe. I knew his father, Ken. So did Bill."

"How?"

"Through the club. We're members of Bellerive. Bill used to play golf with Ken."

"So one of those lawyers got your husband involved with Structured Resolutions?"

"Yes."

"Which one?"

She shook her head. "I'm not sure."

"What did your husband do for Structured Resolutions?"

"Good question." She gave me a weary smile. "He told me he was like a combination Walmart greeter and doorman at a speakeasy. If people wanted in, they had to go through him."

"You mean investors?"

"Yes."

"Did he tell you why they had to go through him?"

"No. Just that they did."

"What kind of investors?" I asked.

"What do you mean?"

"Did he know them? Or were they just off the street?"

"Oh, he knew them. It was all hush-hush, something about the investment opportunities being exclusive, but I'm pretty sure the only ones he dealt with were members of the club."

"Bellerive?"

She nodded.

"Did he get paid for that work?"

"He did, and the money helped tide us over. His company went belly up, but we were able to hang on to the house."

"How much did he get paid?"

"It was usually around thirty thousand dollars a year, but it varied. One year it might be forty, another year twenty-five."

"He did this for about five years?" I asked.

"Yes, right up until he died." She paused. "That's when it got interesting."

"Why do you say that?"

"They delivered what they called his final payment to me a few weeks after the funeral. It was for one-hundred and fifty thousand dollars. A cashier's check."

"How did they deliver it?"

"Personally. Well, not personally by the company. Personally by one of their lawyers."

"Which one?"

"Rob Brenner."

"What did he tell you?"'

"He said that Structured Resolutions thought highly of Bill and wanted to express their sympathies."

"Did he explain the amount?"

"Nope."

"Or what it represented?"

"Nope."

"Did he explain his involvement with the company?"

"Nope. Brenner just said he'd been asked to personally deliver the check along with the company's sympathies."

Beth stood and walked over to the windows.

"Have you had any contact with Structured Resolutions since then?"

"Nope."

I sat back in my chair and took a sip of coffee as I thought over what Beth had told me. She was staring out of the window, her arms crossed over her chest.

"One hundred and fifty thousand dollars," I said.

She nodded, her back to me.

"That's real money," I said.

She turned, her eyes narrowing. "If I had to guess, I'd say it was blood money."

Chapter Forty

After a pause, I said, "Blood money?"

"You heard me."

She strode back over and sat down on the couch, an angry look in her eyes.

"So you think Structured Resolution was connected to your husband's death?"

"I do. I can't prove it, but I do."

"Why?"

"Several things. First off, Bill's passion was hunting. He'd been doing it since he was a teenager. But he was a cautious hunter. He always wore his bright yellow jacket and yellow hat—the ones he claimed you could see even in a thicket. But he wasn't killed in a thicket. I went down to Oxford County. I saw exactly where he was standing when he was shot. One of the county deputies took me out there. It was on the edge of a clearing in the woods. Bill was facing the clearing and wearing that bright yellow jacket and hat. He was shot in the chest, which means he was shot in the open by someone staring across that clearing."

"Do they know how close the shooter was?"

"No. They say he was standing at least two hundred yards away. The only footprints near my husband were the ones of the two hunters who found him."

"What did the authorities say?"

She exhaled slowly and shook her head. "They labeled it a likely accidental homicide. One of three that year in Oxford County, one of fourteen over the past decade."

"Okay."

"Except Bill's was the only one with an unidentified shooter."

"So you don't believe it was an accident?"

"He was at the edge of the clearing and he was shot in the chest." There was anger in her voice now, and in her eyes. "That was no accident. That jacket didn't protect him. It turned him into a target."

She stood and walked into the kitchen, shaking her head. I waited.

After a few minutes, she returned to her seat. Her eyes were red. "I'm sorry," she said.

"You have nothing to apologize for, Beth."

"It gets me upset."

She poured herself another cup of coffee. I waited as she added artificial sweetener and cream, stirred the cup, put the spoon down, took a sip, then another, and set the cup onto the saucer. She looked up at me.

"You called the money blood money," I said. "Why?"

"I think they killed him. I think they saw Bill as a threat and they killed him."

"Who is the they?"

"That outfit he did work for. Structured Resolutions."

"Why would they want Bill dead?"

"Because he started asking awkward questions."

"What kind of questions?"

"Financial ones. I don't know exactly what he asked, but I know he was starting to have doubts about that company and wanted answers to his questions before he would give anyone else at the club access."

"Were people at the club asking questions?"

"Hardly. Bill said they were lining up to get in. And each with a big pile of money. That's what made him nervous. My husband was a good man, Miss Gold. These people at the club were his friends. Bill wanted to make sure they didn't get hurt. 'This'll be on my head,' he told me more than once. 'If this investment turns out to be nothing but smoke and mirrors,' he said, 'I'm the one they'll blame.' He tried to find information on the company on his own but couldn't find a thing. That really bothered him."

"You said he started asking questions."

"He did, but he wasn't getting answers."

"Who did he ask?"

"I don't know." She frowned. "That's what I've been trying to find out."

"How?"

"I hired an investigator about a year ago, but he got nowhere. After six months all he could find out was Rob Brenner was now serving the same role Bill used to have at the country club."

"Did the investigator talk to Brenner?"

"No. I told him not to. Brenner was the one who'd brought me that big check. He hadn't been straight with me that day, and I didn't think he'd be straight with some investigator, either. And by then I knew who to talk to."

"Who?"

"Donald or Len. They were Brenner's bosses. If anyone could get him to answer questions, they could."

"Did you talk to them?"

"To Donald. I tried Len first, but he was out of town on a case. I met with Donald."

"When?"

"About three weeks ago."

"Tell me about it."

"Not much to tell. We met at his office. I told him my suspicions about Bill's death and about the big payment check that Rob Brenner had delivered and the fact that Brenner was now doing what Bill used to do at Bellerive."

"What did Warner say?"

"He promised to look into the matter—both the Oxford County investigation of Bill's death and any information he could find about Structured Resolutions."

"And?"

"Nothing yet. He called last Friday to say he was working on it but that it might take a few more weeks to gather all the information. He told me he would get back with whatever he was able to find out."

"Did you get the sense that Warner knew about Structured Resolutions?"

"Hard to say. He mainly asked questions and took notes."

Chapter Forty-one

We waited as Rebecca Hamel studied the Oxford County Sheriff's Department file on William T. Dayton's death. I'd borrowed Beth Dayton's copy for the meeting. The file included several gruesome color photographs of the victim, both in the field and in the morgue, along with various investigative reports. Rebecca was a hunter, and thus seemed a good person to review the file.

It was Sunday afternoon and we were gathered in Benny's law school office. It was a less visible place for the gathering than my office or home. In addition to Rebecca Hamel and Benny, Stanley Plotkin and Jerry Klunger were here. I'd picked them up on the way to Benny's office.

Rebecca was seated behind Benny's desk. She closed the file and looked up. "She's right."

"You mean Beth?" I said.

Rebecca nodded. "It's suspicious."

I said, "The investigators estimate that the shooter was between two and three hundred yards from Dayton. That's pretty far away."

"Yes and no," she said. "Three hundred yards isn't that far for deer hunting. According to the file, the shooter used a long range cartridge. A .270 Weatherby Mag. Same one my dad and I use on our hunting trips. You don't shoot at anything that far away without a long-range scope mounted on your rifle. At three hundred yards, Mr. Dayton would have been in focus in the scope's cross hairs."

192 Michael A. Kahn

She opened the folder and lifted up a sheet of paper. "According to this, there was no wind that day. If you know what you're doing and your goal was to shoot Mr. Dayton, he'd have been an easy target from that distance."

"You think the shooter meant to shoot him?" Benny asked.

She shrugged. "It was opening day for deer season. That's a big deal in this state. I've gone hunting with my dad on that day. Lots of hunters turn out. Even so, though, looking through a long-range scope, Mr. Dayton would have been pretty hard to mistake for a deer, especially in that bright yellow jacket."

Stanley cleared his throat. We turned toward him.

"We can safely conclude," he announced "that Mr. Dayton's death is suspicious. We can also safely conclude that his suspicions were well-founded."

"Meaning what?" I said.

Stanley craned his neck and turned to Jerry. "Explicate, Mr. Klunger."

Jerry frowned at Stanley. "What?"

"He means explain," Benny said.

"Oh," Jerry said. "Yes. Stanley had me talk to the plaintiffs' lawyers in some of those cases."

"Which cases?" I said.

"The ones on that form."

"You mean the annual statement from Structured Resolutions?" I said.

Jerry looked at Stanley for the answer.

"Precisely," Stanley said.

I turned to Rebecca and Benny. "We have three annual investment statements from Structured Resolutions. I got them in discovery in the sexual harassment suit against Doctor Mason. He's an investor. Each statement includes in a footnote a list of what it calls representative underlying cases where the plaintiffs cashed in their structured settlements for a single payment. The cases are from all over the country. My assistant did a docket search. She confirmed that they were all real cases and they all settled."

I looked back at Jerry. "You actually talked to the plaintiffs' lawyers in those cases?"

"In just four of them," Jerry said.

"Four proved sufficient," Stanley stated.

"Sufficient for what?"

"To establish the essential fact."

"Which is?" I asked

"That Structured Resolutions is a fraudulent enterprise." Benny said. "Tell us about your conversations, Jerry."

"Stanley wrote me a script to follow," Jerry said. "That's what I did."

"What was in the script?" I asked.

"I told each lawyer that I was a graduate student working on a research paper on structured settlements, that I had just a few questions that would take no more than five minutes to answer, and that they would stay...uhm...ani...uhm..."

"Anonymous," Stanley snapped.

"Right. I called eight lawyers and four gave me answers. I had the names of their cases and when they were dismissed. Two of the lawyers told me right off the bat that there wasn't a structured settlement in their case. One even told me that he settled the case for seventy-five thousand dollars. He warned me that information was strictly confidential. The other two lawyers told me there was a structured settlement. My next question on the script was whether their client had sold his structured settlement. One of them had sold his, the other hadn't. The one whose client did sell his structured settlement sold it to a company called..."

Jerry paused, trying to remember.

"Strategic Capital," Stanley announced.

Jerry nodded. "Yes, that was the name."

I leaned back in my chair, trying to absorb that information.

"So," I finally said, "two of four representative structured settlement cases didn't even involve a structured settlement, and neither of the other two was purchased by Structured Resolutions."

"You are correct," Stanley said. "Thus the conclusion that Structured Resolutions is a fraudulent enterprise."

"Which Sari must have discovered," I said.

"As did Bill Dayton," Benny said.

I nodded and turned toward Jerry. "Good work."

Jerry blushed. "Thank you, Miss Gold."

"You, too, Stanley."

"As you may know," Stanley announced, "William Dayton is also the name of one of the two unsuccessful candidates for the Vice-Presidency in the election of 1856. The victor, John Breckenridge, received 174 votes to Mr. Dayton's 114 votes. The third candidate, one Andrew Donelson, received only eight votes. I would be remiss, however, if I did not point out that the William Dayton that is the subject of your inquiry had a middle initial of *T* while the unsuccessful candidate had a middle initial of *L*."

After a moment of silence, Benny said, "We thank you for not being remiss. Back to *our* Bill Dayton: Where the hell are we now?"

"He needed money," I said. "That was their hold over him."

"What's their hold over the other two?" Benny said.

I turned to Rebecca. "Thoughts?"

She frowned. "What do you mean?"

"According to Bill Dayton's wife, he got involved in Structured Resolutions because he needed money. That was their hold over him, although apparently it wasn't strong enough. Assuming that Brian Teever and Rob Brenner are doing that outfit's bidding, where do you think they're vulnerable? Are there any rumors about them at the firm?"

She stared past me at the wall as she thought it over.

I waited.

She shifted her gaze to mine. "Sex."

"What kind of sex?" I asked.

"Just rumors."

"I understand."

Keeping her eyes on mine, ignoring the others in the room, she said, "The year before I joined the firm, Mr. Brenner supposedly had sex with two of the firm's interns."

"Law students?" I asked.

"High school students," she said. "They were part of a summer internship program sponsored by the city schools. Supposedly, Mr. Brenner invited the girls back to his place for dinner. They got drunk and he had sex with them."

"What happened?" I asked.

She shrugged. "No one knows. There's a rumor that the girls got a lawyer and threatened to file charges against him and then it got resolved. All hush hush."

I turned to Benny and raised my eyebrows. "That's leverage."

He nodded.

I looked back at Rebecca. "And Teever. What's his sex issue?"

"The wives of clients."

"Such as Claire Hudson?"

Rebecca frowned. "I haven't heard about that one."

"Sari never mentioned it? That was the estate plan she was working on that included the Structured Resolutions investment."

Rebecca shook her head. "She didn't say anything."

"So Teever has had affairs with the wives of other clients?"

"At least one. That's the rumor." She shrugged. "Supposedly the husband found out and raised hell."

Chapter Forty-two

"They're rumors, Benny. Not proven facts."

"Come on, Rachel. She's an associate, and a sharp one, too. We were once associates at a big law firm. We knew more secrets about that firm than some of the partners."

Benny and I had remained at his office after the meeting. Rebecca Hamel drove Stanley and Jerry home.

"You remember Graham Marshall?" he said.

I smiled. "Hard to forget."

"That's my point. According to the official version, he died of a heart attack at his desk that night while working on an appellate brief. Hell, that's the version that was even published in the *New York Times*. I bet there are still partners at Abbott & Windsor that believe that bullshit. But we associates knew the real story."

Graham Anderson Marshall was a powerful senior partner at Abbott & Windsor. The heart attack that killed him that night occurred in the living room of a condominium overlooking Lake Michigan. At the time of his death he was neither working on a brief nor wearing any. Instead, he was indulging in his fetish for rubber (specifically, a skin-diving suit, crotch unsnapped) and his preference for fellatio, which he was receiving from a high-priced escort named Cindi Reynolds—all of which I was to learn after the fact when retained by his firm to investigate a mysterious grave in a pet cemetery.

"I liked Cindi," I said.

"So does Fox. I understand she co-anchors the five o'clock news in Chicago on Fox 32."

"Wow. Good for her."

"But my point here is that there are good reasons to take these rumors about Teever and Brenner seriously. Especially Teever. You already know he was banging one client's wife."

"Assuming the rumors are true," I said, "then someone else in that law firm has a lot of leverage over those two lawyers. My questions are who and why?"

Benny nodded. "Don't know the who, but we're starting to get a good read on the why. That Stanley is fucking genius."

"Hard to believe the whole thing is a scam."

"Sure starting to sound like it."

"I don't get it," I said. "They're not targeting little old ladies in Dubuque with twenty thousand-dollar savings accounts. They're getting millions of dollars from sophisticated businessmen. And they're doing so with financial statements that Pinky Zuckerman described as opaque."

"I have a two word answer for you: Bernie Madoff. You want two more words? Allen Stanford. Or any of the other hundreds of Ponzi schemers who've bilked billions out of supposedly smart investors."

I sighed. "I suppose."

"I'll be curious to see if we get a bite on that Laclede Club bait we dangled in front of Brenner. That kind of money ought to be damn tempting."

"Which reminds me," I said. "Paul Rogers wouldn't give me the names of the three Bellerive Country Club members he knew had invested in Structured Resolutions, but he told me one was a former president of the club and two had served on the membership committee. In other words, big shots at the club. If Brenner or whoever tries to narrow down the Laclede Club membership for the possible candidates for our mysterious big donor, he's going to end up with two former club presidents and one chair of the membership committee."

"Which means?" Benny said.

I shrugged. "Nothing yet. Something to file away."

Benny leaned forward, his expression serious. "Here's something *not* to file away. Sari Bashir asked questions about Structured Resolutions, Sari Bashir died. Bill Dayton asked questions about Structured Resolutions, Bill Dayton died. You be careful, Rachel."

"I will."

"I'm serious."

"I know you are, Benny. Thanks."

Chapter Forty-three

Benny answered on the second ring. "Talk to me."

"We gotta bite."

"No shit. Who?"

"Len Olsen."

"Olsen? What the fuck?"

"I know. Surprised me, too."

"So tell me."

"Nothing to tell yet. Just got off the phone with him. He's coming by my office at five-fifteen."

"Five-fifteen? Shit. See if he can move it up to four. I teach that antitrust seminar at five."

"No, Benny. It's better this way. Just me and him."

"You sure?"

"Positive."

"What if he tries to pull something?"

"He's not, Benny. I'm not even sure he knows that much about Structured Resolutions. All he said was that he'd heard about our conversation with Rob Brenner and wanted to drop by to share some information."

"That's it?"

"That's it. I asked him what kind of information. He told me he'd explain when he got here."

"I'm not crazy about you meeting him alone in your office."

"I won't be. Jacki is back from vacation. She's in today."

"Good. Be sure she introduces herself." Benny chuckled. "That'll make him behave."

I smiled. "You're probably right."

"No shit. She'd make Darth Vader behave."

Jacki Brand was my law partner. When we first met, Jacki was a Granite City steelworker named Jack Brand who'd quit his day job to pursue his two dreams: to become a lawyer and to become a woman. I hired him/her as my legal assistant at the front end of those pursuits, back when he had just started attending law classes and taking hormone shots and wearing dresses and wigs. Jacki helped keep my law practice organized, and I helped teach her to be a woman. The week after she received her law school diploma, she underwent a surgical procedure to lop off the last dangling evidence of her original gender.

When she passed the bar exam, I changed my firm's name to Rachel Gold & Associates, Attorneys at Law. A year ago, I made her my law partner. I kept it a secret until the new signs and business cards were ready. She left for court that morning from the offices of Rachel Gold & Associates and returned that afternoon to Gold & Brand, Attorneys at Law. You haven't experienced joy and gratitude until you've been swept off your feet in a bear hug by your blubbering six-foot three-inch two-hundred-fifty-pound high-heeled partner.

"By the way," I said, "here's a weird fact. Remember that memo Sari did for Donald Warner? The one on 501(c)(4) organizations?"

"Oh, yeah. Client was some moral majority outfit that didn't exist."

"Exactly. Missouri's New Moral Majority. Well, they do exist."

"I thought you did a Missouri business name search."

"I did. No such entity in Missouri. But I was thinking of Warner this morning. Specifically, his Thursday nights trips across the river, which got me thinking about Illinois and that memo. Guess what? That outfit does exist. It's actually incorporated in Illinois."

"No shit?"

"They were incorporated last year. Their registered agent is Bernadine Peters."

"Who's she?"

"The Illinois Secretary of State's website has an address for her in Belleville, Illinois. I searched that address on Google. It's the offices of Condor Investment Advisors. I called the number and asked for Bernadine Peters."

"And."

"She's the personal assistant to Richie Condor."

"I assume he's the Condor of Condor Investment Advisors."

"He is."

"Did you talk to her?"

"No. I got the information from the receptionist."

"So who's Richie Condor?"

"According to his firm's website, he's a certified financial advisor. Started off at Merrill Lynch. I Googled him. Seems to be a big deal in Belleville. Shows up in articles on charity balls and non-profits. Good looking guy, mid-thirties. The All-American boy except for one odd pairing."

"What?"

"He's active in the Republican party *and* he's openly gay."

"Interesting. But what's Missouri got to do with his politics?"

"Hard to say. Belleville's just across the river. Lot of people over there commute to jobs over here. He could have political interests here, too."

"And all of this means?"

"Maybe nothing. But it's odd that an outfit with that name is incorporated in Illinois."

"Meanwhile, call me after your meeting with Olsen," Benny said.

"Okay."

"I mean it."

"Aye, aye, Captain.

Chapter Forty-four

Benny would have been pleased with the timing. I was on the phone when Len Olsen arrived. Our secretary was gone for the day. Thus Jacki met him in our reception area and escorted him to my office. In her heels, she towered over him.

Finishing my call, I gestured Len toward the chair facing my desk. He looked, as usual, stylishly handsome—a gray pinstriped suit, a blue dress shirt with white collar, and a gold-patterned navy tie. He was carrying a leather day bag with a shoulder strap, which he slid off and set on the ground as he took a seat.

"Sorry," I said. "That was a judge's clerk."

"No problem, dear." He gave me a warm smile. "Judicial clerks always take precedence."

"So," I said, "tell me what brings you hear today."

"Rob filled me in on your conversation over at Wash U."

"Okay."

"According to Rob, you have client—a high net worth client—who is interested in making a large donation to the law school and large investment in Structured Resolutions. Is that accurate?"

"It is."

"Rob told me you wouldn't identify him."

"My client instructed me not to at this stage. Not until he has some more information about that company."

"Rob said you told him he was a member of the Laclede Country Club?"

"That's correct."

"And I suppose we can assume he has a degree from the law school."

I smiled. "I suppose you could suppose that."

Len chuckled. "Not that it really matters. I was just curious about your mystery man."

"Speaking of mystery men, Len, I'm curious about why you're here. What is your connection to Structured Resolutions?"

"Fair question. I actually have two connections: my law firm does some legal work for that company and I am a happy longtime investor."

"What kind of legal work?"

He smiled and shrugged. "That part I can't speak to. Corporate stuff, mostly. International, I think. That kind of transaction work is way beyond my abilities. As you know, I'm—"

"—just a simple country lawyer," I said, completing one of his timeworn sayings.

He chuckled. "It is true, at least compared to the corporate lawyers. We haven't done any litigation for that outfit, so I don't have any deep relationships with any of their folks."

"Who at the firm does the legal work?"

"I'm not sure. I can check with Don."

"Please do that, Len. My client expects me to properly vet this transaction. I need to talk to someone with knowledge of the company."

"Understood. I'll see what I can do, Rachel. But as for knowledge of the investment opportunities with the company, I'm about as good as anyone out there."

"Why is that?"

"I've had money invested with them for nearly a decade and they've more than doubled it. If your client is looking for nice, steady returns without all the angst of the stock market, I don't know of a better option than Structured Resolutions."

"That's good to hear."

"I brought along copies of a few of my quarterly statements over those years. You're welcome to share them with your client."

"That would be quite helpful, Len."

He unclasped his leather day bag, pulled out a manila folder, and handed it to me across the desk. "Here you go."

"Thanks."

There were about thirty pages of documents—a seemingly random set of quarterly statements covering the past nine years. The owner of the account was Leonard Michael Olsen. Over the period covered by the statements, Olsen's original investment of $710,000 had grown to $1,475,129.21

"Those are confidential documents, Rachel. You can show them to your client, but otherwise I'd prefer they remain under wraps. Please stress that with your client, too"

"Okay." I closed the folder and leaned back in my chair. "So how do we get to the next stage?"

"Here's my understanding," Olsen said. "Apparently, things have changed during the years since I invested my money. According to Rob, the fund is technically closed. Occasionally, though, they accept a new investor. I have to warn you, though: the company has gotten pretty selective. They turn away most wannabe investors."

"What are their criteria?"

He shrugged. "They don't tell me, so I can only guess. Obviously, they'll need to know the identity of your investor. Probably some information about him and his finances. But after that, I don't know."

I said, "And obviously we'll need to know a lot more about them before my client commits."

"I understand completely. Let me start the ball rolling, Rachel. I'll check with Don, find out who has the client contact, and see if we can get you in touch with someone who can answer your questions. Meanwhile, feel free to share those quarterly reports with your client." He gave me a friendly wink. "I think he'll be impressed."

Chapter Forty-five

When the video ended, Benny said, "What the fuck is with that wink?"

"It constituted an insincere and thus ineffective attempt," Stanley said, "to initiate a connection with Ms. Gold that would displace or diminish her connection with the fictitious client."

The five of us—Benny, Stanley, Jerry, Jacki Brand, and me—had just finished watching the video of yesterday's meeting with Len Olsen.

When Len had called to see if he could drop by my office, I sat down with Jacki to talk strategy. Specifically, I wanted to ask her to sit in on my meeting with Len. My gut told me that he was going to try to sweet talk me about Structured Resolutions. Though I'd like to think I have a decent BS detector, Len was the wizard of sweet talk, as proven by his impressive string of jury verdicts.

While Jacki was no Stanley Plotkin, she had impressive credentials in the real world of BS detection. During her steelworker years, she—or rather, he—became a poker legend in Granite City, Illinois. His ability to read the tiniest gestures and eye movements of his opponents—the "tells," in poker lingo—convinced several of his poker pals that he had ESP. They eventually convinced him—or, by then, her—to enter a Texas Hold 'Em tournament at the Casino Queen on the East St. Louis side of the Mississippi River. Jacki won the tournament. Indeed, her Texas Hold 'Em winnings helped pay her law school tuition.

"I've got better idea," she'd told me. "He'll feel more comfortable if it's just you and him.

She'd reached into her desk drawer, pulled out what appeared to be an expensive black ballpoint pen, and held it up.

"See this?" she'd said.

"Yes."

She clicked the pen, scribbled something onto the yellow legal pad, and then turned the pad toward me. "I just signed my name."

I gave her a puzzled look. "Okay."

She turned the legal pad back to her and set the pen down on the pad sideways.

"Nice pen, eh?"

"Seems to be."

"Smile," she said, "you're on Candid Camera."

I had stared at the pen, which looked exactly like, well, a pen. I looked up at her. "There's a camera in there?"

She nodded. "It's filming you right now."

Jacki explained. She'd learned about the pen—available at Amazon.com for $29.99—during one of her divorce cases. Her client's husband, suspicious of his wife, had used a similar hidden-camera pen. He'd placed it strategically on the desk in the master bedroom to tape his wife's antics with the pool man, who came (in both senses) once a week to take care of the pool and the wife. Jacki bought one of the pens the next day, just in case a future client might have reason to use it.

She'd showed me how to work it, and the resulting video was remarkably clear.

Four of us were seated in our conference room, and Stanley stood over near the wall. I used the remote to turn off the monitor and looked around the table.

"Thoughts?"

"He's full of shit," Jacki said. "When you asked him who at the firm does the legal work and he said he'd have to check with Donald Warner, that's a bluff I'd call in a heartbeat."

"I would affirm Ms. Brand's conclusion," Stanley said. "However, it should be noted that Mr. Olsen's control of his micro-expressions is noteworthy and would suggest why juries do not appear to detect his insincerity. This is true even for his smiles. While the smile he formed during the wink that so captured Professor Goldberg's attention was indeed an insincere and thus voluntary smile, as is evidenced by the contraction of the zygomatic major muscle alone, the smile during the afore-mentioned reference to the conversation regarding certain legal matters being beyond his abilities gave the full appearance of a sincere and involuntary Duchenne smile in that it included the contraction of both the zygomatic major and the inferior part of orbicularis oculi."

Stanley's pronouncement was met with a moment of silence.

And then Benny raised his hand, palm toward Stanley. "Gort," he said, "Klaatu barada nikto."

"What?" I said.

"Directed by Robert Wise," Stanley announced.

Benny gave him a wink. "Dude."

I rolled my eyes. "Back to business, okay?"

I looked over at the Jacki, and then back to Stanley. "Bottom line—one, is Structured Resolutions a sham? And, two, does Len know it?"

Jacki frowned. "Don't know if it's a sham, but Len knows much more than he's letting on."

"Stanley?" I said.

"Ms. Brand is correct regarding Mr. Olsen's knowledge. Among other things, as Mr. Olsen's facial actions confirm, he is cognizant of the fact that his quarterly statements are fictitious."

Part 4

I am in blood
Stepp'd in so far that should I wade no more
Returning were as tedious as go o'er.

Macbeth
Act III, Scene 4

To quote Macbeth or Marion Barry or maybe both:
"Bitch set me up."

Tony Manghini
Manager of Office Support Services
Warner & Olsen, LLP

Chapter Forty-six

Bertie Tomaso looked up from his papers and smiled at me. "Ah, it is the east, and Rachel is the sun."

"Good afternoon, Romeo."

He placed his hand over his heart. "Have I caught thee, my heavenly jewel? Why, now let me die, for I have lived long enough."

"Good grief, Bertie. Falstaff, too?"

He raised his eyebrows. "I'm impressed, gorgeous."

"You're impressed?" I said. "I better know. I was the English major, not you."

I was standing in the doorway of the office of Roberto "Bertie" Tomaso, a St. Louis police detective, a shameless flirt, and one of the most literate people I know. As he explains, the only advanced degree he's earned is in stakeouts. *Six hours alone in a car*, he once told me, *and even a knucklehead like me can plow through a few chapters of* War and Peace.

He gestured toward the chair facing his desk. "Sit. Let's talk."

I took a seat.

Bertie is a dear friend. He and his wife Sue came to my wedding and to Jonathan's funeral, and, though he is an old-school Catholic raised on the Italian Hill, he came to my house several nights during the week I sat shiva for Jonathan and made a contribution to the St. Louis Holocaust Museum in Jonathan's memory on his first yahrzeit.

In his late fifties, Bertie is short and burly and has one of those dark complexions that make it seem like he just returned from a week on the beach. He has a warm smile and a pair of eyes that can be playful or intimidating, depending upon the situation.

"So," I said, "you reviewed Sari Bashir's file?"

"I did. I talked to both detectives, too."

"And?"

He grimaced and shook his head. "Suicide seems a reasonable conclusion, Rachel. Wasn't robbed. No evidence of sexual assault. According to friends and family, she'd seemed withdrawn the last few days."

"But you can't rule out murder, right?"

He shrugged. "I suppose. The external walls in that parking garage are fairly low. She could have been pushed, but it's more likely she jumped."

"What about the hunting death? Bill Dayton?"

The day after my meeting with Len Olsen—which was two days ago—I'd given my copy of the Oxford County Sheriff's file to Bertie when I asked him to look into Sari's death.

Bertie raised his eyebrows and chuckled. "That's some file."

"Oh?"

"The sheriff's men could star in a remake of the Keystone Cops. I don't have a basis to challenge their conclusion, but they missed some key evidence."

"Such as?"

"They did a so-so job of examining the immediate area around the body, although they didn't secure the area. There were plenty of stray footprints around the body. But that doesn't really matter, since the shooter wasn't standing in the immediate area. According to their own estimates, he was at least two hundred yards away from the victim, apparently in the woods on the other side of the clearing. They never did an evidence sweep over there. Never. We have no idea what the shooter may have left. If nothing else, it might have helped ID him."

"It could have been murder, right?"

"Could have been? Sure. But that would require the shooter to have some detailed knowledge about the victim."

"What do you mean?"

"Think about it, Rachel. It's not like getting into position to shoot a target when he gets out of the car in front of his house, which you know your target does around six o'clock every evening after work. Here, the shooter has to set up in the trees on the far side of the clearing and just wait and hope. How's he know whether Dayton is ever going to step into that clearing? He could sit there all day and never see the man." He shook his head. "Without more, it's hard to move this from the accident column over to murder."

I pressed him some more, but he had answers to each of my questions.

"Here's the bottom line for a cop," he explained. "I'd never be able to get a prosecutor to touch either one of these files based on what you have so far."

"What about the financial stuff?"

"Structured Resolutions? Now that is intriguing."

"But outside your jurisdiction?"

He raised his eyebrows and shrugged. "Maybe eventually. But depending how you look at it, Len Olsen might be a victim, and he's sure local. Sounds like there are other locals, too. Could be interesting. Now I admit that we may have to notify the Feebs at some point, especially if this operation goes interstate or international, but we can start with a little home cooking."

"Who's the chef?"

He raised his fists in front of him with his thumbs pointed toward his chest. "*Moi.*"

"Last time I checked, Bertie, you were in homicide."

"True. But didn't you come to me with suspicions of homicide, Rachel?" He winked. "Just pursuing your lead, my dear."

Chapter Forty-seven

Four days later, I met Stanley, Jerry, and Rebecca at Kaldi's coffeehouse in the DeMun area on my way home from work. It was 5:50, which was during the dinner break for Stanley and Jerry. I wanted to meet them away from downtown and thus minimize the chances of their being seen in my company. Rebecca was able to join us, which was good for two reasons: she could drive them to the meeting, and I had some more hunting information to share with her.

I filled them in on my initial meeting with Bertie Tomaso, including his skepticism about Bill Dayton's death being a premeditated homicide given what he viewed as the fortuitous nature of the shooting.

"Even with the yellow vest?" Rebecca asked.

I nodded. "He told me I was assuming the shooter was a pro. He said there were plenty of dangerous amateurs out there, especially on opening day of the deer season. He said the shooter could have been aiming at a deer, maybe even the same deer Dayton was aiming at, and simply missed."

Rebecca looked skeptical.

"I know," I said. "So I contacted Bill Dayton's widow again. I talked to her this morning. I asked her if any of his lawyer buddies from Warner & Olsen had gone hunting with her husband. The answer is yes."

"Who?" Rebecca asked.

"She recalled three times. Once was an elk hunting trip for clients that the law firm sponsored about five years ago. She wasn't sure of the names or numbers but she thinks there were about a dozen clients and several lawyers from the firm. She's pretty sure Len Olsen was one of them. But the other two hunting trips were down in Oxford County, both times for the opening of deer season. The first time—two years before he died—there were four in the hunting party."

I paused to check my notes.

"There was Dayton, two of his longtime hunting buddies—a real estate developer named Jack Cheever and a dentist named Art McKenzie—and Len Olsen. She knows because they all met at her house at three in the morning for the drive down to Oxford County. Apparently, the goal is to be in position at the break of dawn. Three of the four went the following year. Len Olsen had some sort of conflict, and guess who took his place? Donald Warner."

"What about the year Dayton died?" Rebecca asked.

"Only Dayton and Cheever. The dentist couldn't because he'd had back surgery earlier that month. Olsen had to cancel because he was getting ready for a big jury trial."

"And Mr. Warner?" Rebecca asked.

"Not that year."

"But both years the group went hunting in Oxford County?" Rebecca asked.

I nodded. "Same area, all three years. Dayton had a college buddy who owns a big tract of land down there. That's where he'd been going for more than a decade." I took a sip of coffee. "What's your reaction?

Rebecca thought it over. "Each hunter has his own preferences. If you hunted down there with Mr. Dayton, especially given that he went there every year, you'd have an idea where he liked to set up before dawn and where he might wander after sunrise."

"That's at least something to work with," I said. "I'm meeting again with Tomaso tomorrow. I'll pass this along."

Stanley twisted his neck and then said, "You should also inform your detective of two additional pertinent facts."

I turned to Stanley. "Okay."

"While I cannot speak to Mr. Warner's proficiency with a rifle, Mr. Olsen is not, in Detective Tomaso's derogatory characterization, a dangerous amateur."

"How'd you know?"

"The information is publicly available, Ms. Gold. As disclosed in his law firm biography, Mr. Olsen was an Army Ranger during his tour of duty in Vietnam. Among the skills required for that position is sharpshooting. Accordingly, Mr. Olsen does not fall within the category of a dangerous amateur with a long-range rifle."

"Interesting," I said.

"During your meeting with Detective Tomaso, Ms. Gold, you should also inform him of the location of Mr. Olsen's beach house."

"Mozambique, right?"

"You are correct."

"And where is that again?"

"As I previously informed you, Ms. Gold, the Republic of Mozambique is located in southeast Africa directly below Tanzania. The ocean visible in the photograph on Mr. Olsen's desk is in fact the Indian Ocean."

"Okay, I will pass that along, Stanley."

Stanley snorted. "I should hardly think that your detective will be interested in Mozambique's proximity to the Indian Ocean. He should, however, be interested in the absence of an extradition treaty between the United States of America and the Republic of Mozambique. Given your increasing concerns over Mr. Olsen's potentially felonious conduct, one can assume that the location of his beach house is not entirely, or even principally, the result of Mr. Olsen's desire to body surf in the waters of the Indian Ocean."

Chapter Forty-eight

"Still too many ifs."

"No more than two, Bertie, and maybe just one, namely, *if* he wanted to kill Dayton."

"And *if* the he is Len Olsen or Donald Warner and *if* he decided to kill him and *if* he decided to do it on that hunting trip and *if* he knew where to set up for the shot. And assuming the answer to all those ifs is yes, there's still not a shred of evidence that either of those two men was there that morning or pulled the trigger. And even if we satisfy all those *ifs*, you can be sure we'll never find the weapon. Right?"

"Maybe."

"Then there's the young lady's death—the one that got you dragged into this craziness. Start with Len Olsen. All you have so far, Rachel, is a bunch of ifs, beginning with *if* he decided that he had to kill her and *if* he decided to do it by pushing her off the garage ledge. Those are big ifs, especially since there's not a shred of evidence that Olsen was there. According to that printout you gave me, he wasn't even in the garage that night. Donald Warner was there that night, and I suppose he'd have some sort of motive *if* he's planning to run for the Senate and *if* she had threatened to expose his gay sex life. But there's too many ifs there as well, beginning with *if* she even knew about those liaisons and, if so, *if* she had any reason to threaten him with that knowledge. Why would she even care?"

"That's why I don't think it was Warner."

"And your printout says it wasn't Olsen. And maybe it wasn't anyone, Rachel. Maybe she jumped on her own. It happens."

"So that's it?" I said. "No interest in Olsen or Warner?"

"Well, not entirely."

"Oh?"

"I told you last time that we might need to notify the Feebs if that outfit was operating interstate or international. Well, we did notify them, and now we got federal agents sniffing around from every branch of the damn government except the EPA."

"Really?" I leaned forward. "Tell me."

"Structured Resolutions doesn't seem to check out. Our own folks, including our IT guys, couldn't find anything. You're right about the registered agent. Some old guy with dementia in a nursing home. We talked to him. Totally out of it. Clearly been used solely to satisfy the registered agent requirement. We can't figure out who put him in that position or who filed the forms. As you also discovered, the auditors on those quarterly statements don't exist. Couldn't find a Missouri bank account for the outfit, and the feds can't find a U.S. bank account for the outfit. As near as they can tell, the money coming in from investors gets wire-transferred direct from the investor to a bank down in the Cayman Islands, but it doesn't stay there long. It gets wired out the same day to a bank in Switzerland. They think it leaves Switzerland the same day, but they can't figure out where it goes from there. Part of the problem is all the banking secrecy laws over there, and part of the problem is there hasn't been a deposit for at least a month, so the trail is cold."

"Do the feds think it's a scam?" I asked.

"Definitely. But they don't know what kind of scam or who's pulling it. Other than those two country club finders—Brenner and Teever—and maybe Olsen and Warner, they have nothing to go on."

"So what's the next step?"

"Next step?" Bertie smiled and shrugged. "Remember, Rachel, I'm just a local yokel to them. I used that gal's death and the possibility of St. Louis fraud victims to get my foot in the door—but it's barely in the door. From what I gather, they may try to bring Brenner or Teever in for questioning, see if they can scare one of them into pointing a finger."

"If the finger points to Olsen," I said, "you should mention to your federal amigos that he has a vacation home in Mozambique."

Bertie gave me a curious look. "Okay. Why?"

I told him.

He leaned back in his chair and rubbed his chin. "Interesting."

Chapter Forty-nine

Bertie Tomaso and I met again in his office at the end of the following week. He'd called to see if I could drop by that afternoon.

He'd been running interference for me since our last meeting—in part to keep the federal agents out of my hair and in larger part to make sure that the St. Louis Police Department didn't get squeezed out of the investigation. As he apparently reminded his federal counterparts at every opportunity, the only potential victim anyone had identified to date was Sari Bashir. Even though he saw little basis to change her cause of death, he had reopened her file to use primarily as a placeholder with the feds.

Meanwhile, the federal investigation of Structured Resolutions had stalled.

He gave me an amused grin. "The great and powerful Feebs are getting nowhere."

"Really?"

"They can't find any financial records. They're not ready to label it a criminal enterprise, but if it is, the odds are good that one or more of those four lawyers—Olsen, Warner, Brenner, or Teever—could be a ringleader. The one thing they don't want to do at this stage is spook the ringleader. You'd be surprised how many white-collar criminals have fled to a safe haven with the Feds hot on their tails. Remember Marc Rich, the sleazebag financier that Bill Clinton eventually pardoned?"

"Vaguely."

"He flew to Switzerland the moment he got wind of his pending indictment. That's what they're afraid of here. That Mozambique angle has them nervous."

"Have they interviewed anyone?"

"Rob Brenner. They brought him in for questioning two days ago. But they did it with kid gloves. No hint of any investigation, criminal or otherwise. They assured him it was a routine bit of information-gathering for the regulators. They said that Structured Resolutions had turned up on a few federal tax returns and they were trying to get some basic information on the company. They said Brenner had been identified by the tax return-filer as someone with knowledge."

"And?" I said.

Bertie shook his head. "Nada. Brenner played it well. He claimed he was nothing more than a happy investor who'd been approached by others interested in making an investment. He said all he did was pass along their names to the organization."

"How did he do that?"

"He said he sent an email to the company with some basic information about the would-be investor. That was all. He understood that the company would contact the would-be investor and, if that person met the requirements, allow them to invest."

"Did he give them the company's email address?"

Bertie nodded. "He did. And the feds accessed his private email records and were able to confirm that he had passed along fifteen names over the past two years—all wealthy individuals, all members of his country club. Each of those emails followed the format Brenner had described."

"So where is the company located?"

"They have no idea."

"But they have an email address."

"True. I don't understand the technology side of it, but it's apparently untraceable. Some sort of Internet black hole. The first email gets automatically forwarded to a password-protected email account out of the country, and then gets forwarded to another and another until you eventually lose track."

"So how does the investor get contacted?"

"According to Brenner, you receive a packet of materials via a private courier service, like FedEx or UPS. At least that's how he got contacted. You get the materials, fill out the application form, and then put it in a return envelope."

"A return to where?"

"He doesn't remember. He doesn't think there is a return address, though. Just a customer number."

"So what does he remember?"

"He said he got his approval in the mail, along with wire transfer instructions."

"Which he no longer has," I said.

"Of course. All he can recall is that it was a foreign-sounding bank. Anyway, he wired his money, got a confirmation in the mail, and now gets quarterly statements. They come in the mail from an undisclosed location overseas."

"Do they believe him?" I asked.

Bertie shrugged. "They think he knows more than he's telling."

"But?"

"They don't want to spook the ringleader, so they thanked him and told him he'd been quite helpful. They tried to give him the impression that he'd filled in enough of the blanks for them that they could close the matter and return to Washington."

"So now what?"

He smiled. "Rachel Gold enters, stage left."

"Oh, great. Let me guess: Brian Teever."

"Yes and no."

"Meaning?"

"Their concern is that an official federal interrogation of Teever will be a dead end, same as Brenner. Rather than haul him in and ratchet up the paranoia on the other side, they want a different approach."

"What does that mean?"

"They want the pressure to come from a non-governmental source."

"Explain."

"Assuming this is in fact a Ponzi scheme, the bad guys need to be able to make sure no one panics. One way is to let any skeptics cash in their investments. That way the skeptics get their money, walk away happy, and no one is the wiser."

"How does that help this investigation?"

"When Structured Resolutions refunds the investment, whether by wire transfer or check, it will create a financial trail that the feds can follow back to its source."

"Where do I come in?"

"You know one of the investors."

"Who?"

"That doctor you sued. Jeffrey Mason."

"What about that list of names they got from Brenner's email account?"

"Three problems with that. First, the feds don't know which of those potential investors became actual investors. Second, even if they figured out who was an actual investor, the feds have no idea how to approach them without setting off alarms. And third, even if they found an actual investor and figured out how to approach him in some sort of disguise, the odds are likely that the investor would turn to Brenner, since he was the one who got them access to Structured Resolutions. Your guy, by contrast, got in via Teever."

"He's not my guy, Bertie. I'm suing him. Explain to your FBI guy that Mason has his own lawyer."

"I know that. So do they. They asked me to run the idea by you, hoping you'd think of something clever."

"Me? I thought you were the clever one."

He chuckled. "I'm just the local yokel still trying to figure out how and why a suicide could become a homicide."

I leaned back in my chair. "Dr. Mason."

"Mull it over, gorgeous. Maybe something will come to you."

"I'll try."

As I stood up, it did come to me. I smiled down at Bertie. "Actually…"

Bertie grinned. "I knew it. Tell me."

Chapter Fifty

The Barracuda stared at me. With his black hair slicked back, prominent widow's peak, intense eyes with nearly black irises, and angular face, Barry Kudar's features only reinforced his nickname.

He shook his head. "I don't get it."

"You don't get what?" I said.

"Why do you care? It's my client's money."

I raised my eyebrows. "For now."

"What the hell does that mean?"

"We go to trial in three months." I smiled. "I'm hoping that the jury will decide that your client's money belongs to my client."

"Give it a rest, Rachel. There's no fucking way that's going to happen."

We were meeting in the Barracuda's office. I'd called him yesterday after my meeting with Bertie Tomaso and told him we needed to meet. He agreed to see me today after lunch. At his office, of course. I didn't mind. He was hardly the first macho man I'd had to deal with over the years.

I said, "I didn't come here to argue the merits, Barry. Let's just say that I have as much interest in your client's liquidity as your client does."

"How so?"

"If I get the verdict I hope to get from that jury, I'd much prefer to garnish your client's investment accounts instead of trying to foreclose on his house and his vacation home in Aspen."

"That's ridiculous."

"I'd prefer to call it due diligence. I had a forensic accountant look at your client's assets." I gestured toward the copy of Dr. Mason's quarterly statement from Structured Resolutions that I'd brought to the meeting and set on his desk. "My guy raised some serious questions about that one. Given that your client has more than six million dollars tied up there, I decided I ought to mention it to you."

"What kind of questions?"

"There's no publicly available information on Structured Resolutions," I said. "I don't know who your client's contact is at that company, but he ought to ask some questions."

"Such as?"

"Look at footnote five."

Kudar picked up the statement and studied it. He raised his eyes to mine. "So?"

"That's the only disclosure about the underlying structured settlements, right?"

He looked down at the statement again, and then back at me. "So what?"

"There are nine cases mentioned, right?"

He nodded. "Nine. Right."

"Talk to the lawyers in those cases."

"Why?"

"Ask them about the settlements they supposedly sold to Structured Resolutions."

"Why?"

"Just talk to them."

He looked down at the statement again. "They aren't even listed. Just the case names."

"And the venues of the cases."

He frowned as he studied the footnote. "Just the states, not the venues."

"That's enough information to track them down from the court records."

"Why the hell do I need to talk to them?"

"See if you can get them to tell you about the case that's listed. See what they say about their settlement. See if it raises any questions about your client's investment."

He gestured at the statement. "Read the whole footnote. These are just random examples."

"That's what it says. Nine random examples. Check them out, Barry. See if those examples give you comfort. And then try to talk to the auditors listed on the statement. See if you can even find them."

He stared at me, his eyes narrowing. "What if you're just jerking me around?"

I shrugged. "Then I guess I'm a jerk. But I don't represent your client, Barry. You do. You might want to review the Code of Professional Responsibility. Check out your obligations to your client. Then do whatever you want you. Just know that when I get back to my office I'm going to dictate a detailed memorandum describing our meeting, including everything I told you. For both of our sakes, I hope my accountant's concerns are unfounded."

I stood and looked down at him.

"But," I said, "if there is substance to those concerns, and you ignore them, then you better hope that Dr. Mason's lawyer in the malpractice claim against you doesn't serve me with a subpoena for that memo."

I gave him a wink.

"See you in court, Barry."

Chapter Fifty-one

"Four days in Bermuda?" I said. "Who knew the Sherman Act was so sexy?"

"Sexy?" Benny shook his head. "Odds of me getting laid at an antitrust seminar are about as good as the odds of me getting elected Pope."

"Well, if you have to await the vote of the Cardinals, I can think of worse places than the Fairmont Hamilton Princess Hotel."

Benny and I were having a good-bye lunch. He was leaving in the morning for the annual ABA antitrust seminar, where he was presenting a paper on something having to do with the Robinson-Patman Act, a federal statute as difficult to understand, at least for me, as string theory.

We were at McGurk's Irish Pub in the Soulard area. Fish and chips for me; lots of stuff for Benny, including Mrs. McAteer's potato soup, corned beef and cabbage, toasted ravioli, and now his second pint of Guinness Stout.

He took the last spoon of his soup, washed it down with a gulp of Guinness, leaned back in his chair, semi-smothered a belch, and said, "Guess who called me this morning?"

"The Vatican?"

"That little weasel Brenner."

"Really? And?"

Benny placed his hand over his heart in mock commiseration. "He regretted having to tell me that Structured Resolution was currently closed to new investors. He hoped they might open up again after the first of the year, but he wasn't in a position to predict."

"Did he tell you why they were closed?"

"He said he didn't know. I pressed him. He said he wasn't privy to those kinds of decisions. He claimed his only connection to the company, other than as an investor, was to help potential investors make their initial contact. After that, it was out of his hands. He told me Structured Resolution has occasionally closed to new investors. He apologized and said he wished our donor the best."

"Interesting."

"You think they figured out our spiel was bullshit?"

"Possibly," I said. "If so, though, I would have thought they might try to call our bluff. Find out if we really had a donor."

Benny shrugged. "Maybe they really are closed."

"Or maybe something else is afoot."

"Such as?"

"My meeting with the Barracuda seemed to have an effect."

"No shit? Did he get back to you?"

I laughed. "Kudar? No way he'd get back to me. But he definitely talked to his client. Two days after I met with him, Kudar called Brian Teever and demanded that Structured Resolutions cash out his client."

"He called Teever? How do you know that?"

"Big Brother. The feds have Teever's phone tapped. They recorded the call, according to Bertie."

"That's sure comforting to know. Wonder if they have your phone tapped?"

"Probably."

"So what did Teever tell Mason?"

"He said he'd pass along the request. Kudar called him the next day demanding an answer. Teever didn't have one. Kudar called the following day. Teever told him he'd heard that the company was in the process of closing Dr. Mason's account and that they would wire-transfer the funds into his bank account within seven days."

"When was that?" Benny asked.

"Yesterday."

"That must have given the FBI a chubbie."

"Sounds like it. They claim they will be able to trace a wire transfer back to its source."

"Maybe they'll give you a J. Edgar Hoover Gold Star."

"It gets better."

"Oh?"

"If their goal was to apply pressure, that part is starting to snowball. According to the feds, Teever has now received similar requests from two other investors."

"So the good doctor is talking to his country club buds, eh?"

"Sounds like it. And before long they'll be talking to theirs. If Structured Resolutions really is a Ponzi scheme, we're entering the final phase."

Benny was grinning. "Awesome."

"It could get interesting."

"So who is Teever talking to?"

"Good question. Whoever it is, he isn't talking on that phone. The only other calls they've recorded have nothing to do with Structured Resolutions. If he's using a phone, it's one that's untraceable."

"How do you do that?"

"Bertie told me that you can buy prepaid disposable cell phones at Target, Walmart, wherever. It's apparently what drug dealers do. You make a few calls, dump the phone, and get a new one."

"That's what he's doing?"

"Maybe."

Benny took another gulp of his Guinness and wiped his mouth with his napkin. "So if we're really entering the final phase, what's that mean?"

"They expect the bad guys to cut and run."

"By plane?"

"Probably, although a car is always a possibility. If you get across the border, you might be able to hide out for a while."

"But not forever."

"I don't know. Maybe they lay low for a few weeks and then fly from that country." I shook my head. "I didn't take that class in law school."

Benny took another forkful of corned beef and washed it down with a gulp of Guinness. "For your sake, I'm just glad the feds are involved. Keep you out of harm's way."

"Speaking of the feds, guess who else is sniffing around?"

"Who?"

"The IRS."

"What?"

"Apparently, they've got their own investigation of that Moral Majority outfit."

"The one connected to the guy in Belleville?"

"Yep. Bertie doesn't know the whole story. It started out as a routine audit. The IRS thinks there may be a link to Donald Warner, which might not have been a big deal on its own but with all this other stuff going on, they've ramped it up."

Benny chuckled. "When old Donald finds out, he's going to piss his pants. Those IRS agents are scary. Just ask Al Capone."

"I know."

"Big money involved?"

"Bertie doesn't know that part. He just knows that the IRS is in the mix."

Chapter Fifty-two

Rebecca Hamel nodded. "So it's Mr. Warner."

"Apparently," I said.

"Interesting."

"He wasn't at the top of my list."

"Nor mine."

Rebecca and I were seated on a park bench in Soldiers Memorial Park and facing the Military Museum, a limestone structure with an outer wall of massive four-sided stone columns. In front of us was the entranceway, above which was engraved TO OUR SOLDIER DEAD. Flanking the broad stairway leading up to the entrance were two large stone Art Deco statues of winged horses, each with a martial-looking man or woman at its side.

The park, two blocks west of the Civil Courts Building in downtown St. Louis, was a good place for us to meet. Rebecca had a hearing in Division Four that morning at eleven. We agreed to meet at ten-fifteen. All the surveillance and wiretapping had raised my own paranoia level even though I assumed—or at least hoped—that I was not among the watched. Nevertheless, it seemed prudent to meet somewhere outdoors, and preferably just with Rebecca. The logistics and added risks of trying to include Stanley and Jerry seemed too high, especially since there would be plenty of time for Rebecca to update them on what was going on.

"When did you find out?" she asked.

"Last night. I got a call from Detective Tomaso."

"So it goes down tomorrow night?"

"At the airport," I said. "The flight is at nine. They'll make the arrest before he boards."

"Do they think he'll confess?"

"No. But they feel confident he'll be carrying evidence. Either in a laptop or in his briefcase. Or maybe in his luggage if he checks any, which they expect him to do. They'll have an FBI agent ready to intercept his luggage before it gets loaded onto the plane."

Rebecca frowned. "What do they expect to find?"

"Financial records, passwords, electronic data. Maybe not the whole scheme, but enough to give them access into it. I didn't get details. All Tomaso told me was that the FBI says that an operation of that scale can't be run from one guy's memory and can't be run without a central control."

"You said a flight to Detroit?"

"That's just the first leg. Warner apparently bought that ticket a month ago. Or rather, his secretary bought it for him. He has a client in the Detroit area. He's been going there about once a month for the last few years. Typically, he flies in the night before, has his meetings the next morning, and flies back to St. Louis. What tipped them off apparently happened yesterday. Though he hasn't cancelled the flight back from Detroit, he bought a new ticket that day from Detroit to JFK in New York, and from there to Casablanca."

"Casablanca? Like that movie?"

"Same city."

"Where is it?"

"In Morocco."

Rebecca frowned. "What's there for him?"

"Apparently, what's important is what *isn't* there for him. Morocco has no extradition treaty with the U.S."

"So if he gets there…?"

"He's beyond our government's reach."

She nodded. "Tomorrow night."

"That's the plan. You can tell Stanley and Jerry, but make sure they understand they have to keep it absolutely secret. Detective Tomaso told me on a strictly confidential basis. I'm not supposed to tell anyone, but the three of you have been in this from the beginning. You deserve to know. Tell Stanley and Jerry to assume the government is monitoring their phones and their emails. That means no calls, no emails. For all of us. If you need to tell me something, do it via a text message. And keep it short and cryptic."

"When will you know about the arrest?"

I shrugged. "Probably not until it's announced. I'll call you."

She nodded and checked her watch.

"You better get going," I said. "In my experience, Judge Carter starts on time."

We both stood.

"Good luck in court," I said.

We shook hands.

She smiled. "Thanks, Rachel."

As she walked toward the courthouse, I looked around the park. It was warm for December. There was a homeless man asleep under a nearby tree. Two teenagers were playing catch with a Frisbee. A pudgy man in a brown suit was walking quickly along the pathway in the direction of the courthouse. He had a briefcase in one hand and was holding a cell phone to his ear with the other. He gave me a curt nod as he passed. It sounded like he was talking to his secretary.

No one in the park looked suspicious.

As if you would you know, I reminded myself.

Chapter Fifty-three

"So tonight?" my mother said.

I checked my watch. "In about an hour."

"Oh, Bea will be so proud when she hears."

Bea was Stanley Plotkin's mother.

"A doctor and a rabbi for sons," my mother said, "and now she has a regular Columbus."

"Columbus?"

"That smarty-pants detective on TV. The one played by Peter what's-his-name. Fonda, I think."

"Columbo, Mom. And the actor is Peter Falk."

"That's what I said."

I sighed. "Right."

We were in my kitchen having tea and oatmeal cookies, which my mother had baked with Sam that morning. My son loves cooking with his Bobba Sarah.

My mother had dropped by tonight after her meeting at the Holocaust Museum. I'd already put Sam to bed. I brewed tea while she told me about her day.

I'd been on edge all day thinking about the upcoming event at Lambert-St. Louis International Airport. I'd given Bertie my cell phone number and made him promise to call me as soon as they made the arrest.

"So this Warner, he's not the one you thought," my mother said.

"I was a little surprised. Apparently, so was Stanley."

"Oh?"

I explained the strict confidentiality rule I'd given Rebecca—no communications the government might trace.

"She sent me a text message last night. Three words: *S is skeptical.*"

"S?"

"Stanley. I sent her back one word: *Noted.* She sent another text this morning. Two words: *Very skeptical.* I sent back the same one-word response."

I poured us each some more tea.

My mother said, "So you thought the bad guy was Len Olsen?"

"He just seemed more suspicious. But if you assume that Sari's death was connected to the scheme—that she found out and posed too much of a threat—then I suppose Olsen is in the clear."

"Explain that again."

"He wasn't in the parking garage that night."

"How do the police know that?"

"Computer records. You need to use your cardkey to go from the building to the garage after seven. The computer recorded every user that night. He didn't use his."

"Is that something new?"

"No, Mom. It's been around for a long time. Back when Benny and I were associates at Abbott & Windsor in Chicago, the firm had offices on ten floors, but the only public entrance was on the main floor with the receptionists. The entrances to the other floors were locked. If your office was on that floor, the only way you could open the door was with your cardkey."

"I had no idea."

I smiled. "We assumed that the firm kept track of who stayed late and who came in on Saturdays. That why we made sure we each used our own cardkey late at night, even if we were together and didn't…oh, my God."

"What?"

"Oh, my God." I leaned back in my chair, my mind racing. "He *could* have been there that night."

"Who?"

"How did I miss that?"

"How did you miss what?"

"The cardkey. If two or three people are together, they don't each need to use their cardkey. All you need is for one to open the door and hold it for the others. We did that all the time at Abbott & Windsor when more than one of us got off the elevator in the morning or after lunch."

I paused, trying to visualize that night in the crosswalk.

"Olsen could have walked out with anyone," I said. "Especially Sari. She was the only one parked on that floor. He could have walked her to her car, maybe trying to convince her not to tell anyone."

"But he's not the one flying to Detroit, right?"

"True. The feds are monitoring all the airlines. If he were flying anywhere, there'd be a record of it…unless…"

"Unless what?"

"Unless there isn't a record."

"What do you mean?"

"There wouldn't be a record if he isn't flying commercial."

"How could that be?"

"The law firm owns a plane. Olsen's a pilot. He flies his trial teams to out-of-state courts."

"But wouldn't there still be a record of where he's going to fly it?"

"I doubt it. I don't think you have to file a flight plan with anyone."

I checked my watch: 8:05.

I stood as I tried to formulate some sort of plan. I thought back to that photograph in Olsen's office, the one with him posed in front of the Cessna jet. I tried to visualize it, to remember the sign in the background.

VALLEY PARK AIRPORT

"Mom, can you stay with Sam until I get back?"

"Where do you think you are going, young lady?"

"I'm not sure."

"You should call the police."

"I will. But I'm going to head out there just in case."

"Just in case what?"

I shook my head. "I don't know."

"Rachel, you're not a cop."

"I know, I know." I grabbed my purse. "I'm not going to do anything crazy. I promise."

"*This* is crazy."

"Don't yell. You'll wake Sam."

I walked over to the back door. "I'll call you. I promise."

"He's a man, Rachel. He's bigger than you. What if he really did push that poor girl off the garage?"

I stared at my mother, a smile forming on my lips. "Good point."

I walked over to the stairs to the second floor.

"Yadi," I called in a soft voice.

I heard a slight rustling, and then Yadi appeared at the top of the stairs, his tail wagging.

"Come here, boy."

He clambered down the stairs and sat at my feet.

I patted him on the head. "I need a bodyguard. You game?"

He barked once and followed me back into the kitchen, where I took the leash off the hook.

I gave my mother a wink. "No one's going to mess with me now."

"You call me, Rachel."

I opened the back door. "I promise."

"I love you, darling girl."

"I love you, Mom."

Chapter Fifty-four

It was a thirty-minute drive to Valley Park Airport, home base to many of the corporate jets and other private planes of St. Louis. I tried to reach Bertie Tomaso four different ways on the drive. I didn't know his cell phone number, so first I called his office phone, listened to his out-of-office greeting, and left a message with little hope that he would hear it before tomorrow. Then I called police headquarters and tried to urge a particularly apathetic desk sergeant to contact Bertie and have him call me ASAP. Then I called 911, explained that Detective Tomaso was on a stakeout at Lambert Airport, and asked the operator to have him call me on my cell. That was an especially frustrating call. The 911 operator had no idea who Detective Tomaso was. It took me a moment to realize that my call had been answered by the 911 operator in the suburban town near the highway I was on. I explained to her that Bertie was a St. Louis homicide detective and that it was urgent that he call me ASAP. My cell phone dropped that call before she responded, though presumably her phone had a record of my cell phone number. Last, I called Bertie's home number, hoping to reach his wife Sue, but got their answering machine. I left a message for Sue to have Bertie call me on my cell ASAP.

As I took the exit for the Valley Park Airport, I was still trying to come up with a plan. I had driven there on pure conjecture. It was certainly possible, even probable, that Donald Warner was the ringleader and that the FBI had correctly scoped his escape plan. His specialty, after all, was international corporate finance, and he was definitely in the parking garage the night she died. And maybe some of that Structured Resolutions money had been funneled into that Moral Majority 501(c)(4) outfit in Illinois.

But it also seemed just as possible that the whole Donald Warner airline ticket scenario was a ruse designed to misdirect law-enforcement attention toward Lambert International Airport while twenty-miles to the south a private plane would be taxiing down the runway on the first leg of a journey that required no flight plan, no ticket purchase, and no publicly available information.

And what if I was right? What if Len Olsen was here? What then?

Maybe the best strategy would be to hide until he took off and then try again to contact Bertie. Once he was in the air, he'd be on someone's radar. Literally.

Not much of a plan, I conceded.

I turned onto Airport Boulevard. There were no street lamps. I drove slowly in the darkness toward what appeared to be a two-story air traffic control tower in the distance off to the left. I turned left at the three-way intersection, where the road sign arrow pointed toward AIRPORT. About a hundred yards further down, the road ended in a small parking lot surrounded by a chain-link fence. As I pulled into the lot, I counted five other cars.

I parked in a front-row space facing the chain-link fence and the runway beyond, which ran perpendicular left to right in front of me. It was illuminated by a row of embedded lights running down the middle and bright yellow stripes painted along both sides the entire length.

As I shifted into Park, a twin-engine plane landed, coming in from the left and taxiing past me, its propellers a blur. I shut off the engine and turned toward Yadi, who was seated alongside me, eyes alert.

"Ready?"

He rose into a crouch, his tail wagging. I took the leash, snapped it onto his collar, and opened my door. He followed me out, scrambling down from the car.

It was a chilly night. I stashed my purse under the front seat, zipped up my fleece jacket, put my cell phone in one pocket, closed the car door, and put the car keys in the other pocket.

I glanced around. The other five cars were dark and empty. I looked down at Yadi, who was seated on the asphalt and staring up at me.

"Let's do it."

We walked along the fence to the gate, which was open. We stepped through the gate and onto the concrete walkway that runs the length of the runway. On the far side and facing the runway stood a long line of hangars—at least forty. Between the hangars and the runway on that side was a wide, paved taxiway. About half of the hangar doors were open, their interiors unlit. It was a cloudy night. The only illumination came from a series of tall arc lights facing the hangars and spaced about every three hangars. A few were burned out or turned off, leaving just enough light to make out the dark shapes of the airplanes inside some of the open hangars across from us.

The twin-engine plane that had landed moments before had turned off the runway at the far end and was now taxiing back in our direction, moving along the row of hangars. We watched in the darkness as it passed by and eventually stopped outside a hangar near the other end. I could hear the engines turn off, but it was too far away to see the propellers stop spinning.

I stared at the darkened hangers directly across from us, looking for any movement.

Nothing.

We were largely hidden in the night. The best option seemed to be to start at one end and move down the line of hangars, cautiously, one by one. Hopefully, I told myself, we'll confirm that there's nothing suspicious going on out here.

"Let's go," I whispered to Yadi.

We headed down the walkway toward the end of the runway and then we crossed over. We slowly approached the first hangar, which was open and empty. There was a door on the left front corner of the hangar, and the sign on the door read:

HANGAR 41B
SULLIVAN COAL INC.

The next hangar was closed. The sign on the door read:

HANGAR 40B
SMILOW PRODUCTIONS LLC

The next one was open, a small corporate jet parked inside. The sign on the door read:

HANGAR 39B
LANDAU, MURPHY & MORAN LTD.

We kept moving, slowly, carefully, hangar by hangar. About eight doors further down, Yadi halted, his body rigid.

"What?" I whispered, my own body tensing.

He was staring into the empty hangar as he made a soft growling sound. I held my breath and peered in. I could see nothing. Then I heard a scurrying noise from inside.

"Come on," I whispered, tugging on his leash. "Probably just a rat."

As we passed the parking area, which was now on the far side of the runway, I heard the distant sound of two men talking. We ducked into an open hangar. They were coming down the walkway along the runway. One was carrying what looked like a briefcase and the other had on a backpack. From what I could make it out, they were talking about last week's Rams football game.

I watched as they walked into the parking area and got into an SUV. A moment later the engine started and the headlights came on. The vehicle backed out of its space, turned, and headed out of the parking area. They must have been on the plane that had landed just as we parked.

When the SUV's taillights disappeared into the darkness, we stepped out of the hangar. I paused to check my cell phone. No messages. I shook my head.

C'mon, Bertie.

◇◇◇

It happened suddenly.

We had passed three hangars and had just reached the next one, open and dark, when Yadi leaped forward and started barking. I glanced at the door on the other side of the hangar: WARNER & OLSEN LLP.

From inside the hangar a familiar voice called, "Hello?"

I heard a metallic clatter, and then the sound of something—a small steel door—opening and closing.

Out of the darkness stepped Len Olsen. He squinted at me in the dim light.

"Rachel?"

He was in jeans and a dark leather jacket, hands in the jacket pockets.

Yadi was growling now. I pulled him toward me. "Sit."

He did.

Olsen said, "What are you doing here, Rachel?"

"What are *you* doing here?"

He nodded toward the hangar. "This is the firm's plane."

"That wasn't my question."

"Answer mine first. What are you doing here?"

"Looking for you."

"Why me?"

"You know why."

There was a moment's silence, and then he chuckled.

"Who exactly do you think you are?" he said. "Mrs. Dirty Harry?"

"I'm not here about the money, Len."

"No?"

"You want to rob from the rich? That's between you and them."

He grinned. "They can afford it. Back to my question. Why are you here?"

"Sari Bashir."

He stared at me.

"Why'd you kill her, Len?"

"Rachel, Rachel," he said, shaking his head as if speaking to a child. "The police ruled it a suicide."

I needed to keep him talking, hoping that maybe by now Bertie would have received one of my messages, that maybe, just maybe, the cavalry was finally on its way.

"I asked you a question, Len. Why did you kill her? Had she figured out your scheme?"

He was silent.

"Was she going to turn you in?"

No response.

"Pushing her out of a parking garage?" I said. "That was your plan?"

"Of course not."

"Then why?"

He shrugged. "I guess you could call it spur of the moment."

"I'd call it murder."

"Whatever."

I said, "And she wasn't the first, was she?"

"What are you talking about?"

"You know exactly what I'm talking about."

After a moment, he said, "An unfortunate hunting accident. Happens every year."

He took a step toward me. "While I'd love to stand here and chat, I need to be on my way."

He pulled his right hand out of the jacket.

I was staring at a handgun aimed at me.

"We'll make this quick and painless," he said, lowering the gun toward Yadi. "First your dog."

I stepped in front of Yadi and lowered my hand to where the leash was clipped onto the collar.

"You'll have to shoot me first" I said, my voice unsteady, my hand shaking. "When you do, my dog will make you pay."

And then, from somewhere in the darkness, came a familiar nasal voice.

"Mr. Olsen," the voice announced, "your reference to that 1971 motion picture is both apposite and ironic."

Still pointing the gun at me, Olsen jerked his head toward where the voice seemed to be coming from, which was behind him to the left.

I scanned the darkness in disbelief.

Stanley Plotkin?

"Look back at Ms. Gold," Stanley commanded.

Olsen turned slowly toward me.

"Now, sir," Stanley continued, "lower your gaze. You will see a red dot on your chest hovering directly over your heart."

Olsen did as commanded. There was indeed a bright red dot on his chest.

"That is from a laser sight, sir. It is affixed to a loaded rifle now in possession of an experienced hunter prepared to pull the trigger should you make any rapid motion. I will shortly commence the standard countdown. If you have not set your pistol on the ground in front of you and placed your hands behind your head by the time I reach zero, sir, you will experience what you have represented to Ms. Gold as quick and painless. While I am not sufficiently versed in neuroscience to attest to the painless element, I can assure you that it will be quick. In the interim, be advised that the appropriate law-enforcement officials have been notified. If you listen carefully, sir, you will discern the sounds of their approach."

Stanley paused. I could hear the distant wail of sirens and a deep fluttering noise from somewhere above us to the east.

"Thus," Stanley continued, "to paraphrase Detective Harry Callahan in the motion picture you referenced, as you stare at that red dot on your chest, you've got to ask yourself a question, Mr. Olsen: 'Do I feel lucky?' Well, do you, punk?"

Chapter Fifty-five

"Get yourself a Hollywood agent, woman."

That was Benny's reaction when I filled him in upon his return from Bermuda. He'd already heard the public version, of course. We'd made the front page of the *New York Times* and *USA Today*—or, more precisely, Homeland Security had. There *huh?* was no mention of the three of us during the initial twenty-four-hour news cycle, which featured a forty-two-second video clip of the SWAT team's arrival at Valley Park Airport, complete with helicopters descending onto the tarmac. Filmed on an iPhone by an astonished air traffic controller, it ran hourly on all the cable news networks.

The video was too dark and grainy to identify anyone, which was just fine with me. But the press soon attached us to that evening's events, and as our roles emerged in follow-up stories, I was contacted by two West Coast agents, one claiming to represent an A-list director and the other a major film actress, both interested in story rights—an interest not shared on our end, as I confirmed with Rebecca, Stanley, and Jerry.

"That cell phone call is the perfect touch," Benny said. "I'm telling you, Hollywood loves that ironic shit."

And it did feel ironic even when the call came through, despite the fact that I was, to put it mildly, somewhat stressed at the time. After Len Olsen placed the gun on the ground, Rebecca Hamel stepped out from the darkness behind me, her hunting rifle still aimed at Olsen, the red dot now hovering just above the bridge of his nose. Flustered, I had picked up the handgun and stepped back, pulling Yadi with me. Stanley and Jerry appeared from around the far side of the hangar. Jerry was carrying a flashlight, which he clicked on as he lumbered toward us. He swung the beam of light in an arc, illuminating me and then Olsen and then the hangar, where it was apparent that Olsen had been loading the plane when I arrived.

For what seemed like an eternity, the five of us stood silent—me with the handgun at my side, Rebecca with the rifle cocked, Stanley dwarfed at Jerry's side, Jerry pointing the flashlight at Olsen, and Olsen, hands clasped behind his head, looking down, the red laser dot hovering on the top of his head. More than a month has passed since then, but I still wonder what went through Olsen's mind as he stood there, the sirens growing louder, the fluttering morphing into the thrumming of two descending helicopters.

My cell phone rang just after the SWAT team's ground vehicles—a car and a van—screeched to a halt on the tarmac and the helicopters landed. As the vehicle doors burst open and agents charged out in full battle attire—body armor, night-vision goggles, weapons cocked—I answered the phone.

"Yes?"

"Hey, Rachel, it's Bertie. You can relax, kiddo. We got our man!"

"Really? So did we."

"Huh?"

◇◇◇

Looking back, I was not surprised to learn that Stanley Plotkin had been several steps ahead of me from the moment Rebecca Hamel told him of the impending arrest of Donald Warner. His immediate response to Rebecca was that Warner had been set up. When she pressed him for an explanation, he told her that Warner's only secret was "a familial matter involving sexual orientation."

Although Rebecca was dubious, Stanley came to her office alone that evening—a highly unusual thing for Stanley to do—and implored her to join him and Jerry the following evening at the Valley Park Airport. It would be a pure surveillance mission, he told her. No contact with anyone. Reluctantly, she agreed.

She drove them out to the airport around six that night. As Stanley had requested, she brought her loaded rifle, her night-vision laser site, a flashlight, and the handheld dictation machine the firm provided to all attorneys. Their plan had been to keep the Warner & Olsen hangar under surveillance from a safe distance in the darkness. If Len Olsen showed up, as Stanley predicted he would, Rebecca would move far enough away to be able to safely call her Homeland Security contact, who was her father's hunting buddy and someone she'd known for years.

Olsen showed up after sunset, pulling his Mercedes SUV around behind the hangar. He began unloading enough luggage and other materials to confirm his escape plans. But moments after Rebecca returned from her phone call, I showed up with Yadi.

Fortunately, Stanley had planned for that contingency. By the time Yadi started barking at Olsen, they were all in position—Stanley and Jerry against the left outer edge of the hangar, Stanley with the dictation machine turned to Record and Jerry standing protectively at his side, Rebecca in the darkness behind me, her rifle locked and loaded.

"Feel lucky, punk?" Benny had repeated with amused respect. "That wacky little dude is one awesome motherfucker."

◇◇◇

The media's obsession with Olsen's arrest saved the cops and the FBI from what would have been embarrassing fallout from their arrest of Donald Warner. As the FBI would confirm during a grilling that lasted into the wee hours of the night in an airport interrogation room, Warner had only the vaguest awareness of Structured Resolutions, having just started seeking answers to the questions that Beth Dayton, the dead hunter's widow, had asked him about the company. Nor did he know about any flight from Detroit to Casablanca—a claim of ignorance confirmed by his luggage, which consisted of a briefcase and a carry-on bag containing one change of clothing. Missing was a passport or anything incriminating. The subsequent investigation would reveal that Len Olsen had used the law firm credit card to purchase tickets for Warner's "trip" to Casablanca.

The FBI finished their interrogation at three-thirty that morning. Ten minutes later, a distraught and exhausted Donald Warner looked up to see two Internal Revenue agents enter the room.

And then came the surprise.

Six questions into their examination Warner started crying. But his were tears of frustration and fatigue, not guilt. He did indeed visit that private backroom at the Steamhouse Saloon on some Thursday nights, and on other Thursdays he met in the Belleville offices of Condor Investment Advisors. And while those trips were indeed linked to his relationship with the openly gay Richie Condor, there was nothing sexual about them. Their relationship had grown out of Condor's romantic involvement with Warner's son, Donald, Jr. Warner's love and total acceptance of his son had trumped the strictures of his religion and political party. Those secret Thursday night meetings were strategy sessions with representatives of the lesbian and gay communities who occupied positions of power within the largely Republican corporate world and viewed Warner as a viable Senatorial candidate who could help advance their cause. By the time the IRS agents concluded their questioning that morning, Warner and Missouri's New Moral Majority were in the clear.

Not so for Olsen. The federal judge denied his request for bail on the ground that he was an obvious and literal flight risk. The federal investigation into the Ponzi scheme was ongoing. An acquaintance at the Justice Department told me that almost all of the victims identified were from three St. Louis country clubs, each of which had allegedly rejected Olsen's membership application years ago. The total amount at risk appeared to exceed $100 million, although they were still trying to trace the funds through a series of offshore and foreign accounts found on the hard drive of Olsen's computer, which he'd stowed in the plane before our confrontation.

Ironically, Tony Manghini gets credit for the first breakthrough. With his typical sarcasm, he told me the day after Olsen's arrest, "Sounds like Robin Hood forgot the second half of his mission statement." It took me a moment to figure out what he meant, but it wasn't until I was in the shower the following morning that I grasped its significance. I could understand Olsen's desire to get revenge on the St. Louis elites who'd snubbed him, but you couldn't overlook those Robin Hood posters in his office. Barefoot and wrapped in a towel, I called Bertie from my bedroom. If he was stealing from the rich, I explained, then maybe some of that money found its way to the poor via his Sherwood Forest Fund.

Two days later, Bertie triumphantly announced that he was "the damn Sheriff of Nottingham." He'd passed my suggestion on to the feds, who'd identified contributions to the Sherwood Forest Fund of approximately one million dollars a year for each of the past three years, all via wire transfer from an anonymous donor. The feds tracked those wire transfers back to funds from a Structured Resolutions bank account in Kenya.

Len Olsen wasn't talking to the feds, although apparently his defense lawyers were, perhaps motivated by the fact that Brian Teever and Rob Brenner were definitely talking, both claiming their involvement in the scheme was the result of extortion. My Justice Department source assured me that when the dust settled, whether by verdict or plea bargain, Len Olsen would finally gain admission to a most exclusive club, namely, one of the minimum-security white-collar prison camps known as Club Fed.

The Oxford County hunting fatality case had been reopened, but the evidence was apparently incomplete and afflicted with chain-of-custody issues. Bertie's verdict on that case: DOA.

But he had hope for Sari Bashir's case, which he'd reopened as a possible homicide. The prior autopsy held no clues, and Sari's family had so far refused a request to disinter the body for a second look. Olsen's semi-admissions to me, which Stanley had recorded on the dictation machine, were damaging, but might not rise above reasonable doubt on their own. However, a re-examination of the personal property retained by the police revealed several fingerprints on Sari's purse that matched Olsen's prints, indicating that Olsen had likely tossed her purse off the garage after shoving her off. Again, Olsen wasn't talking, but his lawyers were.

"I'm feeling good about this one," Bertie told me.

As for the wealthy victims of the scheme, Barry Kudar had commenced a class action against Olsen and his law firm on behalf of the investors in what he described, at a press conference he staged on the courthouse steps, as "the most heinous and despicable financial fraud in the history of our great nation and, possibly, the world." It was a typical over-the-top Barracuda blast that might even have offended Charles Ponzi, but it did get him onto *CNN* and *Fox News* that night.

Which left, in my view, the real heroes: Tommy, Tony, Jerry, Rebecca, Benny, and, of course, Stanley. I decided we should have a final dinner in Sari's honor. With me, that would make an odd number. I wanted Malikah Bashir there as well, which would bring us back to an even number—and thus Stanley would be able to join us at the table.

I'm sure Benny would have attended anyway, but his enthusiasm blossomed when I told him that Rebecca would be there. As he explained, "She's tall, she's blond, she's hot, and she can kill and field-dress a fucking elk. That girl is the Uber Shiksa, Rachel—every Jewish boy's fantasy come to life."

I made the arrangements for a Sunday night dinner in a private room at one of my favorite restaurants and worked out the menu with the chef. Although I'd said nothing about attire for the event, I was touched to see that everyone had dressed up for the occasion. The women wore elegant cocktail dresses. Tony Manghini had the lounge lizard vibe going with his shiny black suit, shiny black shirt, shiny black tie, and jewel-encrusted gold cufflinks. Benny was working the professor look: tweed jacket, blue Oxford-cloth shirt, red-and-blue striped bowtie, and, of course, red Jack Purcell basketball shoes. Tommy Flynn's navy blue sports jacket was frayed at the collar and his bright paisley tie was of a width dating back to the 1970s. Jerry Klunger's massive arms and torso were squeezed into a brown sports jacket that looked two sizes too small, and his skinny black tie was obviously a clip-on. Stanley, God bless him, was in his tuxedo.

The meal was great, and everyone was enjoying the evening. As the servers cleared away the dessert plates and refilled the drinks, I tapped a spoon against my water glass a couple of times. The room grew silent. I looked around the table and smiled.

"This is a special night for me," I said. "And I hope for you, too. As some of you know, a few years ago my husband died in a plane crash."

I paused.

"I struggled for a long time to find an answer to his death. In the end, all I could do was accept what I'd always feared, which is that there is no answer. It's the way of the world. Bad things happen to good people for no reason, good things happen to bad people for no reason, and there's nothing you can do about it. But it's different here. When evil things happen to good people, you can try to hold the evil-doer accountable. I know it sounds a corny, but I believe in justice. We can never bring Sari back, but we can seek justice for her. That's what we've done here. All of us, working together. We've helped achieve justice."

I turned to Malikah, whose eyes were red.

I said, "For Sari and for her family, Malikah."

I gazed again around the table. "You guys were amazing."

I tilted my wineglass toward Tony and then Tommy. "Both of you took big career risks to help us get access to key documents and information. Thank you."

Tommy grimaced sheepishly and nodded.

Tony shrugged, grinned, and gestured toward Jerry and Stanley. "Just doing my part for Master Blaster over here."

I turned toward Benny. "You, too, Benny. You helped pull off the fake donor routine that lured out Len Olsen, and you kept me company on our trip to the East Side."

Benny chuckled. "Next time you try to lure me to a strip club with the promise of waiters and dancers in sexy red thongs, I'll be sure to do a little due diligence on the question of gender."

I smiled. "Fair enough."

I turned toward Rebecca. "You risked your life for Sari, Rebecca. And you saved my life. Truly. You are a brave woman. You deserve your own Medal of Honor."

Rebecca smiled and nodded toward Stanley. "Just following orders."

"Which brings us," I said to the group, "to the two men who were there at the beginning."

I turned to Jerry and Stanley. Jerry flushed bright red and lowered his eyes. Stanley began stretching his neck this way and that.

"Jerry," I said, "without you at Stanley's side, none of this would have happened. You helped make justice possible, and we all salute you."

"Here, here!" several in the group shouted, raising their wineglasses.

"Speech!" Tony shouted. "Come on, Sumo."

After a moment, Jerry looked up, still bright red. "Thanks, Miss Gold. I'm just proud to be here with all of you. We did a really good thing."

"And we're proud of you, Jerry," I said.

I looked around table. "If I may borrow from the Book of Genesis, in the beginning there was the word, and the word here was from Stanley—and only Stanley."

I turned to him. "Stanley, you saw what no one else saw, and you decided to act on it."

Stanley craned his head toward the ceiling.

I said, "Your determination started everything rolling. Back in my car after Sari's memorial service, back when you said those words, when you told me that Sari's death was not a suicide, I didn't believe you. When you showed me your evidence—that lip balm and the broken heel—I thought you were crazy."

Stanley was still staring at the ceiling, slowly tilting his head from side to side.

"You weren't crazy, Stanley, and you weren't wrong. You're the reason we're here tonight."

I held up my glass. "I propose a toast to Stanley—to the man who got all this started."

"Here, here!" the group shouted, all eyes on Stanley.

In the ensuing silence, Stanley slowly lowered his gaze until his eyes met mine. After a moment, he spoke.

"Ms. Bashir accepted me as I am. She was my friend, and she was murdered. That, Ms. Gold, is why I said those words to you after the memorial service. You were the right person to correct an injustice."

Stanley paused to take a sip of his water. The room was silent.

Leveling his gaze at me again, he said, "I am not possessed of oratorical skills. I turn to one who was so possessed. He, too, was a lawyer. He was also a cleric and poet. His name is John Donne. He happened to die on Mr. Manghini's birthday, albeit 357 years before Mr. Manghini's birth. Near the end of his life, Mr. Donne published a book of meditations entitled *Devotions Upon Emergent Occasions*. The third paragraph of Meditation Seventeen opens with the well-known phrase, 'No man is an island.' In selecting you, I relied upon the final sentence of that paragraph. That sentence captures your essence, Ms. Gold. Jerry shall read that sentence aloud in your honor."

While Stanley was speaking, Jerry had pulled a folded sheet of paper out of his jacket pocket. He opened it now and cleared his throat

"Any man's death diminishes me," Jerry read, "because I am involved in mankind, and therefore never send to know for whom the bell tolls; it tolls for thee."

Stanley said, "We thank you, Ms. Gold. You understood for whom the bell tolled."

To receive a free catalog of Poisoned Pen Press titles, please contact us in one of the following ways:

Phone: 1-800-421-3976
Facsimile: 1-480-949-1707
Email: info@poisonedpenpress.com
Website: www.poisonedpenpress.com

Poisoned Pen Press
6962 E. First Ave. Ste 103
Scottsdale, AZ 85251